Valeria Vose

"Here is that rare jewel—a spellbinding literary page-turner. It's hard not to love its desperate and fascinating heroine—Mallie, Memphis mother, ex-belle, and artist—caught at a point of extreme crisis. You literally can't put this book down... Beautifully written by Alice Bingham Gorman, this everywoman's journey is a trip well worth taking."

— LEE SMITH, author of *The Last Girls*
and *Dimestore: A Writer's Life*

"Alice Gorman has written for us a realistic, personal and deeply moving account of one woman's journey into empowerment. This fictional work offers a red-alert to everyone in all churches about pastoral boundaries and professional conduct."

— THE RT. REV. CHILTON R. KNUDSEN, former Bishop
of Maine, currently Assistant Bishop of Maryland,
author of *So You Think You Don't Know One:
Addiction and Recovery in Clergy and Congregations*

"Written with psychological insight and spiritual sensitivity, Gorman's novel challenges and inspires."

— RONI BETH TOWER, PhD, ABPP, clinical psychologist,
author of *Miracle at Midlife: A Transatlantic Romance.*

"No wonder I feel such a connection with Alice Gorman! Who has not suffered devastating loss and discouragement? As writers, both Alice Gorman and I want to say: *Know yourself;* take that knowledge to create a new, ever more meaningful life *for yourself.*"

—SENA JETER NASLUND, author of *Ahab's Wife*, and *The
Stargazer and Abundance: A Novel of Marie Antoinette*

For Eleanor, Grace, and Charles
my family, my teachers, my friends

The time will come
when, with elation
you will greet yourself arriving
at your own door, in your own mirror
and each will smile at the other's welcome,

DEREK WALCOTT

Chapter One

allie had waited as long as she could. Larry was late, as usual. The spindly hands on the wall clock pointed to 6:25. She had to start dinner. Troy and David—it was Troy's twelfth birthday—and three sleepover friends were bolting in and out of the kitchen, grabbing half-empty bags of crackers, pretzels and cookies from the food cabinet, moaning that they might starve to death within minutes.

"Back outside, boys," Mallie said, her anxiety mounting—Larry had promised to be home by five. Where was he? Her suspicions, lying just beneath the surface, were rising.

Within minutes, the scrunch of gravel in the driveway told her that her husband was home. From the kitchen window—one of those rare Memphis evenings in November warm enough to allow an open window—she watched Troy and David jump on their father like monkey babies, Larry half-hugging, half-boxing his two sons, then high-fiving Troy's friends. She sighed and lit the gas under the frying pan.

"Hey, Mallie," Larry called to her from the doorway, dropping his leather briefcase with a familiar thump on the wooden floor. "Sorry to be late." A simple apology. None of his usual preemptive explanations. He walked around the butcher block in the center of the square room and kissed the back of her head. "How about a drink?" he said.

She turned around, holding the spatula between them. Their eyes met for a second. "No thanks," she said, her voice flat, as if it should be obvious to him that she had no time for drinking.

He walked over to the cabinet above the refrigerator and pulled out the scotch bottle. "Well, I need one," he said, as if talking to himself as well as to her. He filled his glass three-quarters full—no jigger—then added a little soda water and ice. Without further words, drink in hand, he left the kitchen.

Both her hands were occupied filling the boys' dinner plates when the phone rang. She wished Larry would answer it, but she knew that would never happen. He was already sitting in his comfortable, dark leather chair in the library, his scotch and soda on the table beside him, his newspaper and magazines spread over the ottoman in front of him, the television in the corner set on "CBS News with Walter Cronkite." It was the mid-seventies. Larry would never turn off "Uncle Walter"—the name everyone called the trusted news anchor—to get up and answer the phone. After four rings, Mallie put the plate down on the counter and picked up the receiver in the kitchen.

"Hello?" she said, tucking the phone between her shoulder and her ear. Who would call at the dinner hour?

"Mallie?" A low, deliberate, woman's voice spoke her name and sent chills through her whole body. "Is this Mallie Vose?" the voice repeated.

Mallie gripped the receiver in her hand, squinting her eyes, trying to picture someone from the sound of her voice. "Who is this?" she asked. "Who do you want to speak to?"

"I want you to know I won't embarrass you when I see you on the street," the woman said. She enunciated each word as if speaking to a child. Then she made a choking sound. "I'm not a bad person. I never meant to hurt you."

"Wait a minute," Mallie said. She tried to sound authoritative. She didn't feel authoritative. Thoughts—questions—were whirling around in her brain. One thing she knew for sure: the call was about Larry. She knew that much.

"Larry!" she yelled, covering the receiver with her left hand.

"Who's that, Mom?" Troy asked.

"It's a call for your father." Mallie gestured her son toward the breakfast room, where the other boys had started eating, then closed the glass-paneled door behind him.

"Larry!" she called out again, louder.

Seconds later, Larry walked into the kitchen. "What's up?" he asked, his tie hanging loose, his sleeves rolled up, a look of innocent curiosity on his face. "Are you okay?"

"This call's for you," Mallie said, her voice indignant as she held the receiver out to him. He turned his back to her and cradled the phone under his chin. Taking a few steps away from her, he whispered something into the receiver before he said, loudly enough for his wife to hear, "We'll discuss this at the office." He brushed past Mallie and hung up the receiver, shrugging his shoulders, as if to say the call had been a mere nuisance to him and none of her concern. "Sorry about that," he said. "It was nothing."

Larry walked back to the library, leaving Mallie standing alone in the kitchen. For several minutes she felt paralyzed, her nerve center jammed with accusatory voices. *Stop pretending you didn't know! For months you've known Larry was involved with another woman. Face it! You knew!* Mallie leaned against a kitchen cabinet, listening to the boys chatter in the breakfast room. She could not stop the chatter in her head. Who was that woman? The voice was not at all familiar. She shook her head, as if trying to slough off the past, all the women who had come and gone in Larry's life, all the situations he had explained away as "nothing." Whoever the woman was, whatever she meant by "not embarrassing her"—such a strange thing to say—Mallie would have to deal with it later.

She had a birthday cake to deal with—and a messy kitchen. She had promised Troy before his friends arrived that there would be no candles and no birthday singing. He was too old for that. "Just the cake, Mom," he pleaded. "Promise?" She began tidying up the kitchen while the boys finished their hamburgers.

After David brought the first of the dirty plates in to the kitchen, she gave him the chocolate cake to carry into the breakfast room. She followed him, handing Troy the silver cake knife. No candles, only a small etched football and a goal post that said "Happy Birthday" in yellow icing. Troy smiled. He was proud of being the quarterback on the Holy Trinity lower school football team.

"Dibs on first piece," David said. His voice—the youngest of the group by nearly two years—still bore the pre-adolescent high pitch.

"Not a chance, Bozo," Troy said. The other boys laughed. David rolled his eyes. He was accustomed to being dressed down by his older brother.

Mallie went back to the kitchen, taking the rest of the empty plates with her and piling them together on the counter. She stood in front of the sink, watching the blackened, greasy beef particles from the old iron skillet swirl over the white porcelain surface and flush down the drain. She banged the aluminum Tater Tot pan with the scrub brush, then looked up and checked the clock. Seven thirty. It seemed that the boys would never finish the birthday cake. She shook her head attempting to quell the sound of the woman's voice, the strange things she said and to clear her mind of Larry's cavalier attitude that once again dismissed the call as "nothing." It made her feel as if she were nothing. If it had not been Troy's birthday and if his friends had not been there, Mallie would have accused Larry instantly. No, she would never have accused him in front of her sons—even without friends there. But now she knew what she had to do.

Chapter Two

After Mallie put the last plate in the dishwasher and was certain that the boys were settled in the basement playroom, she took a deep breath and marched into the library. The television was still on. Larry was reading *Time* magazine, his feet on the ottoman in front of him. He did not hear her—or chose to ignore her. She snapped off the TV and stopped a few feet in front of him.

"I need to talk to you," she said. "Now."

The "now" declaration was unlike her. Through the years of intermittent threatening incidents involving other women, all of which Larry explained away, or at least dismissed as inconsequential, Mallie had listened with the passivity of someone waiting—wanting—to be proven wrong. The way he looked at her whenever she accused him, his brow furrowed in earnestness, his gray-green eyes intent upon her, his gentle voice, the way he called her "darling, my dearest," the soft way he touched her face, as if she were his most prized possession—all of it always convinced her that there was no one more important in his life. Since her childhood Mallie had believed that her marriage would be the centerpiece of her life. Like her mother, she would do whatever was necessary to be a good wife. She would tolerate any difficulties that might arise with her husband. That night in the kitchen, from the moment Larry turned his back to her and whispered into the phone, she had had enough. She took another deep breath. "I need to know what's going on. Who was that woman?"

Larry put the magazine down. "What?" he said. This time his brow was furrowed into a defiant groove. "What are you talking about?"

Still standing over him, Mallie said, "I don't know who that woman on the phone was, but you've been lying to me, Larry."

Without hesitation, as if he had been poised for her attack, he looked straight at her and began a litany of explanations. "Okay. Her name's Julie Mason. She's in public relations. I'm in sales. We work together. There's nothing to it, Mallie. It's business. I don't know why she called here. She wasn't making any sense."

"I don't believe you." Mallie stood her ground in front of him, her arms wrapped tight around her body. She felt detached from herself, as if another person inside her was finally shaking loose and demanding to speak. "You can either tell me the truth, or you can keep on lying—and it's over." To her surprise, she heard herself threatening him, telling him that their marriage might be over.

Larry sat immobile, upright in his chair, wide-eyed like a child who never dreamed he would be caught.

The phone rang again. "You answer it," Mallie said. She took two steps back to allow Larry to take his feet off the ottoman and rise from his chair. For few seconds they stared at each other, an unspoken dare between them.

On the fifth ring he stood up, walked past her and around the corner of the library into the telephone alcove. Mallie sat on the small sofa across from Larry's chair. Her breath was shallow, her body tight. She felt certain the caller was the same woman. She couldn't hear what Larry was saying. After several minutes he came back into the library and stood against the doorway.

"That was Karen," he said. "She's a friend of Julie's." His voice was low and faltering as if he were in a confessional booth. "She's called an ambulance. Julie's taken an overdose of something— Valium, Karen thinks."

Mallie stared at him, unable to speak.

"Julie's barely conscious. Karen wants me to meet them at the hospital."

Mallie dropped her head and closed her eyes. Oh my God. An overdose. The hospital. Suicide. Nothing could have prepared her for all that. She felt heat, terror rising in her chest. No words would come, nothing.

After a few seconds of silence, Larry took a step toward her. In a pleading voice he said, "Mallie, will you go with me?"

"To the hospital?" She swung her head up to look at him. She was horrified. She could not imagine going to the hospital with him—could not imagine walking into that situation, seeing whoever that woman was and her friend.

"I need you with me," Larry said. He lowered his eyes as he spoke; his words sounded muffled. He shifted from one foot to the other, as if he were trying to hold his balance.

Mallie shook her head. She couldn't. Impossible. In a barely audible voice she said, "This is your problem, Larry."

He didn't move or speak.

The long silence between them pressed on her heart. Larry finally turned and walked toward the side door.

For hours, or what seemed like hours, Mallie sat alone in the library, a haze of helplessness and despair spreading over her. This was not the way her life was supposed to be. Every image of herself—the person she thought she was, the good girl, the good wife with the perfect loving family—all of it was coming unraveled. The wall of respect that had surrounded her family for generations was crumbling. She would be exposed. Naked. The whole world would see her—her real self. She was inadequate, a failed wife. She had a failed marriage. Her husband had other women. Now her parents and her friends—even her own boys, whom she had tried so hard to protect—would know the truth. Larry had promised her he would never let it happen again. No more women. He loved her. The women meant nothing to him.

She had wanted to believe him, but during the recent months an insidious fear had jolted her awake at night, jumped up in front of her at unexpected moments during the day. His constant lateness. His business trips out of town, too often extending over the weekend. His compulsive jogging for long stretches at odd hours, sometimes at night. She shuddered. The woman's voice in her head felt like poison seeping through her veins. She tried to stop imagining the woman in the hospital, her stomach being pumped—Larry standing by her bed. Was she blonde? Young? Younger than Mallie? It was November of 1976. In April—just four months away—Mallie would be forty. People still told her she was beautiful. There had been a time when Larry told her she was beautiful. What difference did that make now? There was another woman—she had heard her voice. The woman had called her "Mallie." What if the woman died? It would serve Larry right if she died. She wondered how it was possible she could feel so little concern for a human being who had just tried to kill herself. The whole mess was Larry's fault. Billows of anger filled her mind like smoke overpowering a room. She wanted to scream in his face. How could he have done this to her? To their family? But Larry wasn't there to hear her. He had left her to go to the hospital to be with the woman. His parting plea echoed in her head. Maybe she should she have gone with him. He had said he needed her. No, for God's sake, no. Stop it, Mallie. She slumped deeper into the little sofa and closed her eyes. She must not let herself think about Larry's broken promises, or the woman, or what might happen now. There was nothing she could do about any of it. She would have to wait. She forced herself to stand up and walk steadily down to the basement.

All five boys were watching *King Kong* on television, sprawled over the dark blue velveteen La-Z-Boy-style furniture, their gangly legs crossed on top of the round coffee table like crab legs on a platter.

"Promise me you'll go to bed by eleven thirty," Mallie said. "Will you?"

She knew they had a holiday for teachers' meetings the next day so they would want to stay up longer than usual and sleep late in the morning. They assured her with nods and mumbles, barely taking their eyes from the action on the screen.

Mallie went up to her room and ran a hot bath, as hot as she could stand it. She sank down into the water and closed her eyes. The heat surrounded her and penetrated her skin. Peace. Momentary peace. She wanted to stay there forever. As the water cooled down, Mallie looked up at her silky pink nightgown hanging on the back of the bathroom door. She thought of the advice she had read in an Ann Landers column about not wearing pajamas, about wearing a sexy nightgown that would appeal to her husband. What a joke. She wondered if Larry ever noticed her nightgowns. After brushing her teeth, she decided not to bother with the nightly moisturizer. She tucked herself under her blankets and fell into a fitful sleep. Around midnight she awoke and tiptoed down the hallway to be certain the boys had gone to bed.

At some point during the pre-dawn hours Mallie was aware that Larry was on the other side of their king size bed. She kept her back turned to him. Fleeting thoughts of what might have transpired at the hospital crossed her mind. She would find out soon enough. She willed herself back to sleep.

Chapter Three

At the first light of day, Mallie woke to see Larry standing next to her side of the bed, dressed for work. His starched white shirt, his dark blue fleur-de-lis tie, his gray suit gave no indication of what had happened the night before. He bent his head toward her. She could see that he had tears in his eyes.

"I'm so sorry, Mallie—so sorry," he said, his voice barely above a whisper. He stood looking at her, shaking his head.

Mallie watched her husband as if he were a stranger in their bedroom.

"The reason Julie called you last night was because I told her late yesterday afternoon it was over—that I wouldn't see her again." He stopped and took a breath. "I had no idea she'd call you—that she'd take those pills. She's okay. They got her in time. She's home." He choked the words. "I'm in a really bad situation. I need help."

Mallie stared at Larry, his blonde wavy hair more streaked with gray than she had realized, his erect athletic body slumped, as if his shoulders carried an unbearable weight. His bent head. His tears. In spite of herself and the anger that she had felt throughout the night, her heart went out to him, the way it would to one of her boys who was hurt or sick. She had never seen Larry like that—he looked broken. As if the thought had been waiting in her mind for months, she suggested that he might see the Reverend Thomas Matthews. Her friend Jenny Bolton, a deacon in the Episcopal Church, had told her that Father Matthews was a kind, empathetic counselor who worked with married couples in trouble—and that his counseling was free through the church. Mallie remembered Jenny telling her about a couple they both knew who had come back from the brink of divorce through counseling. Mallie had filed away the name of Father Matthews.

"He's a priest, a chaplain at St. Michael's Episcopal Chapel," Mallie said to her husband. "He counsels people in trouble."

"I'll see anybody you suggest," Larry said. "Will you call him?"

She agreed to make the contact. He leaned down and kissed the side of her face.

∽๏

At nine o'clock, before her nerve wavered or the boys came down for breakfast, Mallie steeled herself and dialed the number for St. Michael's. With the receiver pressed close to her ear, she dropped to the kitchen floor, drew her knees up and closed her eyes. She believed that her whole life depended on that call. A measured masculine voice on an answering machine requested that she leave a message for Tom Matthews, not Father Matthews or the Reverend Thomas Matthews, as she had expected, just Tom Matthews.

She left her name and number, asking that he call back as soon as possible. Leaning against the cabinet, she thought about the Reverend Thomas Matthews. She had met him once at Jenny's ordination to the deaconate the year before. She remembered that in the whole line of priests, he was the tallest and most distinguished. There was an intensity about him, a catlike grace in his step that contradicted his obvious signs of age: white hair as thick as snowdrifts, a craggy face with a long jawline as solid as a ship's prow. She sensed a certain mystery about him. He wasn't from Memphis or anywhere in the South. She felt fairly certain of that. She couldn't remember seeing him laugh, or openly hug anyone—none of the affable southern sociability traits that characterized the other priests around town. Maybe he came from New England or the Midwest. From what she had heard, he was known around Memphis as an intellectual and an unconventional priest. After all her years as a devoted Catholic child and her adult years as a searching Episcopalian, she was definitely in a place of questioning her religious convictions. Larry had been raised Unitarian and cared little about any church. The idea of a priest who was "intellectual and unconventional" seemed to offer the right combination, the right possibilities.

Within twenty minutes, the priest returned the call. Mallie was still sitting on the floor. She started to speak to him about the situation with Larry and discovered that she was stammering. How unlike her! She felt tongue-tied. She realized that it was the first time she had admitted to anyone—anyone other than her sister Anne or her friend Jenny—that there was trouble in her marriage. Without giving any specific details—certainly nothing about the suicide attempt—Mallie managed to convey to Father Matthews her appreciation of his counseling practice and a request for an appointment for Larry.

"Of course, I will see him," the priest said. "I'd be happy to meet with your husband." His voice was warm and reassuring, a balm to Mallie's agitation. He confirmed a time to meet with Larry at St. Michael's Chapel on Friday afternoon at three.

She hung up the receiver with an audible sigh of relief. She believed she had placed the problem in someone else's hands, maybe into the hands of the Lord—a concept from her childhood trust in God that had diminished through the years.

Chapter Four

A ll day Friday Mallie's thoughts drifted in suspension from her body. Her mind played "What if?" games while her body drove the carpool, rushed through the grocery store picking up an extra can of Spaghetti-O's and a bag of Oreo cookies, watered the plants, and packed her clothes for a previously scheduled duck hunting weekend. It seemed easier to her to go ahead with the weekend as planned, rather than make lame excuses to their friends, and besides, if she and Larry were with other people all weekend, they would not have to face each other at home alone—no matter what might transpire in Father Matthews's study.

The plan was simple. LeeAnn, the college student daughter of a friend from down the street, would come late Friday afternoon and spend the weekend with the boys. She would drive them to the football game on Saturday and remind them to feed Bingo, David's beloved yellow Labrador retriever. After Larry's appointment with Father Matthews, he would pick Mallie up at home and drive the two of them over to Arkansas for their hunting house party weekend.

∽

At five thirty, Mallie slipped into her side of the car. She sensed instantly that Larry's mood had completely changed. The sunny expression on his face was a transformation from the contrite gloom that he had worn since Tuesday morning. For three days they had barely spoken in the evenings, and they had slept—or feigned sleep—on opposite sides of the bed.

"Hi, peachie," Larry said, as she shut the car door.

Peachie? Mallie was shocked, speechless. He had not called her "peachie" in as long as she could remember. She watched him loosen his tie and pat her knee. Something extraordinary must have happened in Father Matthews's study. The "what if" questions became "what happened?"

Larry turned the car around in the driveway and headed toward the highway.

"So, how was your time with Father Matthews?" Mallie asked, trying to keep from sounding unnerved as she tried to imagine what might have caused his extreme mood swing.

"Great!" Larry said. "It was really great. Tom's a really bright guy. Straightforward. I liked him."

He drove without taking his eyes from the road, but Mallie could see that he was smiling. He cocked his head toward his right shoulder, his way of alerting her that he was about to make an important point. "Tom said we have a communication problem."

"He said *what?*" Mallie could barely get the words out. What on earth could the priest possibly have meant?

"You know—*communication*," Larry said. "He said our big problem's communication. He wants to meet with both of us together next week in his study. He's sure we can work things out."

Mallie felt dizzy. Incredible, she thought, insane. She had a flash of that scene from *Cool Hand Luke*—"What we have here is a failure to communicate." She tried to keep her voice steady. "What did you tell him?"

"Well, I told him about the stupid arguments we have at the breakfast table about the grapefruit. You know, about how mad you get when I click my teeth against the spoon eating grapefruit. About the pain-in-the-ass deal of going to your parents every Wednesday night for dinner. About how I thought we'd definitely decided to go skiing in Sun Valley with the boys for Christmas, and you called me at work and said to cancel everything—we weren't going—we couldn't afford it. All the same old, same old."

"That's all you told him?" Mallie knew her voice sounded accusatory. Not that those things were not true. They were the dust on the tabletops, not the pile of garbage in the middle of the floor.

"No, I told him some other stuff, too," Larry said. Facing directly into the setting western sun, he covered his squinting eyes with his Ray-Bans. "He said he thought the specific issues weren't so important—ours is basically a communication problem."

Mallie wanted to blast Father Matthews—or Tom Matthews—or whatever he called himself. How dare he? Waves of nausea rose in her throat. How dare he tell her husband they had a *communication problem* when he had heard only one side? And, obviously, not even the whole truth from one side. What about her side? What about all of Larry's denials and excuses for years? What about Monday night and the phone call? The attempted suicide? The hospital? And Larry's admission of his need for help? What kind of *communication problem* was that? She was crushed. She had pinned her hopes on Father Matthews. As they sat in the car, bound for Arkansas, Larry flicking the radio from station to station, her hopes were gone. The gulf between them was wider than before.

They crossed over the Harahan Bridge, the Mississippi River roiling beneath them, the Memphis skyline in silhouette behind them, the flat, winter-brown fields of Arkansas spread out ahead. Mallie stared out the side window, her skin crawling with frustration. She felt as if she were bound for hell. Of all the perfect ironies, they were headed for a duck hunting club called Paradise Lodge. Members referred to it simply as Paradise.

"Better make a run into Sportsman's One-Stop," Larry said, as they drove into West Memphis, the first town on the Arkansas side of the Mississippi River. Strip malls with brightly colored neon signs lined both sides of the highway. Eighteen-wheelers stood like circus elephants, side by side in front of the truck stops. "Everything will be shut down in Stuttgart by the time we get there tonight."

Mallie knew he was right. She had been going to Stuttgart on hunting weekends with her father, Samuel G. Malcolm II, since she was twelve. Before her father and a group of his friends started the Eden Lake Club, closer to Memphis, he had been a member of Paradise. She was familiar with the Sportsman's One-Stop. It had always been too late at night to get a hunting license in Stuttgart and no time before the early morning hunt. Like her father, Larry would want to be up at five a.m. to greet the guides. A Yankee moving to the South when he married Mallie, Larry had taken to hunting with the passion of a religious convert.

"Okay," she said. The weekend routine was so familiar that she slid complacently back into it—in spite of a nagging voice inside that wanted to stop right that minute and confront Larry with all her questions about his time with Father Matthews, all of her fears about the future of their marriage. But she knew it wouldn't do any good to confront him. He would be defensive, probably lie to her, and they would be even later getting to Stuttgart. *Just hold on*, she repeatedly told herself, *go along with him, get through the weekend.*

She wasn't the least bit hungry but agreed to stop at the Kentucky Fried Chicken drive-in. At least it meant she wouldn't have to warm up any leftovers at that hour. Larry drove while they opened the red and white striped boxes on their laps and listened to soft rock music on WMC-FM radio. Under a moonless sky, only the headlights and an occasional distant house light relieved the darkness of the straight, two-lane macadam highway.

She picked at the chicken breast and wondered how in the world she would keep up a pretense of normalcy in front of her friends through the whole weekend. One thing she could count on: Larry would sleep through the afternoon, following the early morning hunt and a Bloody Mary before lunch. She would play bridge with the other three women and go to bed early. He would stay up late playing poker with his friends. Their only time together would be in the mornings in the duck blind, but there would always be a guide nearby. There would be no chance for any intimate conversation.

Chapter Five

I n the predawn, Lucille, the longtime cook from Stuttgart, had already opened the kitchen and prepared breakfast. The three hunting guides, Shorty, Bobby Ray and Popeye, poured themselves mugs of hot coffee from the sideboard and pulled extra chairs up to the long rectangular table in the living room. A fire crackled and spat out sparks behind the wrought-iron screen on the wide stone hearth. Mallie and Cindy Morgan were the only women present; the other two wives preferred to sleep in. Larry, Ben Morgan, Gus Ballard, and Jamie McMahon, in various stages of hunting attire—Gus was still in his long red flannel pajama top—were helping themselves to loaded plates of scrambled eggs, hot greasy bacon, buttermilk biscuits and grits.

"Hey, big man," Ben Morgan said, standing up to greet Bobby Ray, his longtime favorite guide. He gave the guide's shoulder a friendly push. "What's goin' on out there?"

It was the standard question concerning the weather condition, the water levels, and the potential for a good shoot. Affable Ben was a vice-president of the Union Planters National Bank, a position he inherited from his father and grandfather. Advancement to president was inevitable. He had been Larry's first male friend in Memphis and had insisted that Larry become a member of the Paradise hunters group. Mallie had known Ben since childhood and, in fact, had been duck hunting with him and their fathers before she ever met Larry. Ben had flaming red hair, slightly muted by a few gray strands at the temples. From the time he turned sixteen, he had been in love with Cindy—Gus Ballard's sister, the redheaded girl he eventually married. As they grew older together, they looked more like twins than husband and wife.

"We got 'em today," Bobby Ray said. He was the oldest of the guides, his face as weathered as an old hunting boot. "'Bout forty degrees, overcast, plenty a water in the ponds. Lotta hungry birds flyin' south."

"How about Mojo?" Ben asked. "He still up to it?"

"That ol' dog'll fall out dead someday pickin' up birds," Bobby Ray said. His chocolate lab was getting past his prime, but he was still the best swimmer, the best finder of crippled ducks in Arkansas County.

Ben loved to tell newcomers the story of Mojo breaking ice to swim after a cripple one January morning when none of the other labs would get out of the boat, never mind put their paws in the icy water.

Ben assigned a guide to each couple, sending Mallie and Larry out with Popeye—as Mallie had requested. She and her father had hunted with Popeye from the time that she was a teenager. Through the years, his long, lean frame had bent over like an old cypress tree, but his reputation as a champion duck caller endured. Gus and Jamie went with Shorty, which left Ben and Cindy with Bobby Ray.

"Get them waders on, folks; we're ready to go," Popeye said.

The group divided into pairs and walked towards the waiting pickup trucks. Like soldiers going to battle, all were dressed in camouflage slickers and dark green waders. Each person carried a gun. The guides took the guns and boxes of shells and stacked them on the flatbed in the back of the truck. The dogs—Mojo, Babe and Dory—were tethered to the cabin windows and panted with anticipation.

Mallie sat close to Popeye, leaving room for Larry on the other side of a large rip in the old plastic seat covering, a dangerous spring about to poke through. A ride from hell, Mallie remembered from all her previous experiences. Bumps all the way. The narrow dirt road into the hunting area was rutted with water-filled potholes, and none of the pickups had much suspension or padding.

"You have enough room?" Larry asked.

"Fine," she said without looking at him. *As if he really cared*, she thought. She wondered why she had decided to go out. She could have slept in with the other women. Habit, maybe. It was what she had always done.

"How do you feel about that Georgia peanut farmer winning the election and becoming President of the United States?" Larry asked Popeye.

"He's okay with me," Popeye said. "I like his talk and they say he can catch a big brim just looking at the water."

Mallie knew her husband and her father had nothing but disdain for Jimmy Carter's liberal views. Sam Malcolm had been a staunch Southern Democrat until LBJ and the civil rights legislation. Sometime in the early seventies he switched to being a Republican. Larry's Rhode Island family had always been Republican. She knew Popeye's declaration of support for Jimmy Carter would end Larry's conversation with him about politics.

At a juncture in the road, the trucks separated, each guide taking a different route toward a particular pond. A single jon boat would be pulled up into the high grass at a place of entry.

"In you go, Mallie," Popeye said. He held her hand and led her toward the metal strut in the bow of the boat. "In the middle, sir," he directed Larry. He had not known Larry for all the years that he had known Mallie. She suspected that all the guides had some reservations about her husband's being a Yankee.

"Get on in there, girl." He popped Dory, his black Labrador retriever, on the backside, pushing her toward the space in the bottom of the boat between them. He shoved the long aluminum boat off the bank, jumped in and knelt onto the rear strut. On the fourth tug of the motor cord from his muscular right arm, the nine-horsepower Evinrude outboard spluttered and roared, then settled into a loud purr. He sat down, steering the long handle, and threading his way slowly through the canals into the open water.

Paradise leased thousands of acres of flooded land each year. Rice, millet and milo grew like weeds, creating the perfect feed for the ducks and the occasional geese flying south from Canada for the winter. Patches of woods and tall grasses provided the covering for the blinds. Decoys were carefully placed in small clusters in the open water to seduce the ducks into range in front of them. The idea was for the hunters to be tucked into the blinds just before sun-up. The guides usually stood close by on a high spot in the woods and did the calling. The real lure was the sound of a master duck caller. Popeye could blow that small wooden cylinder loud enough to break a flock of ducks flying in a V formation some six hundred yards away. If they started to come in and circle, he could perfectly mimic the low wobble of a duck feeding, guttural sounds like a man drowning.

After Mallie and Larry were settled into the blind, seated on the wide wooden bench across the back, Larry pulled out his thermos of hot coffee. "Want some?" he asked.

She shook her head. She tried not to drink anything in the blind. It was too much trouble to deal with all of the layers of clothes in the woods if she had to pee.

He took a flat silver flask of brandy out of his inside pocket and poured it into the steaming coffee mug. "This should warm things up," he said. "Sure you don't want any?"

"No, thanks." She thought of the countless mornings that she had sat in the same spot with her father, watching him slug bourbon from a nearly identical flask. Sometimes he didn't bother with the coffee.

She propped her 20-gauge shotgun against the seat between them and leaned forward in the blind. Through the wide opening, where they could spot the ducks flying high in the sky, and from which they would fire at the unsuspecting birds, she watched the soft pink light rising above the horizon line. It was her favorite time of the early morning hunt, the peaceful beginning before a shot was fired. In her art classes at school, she had painted the scene many times.

"Single circling," Popeye said, his voice a raspy whisper between calls.

Mallie lowered her head, reaching gingerly for her gun. Any quick movement or an exposed human face too close to the opening could spook a duck. A single was particularly skittish.

From beneath her hat brim, she followed the duck's flight path with her eyes, around and around again—then as Popeye switched seamlessly from his high, bleating calls to the low gurgling, feeding sounds, she heard the duck's wing-flapping descent toward the middle of the decoys. She would wait for Larry to shoot first. She had never really enjoyed firing her gun.

"Take it, Mallie." Larry abruptly whispered to her.

Without thinking, she stood and raised her gun to her shoulder. The mallard in her sight, she pulled the trigger twice. The duck twitched, falling to one side—then the splat of impact indicated a dead hit. A second later, its dark body splayed out on the surface of the water, the duck tried to flap one wing and lurched slightly forward.

"Oh my God," Mallie said. "It's still alive."

It had always been her horror to cripple a duck. On her first hunt she had been sick to her stomach when her father had wrung a wounded duck's neck in front of her. "Far kinder to kill it instantly," her father had said.

The more the struggling bird tried to move away, the more miserable Mallie felt. It was as if she herself were the wounded creature. She willed it to get up and fly away. *Please God, make it fly.* But she knew that was not possible. The lone drake—its metallic green feathers designating its male sex—had trusted the compelling sound of Popeye's duck calls and been fooled by the benevolent sight of the decoys. It had been mortally wounded by her hand.

"Get 'em, Dory," Popeye ordered his lab. The dog splashed into the water with all four feet and paddled toward the doomed duck.

Mallie turned away as Dory swam back across the open water to Popeye with the limp bird locked in her mouth.

"Good girl," Popeye said, taking the duck in his hand and warning Mallie not to look. Quickly and soundlessly, he wrenched its neck and tossed the lifeless body on the ground behind him.

Mallie sat back on the bench and put her gun down. "You take the rest," she said to Larry without looking at him. "I'm finished."

"What's the matter, peachie?" he said. "You've seen cripples before."

"I've had enough," she said. She didn't want to explain that she felt a part of her was lying on the ground.

Larry eventually killed three more mallards to reach their legal limit of keepers for the day. All three of them got into the boat to head for the truck. Popeye dropped Mallie and Larry off at Paradise and took the ducks home with him to have them picked, tagged and bagged for the Voses' trip back to Memphis.

Ben and Gus had finished early and were already drinking Bloody Marys and telling tales of the morning's shoot. The two women who had slept in were playing gin rummy, waiting for Cindy and Mallie to start the afternoon bridge game. Complaining of a headache, Mallie told her friends she needed to take a nap and that she would join them later.

Her room was still dark with the blinds closed. She crawled under the quilt with her clothes on to hide, to sleep, to forget.

But her mind would not leave her alone. There seemed to be no answers to her badgering questions about Larry, her frustration with Father Matthews. She had counted on the priest to help her. Jenny had said he was a wonderful, wise counselor. There was no wisdom in telling Larry that their marriage problems were about communication. Over and over she replayed the record of Larry's lies. She heard the woman's voice on the phone, thought about the suicide attempt. All of Mallie's fears collided like dodge-em cars in her head. Finally she slept.

As if an electrical jolt had woken her, she had an idea. On Monday morning, she would call Father Matthews and make an appointment to see him by herself. She would tell him everything Larry had obviously neglected to tell him. She would make him understand what was really going on in their marriage. Surely then he would see the real picture and help her. She nestled down into the soft mattress, knowing that she could get through the rest of the weekend.

Chapter Six

Monday morning, after Larry left for work and the boys had gone to school, Mallie phoned St. Michael's Episcopal Chapel. It was close to ten before the priest returned the call.

"Mallie, it's Tom Matthews," he said in a courteous, steady voice. "What can I do for you?"

Accumulated anger caused tightness in her throat; she wanted to accuse him: *You've already done enough damage*. Instead, she said, "Thanks for calling me back." She hesitated, then spoke carefully, "I need to see you, Father Matthews. I'd like to see you alone before Larry and I come for counseling together." She tried to sound calm.

"Of course," the priest said. "That's a good idea. Any chance you could come in this afternoon?"

She felt a rush of relief. "Yes," she said quickly.

"How about two o'clock?" he said. "And, by the way, Mallie, please call me Tom."

"I'll be there," she said. "Thank you." She hung up the phone and tossed her head, feeling her mane of dark brown hair swishing just above her shoulders and settling back in its natural pageboy. The tension in the muscles of her face released, her rigid spine bent in a gesture of gratitude. Thank God, she thought, she would have her chance to set things straight.

☞

St. Michael's Episcopal Chapel was tucked into a wooded lot in Victorian Village, an area of historic preservation in Memphis. Located near the medical center, it remained one of the only downtown residential neighborhoods in the mid-seventies still standing from the fifties blitz of urban renewal. To a casual observer, it was difficult to tell that the building was a chapel. Without the small pewter cross that was mounted next to the front door, the low modern rectangular structure could have been a residence. The sanctuary faced the back yard. To an architecture buff, the design was at least a century out of sync with its stately rococo Victorian neighbors. In further contrast to their manicured lawns and gardens, the grounds of the chapel were often neglected and overgrown.

St. Michael's had been conceived by Bishop Wagner, the progressive bishop of the West Tennessee diocese, to fill a need, as he saw it, for medical students and faculty who wanted pastoral counseling, and who, over time, might choose to attend Sunday services—perhaps even to join Episcopal confirmation classes. It was said that he had brought the Reverend Thomas Matthews in from a parish in Indiana. In less than two years of operation, both the chapel and its chaplain had developed a respected, albeit theologically liberal, reputation.

As Mallie walked through the front door, a woman she assumed was the chaplain's secretary looked up from her desk and smiled.

"You must be Mallie Vose," she said. "I'm Terry. Tom's got someone in his office, and he's running a little late." She was a pert, carrot-haired woman with a pencil stuck behind her ear. A pair of green hightop tennis shoes on her feet stuck out from under the desk. "Won't you have a seat? Can I get you a Coke?"

Except for the filigreed gold cross on a chain around her neck, the woman seemed an unlikely secretary for an Episcopal priest. Too casual, too much of an aging hippie. "No thanks," Mallie said, reaching over the desk to take Terry's hand. "Nice to meet you."

Behind Terry's desk a brass plate on a heavy mahogany door read Chaplain's Study. Mallie had an instant flash of Larry slouching through that door on Friday afternoon to meet Tom Matthews— she recalled the priest asking her on the phone that morning to call him "Tom" rather than "Father." Obviously from Larry's behavior in the car, he had walked out a completely different person.

"Mallie's such an unusual name," Terry said. "Is it a nickname?"

"You're not the first person to ask," Mallie said. "My real name is Valeria. I'm named for my grandmother and my Aunt Valeria, my father's sister. I've always felt strange about the name Valeria. It sounds so formal and grownup—not like me at all. My father always said I should be honored to carry that name. My maiden name was Malcolm. A boy in fourth grade started calling me Mallie. I liked it better."

Terry smiled. "I know what you mean. My real name's Theresa—I'm named for a saint. Terry suits me better." She spoke with an ease that made Mallie feel comfortable. "*Valeria* does sound like a lot to live up to." She lifted her nose in mock sophistication. "But I have to say, it's a beautiful name. Is this your first visit to St. Michael's?"

"It is," Mallie said. She turned to look around at the big, over-stuffed couches, the card table and the stone fireplace in the sitting room. It didn't seem like a church at all. "I'm a member at Holy Trinity," she added, in case Terry might question whether or not she was an Episcopalian. "May I see the sanctuary?"

"Of course." Terry bounced up from behind her desk and ushered Mallie through the side doorway of the sanctuary.

It was small, probably no more than twelve or fourteen pews on either side of a wide center aisle, soft white walls with rough-hewn wooden beams, brick floors and a window behind the pulpit that framed the sculptural winter branches of a spreading oak tree. Mallie was touched by the simplicity and serenity. She decided to kneel in one of the back pews. It occurred to her to say a prayer.

Mallie closed her eyes and tried to let go of her skepticism of religion. What had once been so important and meaningful in her life had been on a jagged path of disillusion for years. She had been a devout Roman Catholic child. The whole Malcolm family was Roman Catholic, originally from County Clare in Ireland. Neither of her parents ever went to church except for Christmas and Easter, but as early as she could remember, her grandmother, Nannie Malcolm, had taken her to Mass on Sunday mornings. Mallie had made her First Communion when she was seven and carried rosary beads in her purse for years.

By the middle of her freshman year at Sweet Briar College, Mallie had begun to question the basic tenets of Catholicism—partially in response to her philosophy and psychology courses. Kant. Hegel. Freud. Jung. Confronting the issue of "absolute truth." There was no way there could be "absolute truth" in such a complex world, she thought. Shortly thereafter, she began to have doubts about the divinity and the omnipotence of the Pope. So much of the Catholic teaching seemed out of sync with the modern world. The sin of birth control, of divorce. Even as she questioned what sin really was, and as remote as birth control and divorce were from her personal life, she could not see those things as punishable by God, no matter who or what God really was.

The final blow to her beliefs was struck when she spent the fall semester during her junior year in college taking painting classes at the Villa Mercedes in Florence, Italy. She was appalled by the juxtaposition of the opulent cathedrals surrounded by dingy buildings on dirty streets. All the beauty and comfort of the Catholic Church that she had so loved as a child disappeared as she watched the clusters of weary women holding bedraggled, bandaged children in their arms, begging for money on the church steps. Going into Mass one morning, she happened to see a man in a collar—was he a priest, or a man pretending to be a priest?—outside the church open a flap of his oversized black coat that held packages of cigarettes in layered pockets. Several other men surrounded him, haggling over the price. The sacredness was gone for her. She stopped going to Mass.

When she had been in Italy just long enough to feel slightly homesick, one of her roommates talked her in to going to a service at St. James Episcopal Church, known as the American Church in Florence. That morning the choir came marching in behind the American flag and the Episcopal flag, singing "God Bless America." Tears welled in Mallie's eyes. Instantly, she felt at home. So much of the liturgy and the prayers were the same as those she knew so well from the Catholic service, but they were spoken in English. The hymns and the camaraderie afterward appealed to her. She and her roommate joined the choir, mostly made up of expat Americans. After attending the American Church nearly every Sunday while she was in Italy, it had been an easy decision for Mallie to take Episcopal confirmation classes when she returned home to Memphis. She and Larry were married in the Episcopal Church.

Through the years, and particularly after Sammy, her first child, was born, she found that Sunday morning was her only time for herself. While Larry played tennis, she could actually read a book, occasionally without interruption. Then she had two more boys. She had no time for herself, even on Sunday. When the boys were old enough to go to Sunday school at Holy Trinity, she tried going to the nine a.m. service. She began to get distracted by phrases in the *Book of Common Prayer* like "angels and archangels and all the company of heaven." She could not stop the visions of adorable cupids floating around in the heavens. It all seemed so detached and superfluous. Also, she felt as if all the parishioners were the same Saturday night at the Country Club crowd dressed in their

Sunday clothes. There was nothing spiritually meaningful there for her, so once again, she stopped going to church.

On her knees with her eyes closed in the quiet of St. Michael's Chapel, the memory of her Catholic childhood devotion and the comfort of the faith she had once found in the Episcopal Church in Italy came back to her. She was aware that in the busyness of her family life, something important to her had been missing. Maybe she should try going to church again. She looked up to see Terry still standing, waiting for her in the doorway.

"Are there services in this chapel on Sunday?" Mallie asked.

"Oh, yes," Terry said. "It's usually filled up with nurses and medical students. Besides his pastoral counseling, Tom's the chaplain to the University of Tennessee Medical School, you know."

"Do other people from outside the medical community ever come to the service?"

"Of course," Terry said. "Tom's got a big following—often including some of the people he's counseling." She turned quickly back toward her desk. "I think I hear him." She motioned for Mallie to follow her.

Chapter Seven

Mallie felt an anxious rise in her pulse when she saw Father Matthews standing in the entrance to his study. He was even taller than she remembered and far more handsome, not as old. His craggy face softened when he smiled. He wore a gray tweed jacket over his dark shirt and white-banded collar.

"Hello, Mallie," the priest said. His voice in person had a sensuous resonance; it seemed to enter her skin. He did not move but stretched out his hand to greet her. "Forgive me for running late. It's an occupational hazard of mine. Come on in." He took her hand and guided her past him into his office.

His study looked like a scholar's library: dark brown wood paneling that surrounded burgeoning book shelves and an aging Oriental rug across the center. Books covered every surface: the shelves, his desk, the couch, the floor. He pointed to an empty chair near the corner of his desk. "Have a seat," he said. "Or maybe you'd be more comfortable on the couch. I could move the books."

"This is fine," Mallie said. She sat down on the edge of the chair.

Father Matthews pulled another chair out from behind his desk and sat slightly across from her. "So, tell me why you're here. You sounded somewhat distressed on the phone." His tone was formal but kind.

Underneath his thick, dark rimmed glasses, she could see the softness of his gray-blue eyes. A rush of anger returned to her throat. *You should know why I'm here!* She tried to speak, but no words would come out.

He reached over and took her hand. "Take a breath," he said. His hand was warm and strong.

She shut her eyes, a reflex to hold back tears. "I'm so sorry. I didn't want to do this."

"You haven't done anything, Mallie," he said. "You're safe here. Take your time." He let go of her hand and sat back in his chair, an indication that he had all the time in the world.

She waited for what seemed like an eternity. Finally she took another breath and began to speak. "I can't believe you told Larry our only problem was *communication*. I can't believe—did you really say that to him?"

"All marriages have problems of communication," the priest said quickly. "It's part of human relationships. I guess you could say all *people* have problems with communication."

"But didn't Larry tell you anything about the women in his life—about Julie?"

"No," he said. He crossed his arms, not changing his expression. "He didn't mention any other women. Who's Julie?"

Oh God, Mallie shuddered. *Of course, he didn't.* "I guess I should tell it from the beginning." She looked hard at Father Matthews to be certain she had his approval.

"You can say whatever you need to say in this room," he said. His voice was gentle, assuring, without any tinge of judgment. He folded his hands in his lap.

Mallie held her eyes closed for a few seconds. Could she really tell him her secrets, all those things she had been hiding for so long? She had never talked to a priest—Catholic or Episcopalian—about anything personal. Yet here she was about to tell Father Matthews about her husband's affairs—the attempted suicide—and her terrifying fear of what might happen to her, to her marriage. She wanted to trust Father Matthews. If she did not tell someone about the lies in her life, Mallie felt as if she might shatter into a thousand pieces. She cleared her throat. "I thought we had a perfect marriage for the first two years. Ups and downs—disagreements, of course—but nothing major. The first time we were separated for longer than a few days at a time was in 1962, the summer after Sammy was born. Sammy's our first son—he's away at St. George's School in Rhode Island. Anyway, that summer Larry was sent out to California for a week of sales calls."

She stopped, realizing she needed to explain to the priest about Larry's job. Right after they were married, Larry went to work for her father at Malcolm Brothers Hardware, a wholesale distributor company that her grandfather started in the 1920s. Her father had told her husband that if he worked really hard he might someday be president. For the first two years Larry stayed close to home, traveling as a sales rep to Arkansas and Mississippi, then as the company began to grow, he was sent all over the country.

"So, on that particular business trip to California," she said, "he stopped in Seattle over the weekend to be an usher in a Princeton friend's wedding. I took Sammy—just a baby at the time—to our little cabin on my parents' property at Pickwick Lake.

"I picked up the telephone on Sunday afternoon. It was long distance—a woman's voice asking to speak to Larry. I thought maybe the call might have had something to do with one of his clients, so I said, 'This is Mallie Vose. Is there a message you'd like to leave for my husband?'"

Mallie took a deep breath before she spoke again. "There was silence on the other end of the line. Then the woman said, 'Oh, my God, I thought you might be his mother. I didn't know he was married. Please forgive me.' And she hung up."

Saying those words, recalling the memory, caused Mallie's throat to tighten.

The priest sat quietly waiting for her to speak again. After a few moments of silence, he said, "How did that call make you feel?"

Mallie put her hand over her eyes, then dropped it in her lap. "I remember staring at that little black telephone as if it were a snake that had bitten me. I knew instantly that Larry had lied to someone. I didn't want to believe it. I tried to convince myself that the woman had misunderstood—Larry couldn't have told her he wasn't married—he wouldn't do that. But I knew. I knew."

"So, how did you handle the situation?" the priest asked.

"I packed up Sammy and went home. I didn't say anything to anyone about it. I kept trying to convince myself there must be some explanation. I tried to stay busy and not think about it until Larry got home. But I began having terrible cramps in my stomach; I couldn't eat."

"How long was he away?"

"Four more days," she said. "When he finally walked in the door—it was a Thursday night, as I remember—I didn't want him to touch me. When he started towards me, I blurted out the story of the phone call."

She hesitated. The priest said, "And then?"

Mallie shook her head. "He started laughing." The remembrance of his laughter seemed even more absurd to her as she repeated it to Father Matthews. "I mean it, he was laughing. I was so shocked at the time."

"What did he say?"

"He stood right in front of me and said, 'Oh Mallie, I'm so sorry. It had to have been that former Miss Washington I sat next to at the bridal dinner in Seattle. It was nothing. I can't believe she called. My friends said she had a crush on me and they thought it would be a lark if I didn't tell her I was married—you know, sort of a joke for a night. When the dinner was over, I told her if she ever wanted to talk to pick up the phone, but I never thought she'd actually call. I must have given her the Pickwick number. We'd all had a lot to drink.'"

"Did you believe him?" the priest said.

Mallie shook her head, as if in retelling the story, she couldn't believe she had been so gullible. "He convinced me the woman meant nothing to him. He assured me nothing like that would ever happen again." She sat back in her chair. "That was sixteen years ago."

"But it wasn't the only time such an incident took place. Is that right?" The priest obviously knew the answer to his question.

"Right," she said, hearing the sarcasm in her own voice. "There've been more *incidents* than I can count. Anonymous, threatening letters. One woman's letter said that Larry had rented an apartment in some new building in downtown Memphis and was sleeping with her daughter. There was another with a newspaper clipping about a wife catching her husband in bed with another woman. That one included a note that suggested I needed to hire a lawyer. I told Larry about them. He always had an explanation. It was only after this last time, after Julie—a woman in his office he's obviously been having an affair with—called me on the phone and then tried to kill herself—"

"Tried to kill herself?" The priest leaned forward and interrupted her in mid-sentence. "What do you mean? What happened?"

"She took an overdose—her friend called our house—Larry went to the hospital. She's okay. He says she's okay." Mallie took another breath, a sigh. "But I knew I couldn't pretend anymore. That night I felt like everything was over. My marriage, my reputation, everything. When Larry asked for help and you agreed to see him, I thought maybe there was some hope." She held back tears. "And you told him our problem was *communication*."

The priest shook his head. "I could only deal with the facts as he told them to me." He sounded sincerely apologetic, as if he wished he had known more of the real situation when he met with Larry. "It must have been an extremely difficult time for you. Suicide's a very serious matter."

"I knew I had to see you by myself," Mallie said.

"Good." The priest leaned forward in his chair, nodding to her. "You made a good decision. Whether you know it or not, you've made a decision to live—no matter what Larry does—or ever did—or what might happen to your marriage."

Mallie closed her eyes. What did that mean—a decision to live? All she could see were Larry's tears, his slumping body and his cry for help. She didn't want a divorce—surely it wouldn't come to that—but she didn't want to live with lies and other women anymore either.

"I'm glad you came today," the priest said.

Thank God. Mallie felt a deep relief. She had done the right thing by seeing him alone. He understood. She trusted him. "Father Matthews, do you think there's any hope for our marriage?"

Taking an instructor's stance, he said, "When a broken marriage is healed, it's often stronger than one that's never been broken."

She nodded her agreement. She had broken her right leg in her early thirties, when she and Larry were on a trip to New Orleans. It had taken nearly a year to heal, but it was stronger than her left leg.

"I think I should meet with the two of you individually for some period of time before I meet with you as a couple," the priest said.

Mallie felt another rush of relief. She liked the idea of meeting with him alone again.

"And, if you wouldn't mind," he said, "I'd prefer that you called me Tom rather than 'Father.' I think it would work better for both of us in an ongoing counseling situation."

"Forgive me," Mallie said. "'Father' is a habit from my Catholic childhood. I've always thought of priests as 'Father.' But I will—I'd like to call you Tom." She couldn't imagine being able to talk to any of the Catholic priests that she had known in the past the way she talked to him.

He took out a small black leather book and a pen from his shirt pocket. "Great," he said. "That's settled. Could you come here at this same time next Tuesday?"

Mallie reached into the confusion of her purse for her own date book. Makeup. Hairbrush. Checkbook. Bills to be mailed. School activities schedule. Kleenex. A little yellow box of Chiclets. She studied her calendar: a book club meeting every other Tuesday morning, carpools every afternoon except Tuesdays and Thursdays. Tennis. Board meetings. "Two o'clock Tuesday would be fine," she said.

After he gave her a few guidelines of what to share with Larry during the week—and what not to share: nothing about their individual counseling sessions, nothing about Julie or the attempted suicide—they both stood in recognition that the session was over. Tom put his arms around her and gave her a firm, warm hug. "This was a good beginning, Mallie," he said.

She closed her eyes and for a second she wanted to melt into Tom Matthews. Not since she first knew Larry had she felt that a man could be so immediately empathetic, so accepting of her. He pulled away, then lightly kissed her on the side of her forehead. She looked at his face. Behind the glasses she saw an expression of compassion. She had definitely come to the right person. "Thank you," she said. "Thank you so much."

He patted her shoulder as she turned to leave. "God bless you, Mallie," he said. "See you next week."

Chapter Eight

n the week that followed, Mallie was surprised at the number of times she thought of Tom Matthews. She found that she was not only holding mental conversations with him, telling him what she was thinking and feeling, her doubts and fears about the future of her marriage, her painful past experiences with Larry's infidelities—expecting the priest's positive response—but she was also looking forward to another hug at the end of the session. The way he held her and said "God bless you" had filled her with warmth, a sense of worth. He cared about her. She wanted more of it. By the time two p.m. Tuesday afternoon came around, she felt both excited and anxious. Would he be the patient listener, the consoling person she remembered him to be? Surely their second session would be at least as meaningful to her as the first one.

When Mallie walked into St. Michael's, Terry greeted her with the same open, positive smile. "Hi there," she said, looking up from her typewriter. "As usual, I'm afraid he's a little late." She nodded toward the closed door of the chaplain's study. "I don't think he'll be much longer."

"I love your shoes," Mallie said, referring to Terry's green tennis shoes peeking out from under her desk. In her mind those shoes seemed so out of place in the chapel. Mallie could never have worn anything like that, but rather than say nothing or ask a question about why someone did something she considered odd, she often called attention to the situation by paying a compliment. It was a southern trait she knew about herself—the desire to please, to always say something nice, even if she knew it was not wholly true.

Terry smiled. "I started wearing them when I had foot surgery a few years ago. Now they're like my old friends."

Before they could continue the conversation, the door opened and Tom Matthews appeared, shaking his head. "So sorry to keep you waiting." He beckoned to Mallie to follow him into his study. "Good to see you," he said, giving her a quick hug as he closed the door behind them. "Come. Have a seat. Tell me about your week."

Mallie took a deep breath, sorting out quickly what she wanted to say. She wanted to please the priest. "Well, we did what you suggested. It was hard—at least for me—but Larry and I didn't talk about anything having to do with Julie or the suicide attempt. Nothing about either of our counseling sessions."

"What did you talk about?" he asked.

"The boys mostly. David's training Bingo to fetch—he's our two-year-old yellow lab— so he and his father can take him hunting. Larry took them both out to Shelby Forest on Saturday to try Bingo out in the lake. I went to one of Troy's football games. We talked about that. We tried to keep things as normal as possible, just as you recommended."

"And how did you feel about your time alone with Larry?"

"It was awkward," she said. "Really strange. It's as if we're walking around each other in the same house but it's not the same. We're not the same." Mallie felt some confusion over telling Tom her real feelings. The truth was that she had experienced moments when she looked at Larry and no longer felt that she wanted to try to make her marriage work. She certainly didn't want to be divorced, but she could not imagine going through the rest of her life not trusting her husband, constantly worried about other women and his lies. She had given her vow to God as well as to Larry when they were married. The idea of wanting to break it, to have a different life, made her feel like a bad person. As much as she wanted to be truthful with Tom about her feelings, she didn't want him to think she was a bad person. She didn't want to think that about herself. "When I look at Larry, sometimes I feel as if something has gone away, or maybe died. I just don't feel anything, any attraction to Larry anymore."

"Do you remember what it was that attracted you to Larry in the first place?" Tom asked. "Can you talk about that?"

"Oh Tom," she sighed as she spoke. "He was so handsome. So much fun to be with. Such a good dancer. He was so attentive to me—and he had such big ideas of what he wanted to do in life. I'd never met anyone like him, certainly no one I knew growing up in Memphis."

"Larry wasn't from Memphis?" Tom asked.

"No, no," Mallie said, shaking her head, as if it were so obvious that Larry wasn't southern. She was surprised Tom didn't recognize it—particularly since he was not southern himself. "Larry's from Providence, Rhode Island. He didn't move to Memphis until after we were married."

"Then how did you meet him?" Tom asked.

"At a debut party in New York City during Christmas vacation," Mallie said. His question opened a book of memories she had long since closed. The tradition of families giving elaborate parties based on the idea of "making a debut into society" was very prevalent among her friends in the North as well as the South at that time. "My roommate at Sweet Briar lived in New York and invited me to spend a few days with her before going home to Memphis."

"Tell me about it," the priest said.

Mallie's story of spotting Larry across a balloon-festooned ballroom of the Union Club came alive for both of them as she told it to Tom Matthews. "I watched him dance with one of my friends and decided he was not only the handsomest boy at the party—movie-star handsome, a blond Cary Grant—but he was also as graceful as Gene Kelly. I asked a friend who he was. She said everyone knew Larry Vose. She was surprised I didn't know him. He was apparently a famous Princeton lacrosse star. The amazing thing was that he walked right up to me a few minutes later and said 'Hi, I'm Larry Vose. You want to dance?'"

"Well, he obviously spotted you, too," Tom Matthews said, implying that she must have been one of the standout beautiful girls at the party.

Mallie smiled. "I felt like Leslie Caron when we danced; he was so easy to follow. When we sat down to talk, it turned out we had so much in common. Besides loving to dance, we both smoked Pall Mall cigarettes, although I never liked smoking. I just pretended I did to be sophisticated. He knew my cousin Margie Montell from Chicago. They were on a ship together when Larry's lacrosse team went to England and Margie was on a European tour with my Aunt Peggy. Larry and I talked and talked and he never danced with anyone else that night. I felt as though we had known each other always. I thought I was in heaven."

She rolled her eyes at Tom Matthews, as if to admit what a fool she had been. In spite of all her current feelings of contradiction and confusion—her lost trust—she knew she had fallen completely in love with Larry that night in New York. For days, weeks after meeting him, she couldn't stop seeing his face in her mind's eye. His gray-green eyes, long dark eyelashes, his small, perfect ears and his smile—slightly crooked—his whole face crinkled when he smiled. His unruly blond hair looked as if it might need a currycomb, and one of his straight white teeth lapped slightly over the other, a tiny identifying imperfection.

"We began writing letters to each other every day," Mallie said. "I could hardly wait to go to my box and see his handwriting. I went to Princeton for weekends. He came to Sweet Briar. He asked me to marry him before I ever met his parents or he met mine."

"That was quite a fast courtship," Tom Matthews said.

"The problem was that he was a senior about to graduate; I was a sophomore, an art major. I had signed up for a semester in Florence, Italy, to study painting during my junior year. It had been my dream before I met Larry. But then, after that, I didn't want to go. I could hardly bear to leave him."

"What did you do?" Tom asked.

"Fortunately, my parents—particularly my mother—insisted that I go. I agreed on the condition they would allow me to drop out of college and get married in June, at the end of my junior year."

Tom Matthews shook his head. He asked her how she felt all these years later about leaving college before graduating. Mallie said that nothing could have stopped her from wanting to marry Larry, not even her art.

"It never mattered to me that I didn't finish," Mallie said. "I wasn't an academic. From the time I was a child, I just wanted to be married and have a family."

"How was your time in Florence?" Tom asked. "Were you able to enjoy your painting classes?"

"Oh yes," Mallie said without hesitation. "It's hard to imagine now but I really believed that I was an artist in Florence." She had instant recall of her days at the Villa Mercedes. "I lived and breathed my work. My fingernails were black from charcoal. I had paint on all my clothes. When I wasn't in the studio, I spent hours wandering the streets of Florence, in and out of the churches and the Uffizi Gallery. It was bliss. At times I even forgot about Larry." She closed her eyes. "I'm afraid I've lost whatever talent I had. I'm not really an artist anymore."

"An artist is always an artist," Tom said. "It's a gift you're born with. Why did you stop painting?"

What a question, Mallie thought. She wanted to laugh. There was not a moment in her life when she could find the time to paint. She had delivered three boys in less than five years and essentially raised them alone. Larry had traveled as a salesman for the hardware company three weeks out of four for years. She closed her eyes for a moment. Besides her lack of time, Mallie thought, there was really no place in the house to set up an easel or a large table. She had stored all of her Italian brushes and colored pencils, her palette, and her old drawing pads in a corner of the attic. "I've done a thousand paintings in my head," she said. "It's my escape. Sometimes I realize I've been dreaming of painting for hours. I can even smell it."

Tom shook his head. "With the boys in school, surely you could find the time now."

The idea had often, fleetingly, crossed her mind. "I haven't picked up a pencil or a brush in years," she said. "I don't know if I still could. Now I'm just a board member of the Art Academy." She thought of her monthly meetings, the trouble it took to get a babysitter to look after the boys while she went to listen to men and women, mostly older than she, some of whom she had known as her parents' friends, talk about how to raise money. Although it made her feel important to be there, she knew in her heart she didn't belong there—she and Larry were in no position to be financial contributors—but she was also aware that the Academy expected her to be a conduit to her father and to Malcolm Brothers' resources.

"Okay, so if Larry was from Rhode Island, how did you end up living in Memphis?" Tom asked.

Mallie explained that from Larry's first visit to Memphis, he had loved her family and friends, the relatively warm winter that would allow him to play golf most Saturdays, and, of course, the hunting opportunities—duck, quail, dove, wild turkey—so close by in Arkansas and Mississippi. "When we got engaged," she said, "my father offered Larry a job at Malcolm Brothers and he accepted."

"Were you happy about that?" Tom asked.

Mallie considered his question. Part of her had imagined that

Larry would work in Providence or New York and she had felt a certain excitement about that. Another part of her felt comfortable with the idea that they would have a life like her parents. She wondered if, at the time, she had really felt she had a right to offer her opinion. It had been her husband's right to decide what he did for a living and where he did it.

"I think I was happy about it," Mallie said. "My father and Larry got along so well in those days. I thought it was a great opportunity for him. Since I didn't have a brother, the idea was that he would someday follow my father as president of the company. And everyone—all my friends—liked Larry. It felt so natural to me."

Mallie saw flashes of the early days of her marriage. The night she had tried to cook fried chicken—the burnt outside and raw inside—her tears, Larry's sympathy, his immediate response of taking her out to dinner. The blue velvet robe he gave her for their first Christmas together. The sex—the awakening, the thrill she felt from his touch. All she had wanted in those days was to be with Larry.

"What was your married life in Memphis like?" Tom asked.

Mallie thought about his question. As best she remembered it, life had been easy in Memphis in the early sixties. Or so it seemed at the time. Friendships were passed down from generation to generation and the old families still ruled. She was from an old family and Larry, as her husband, was immediately accepted. There was so much tradition about the way they lived, going to her parents' house for dinner on Wednesday nights, just as her parents had once gone to her grandparents' house when she was growing up, dressing up the boys to go to an annual social party on Christmas morning, joining the right secret society during the Memphis Cotton Carnival. Larry fit right in and seemed to enjoy all of it. He was given a junior membership in the Memphis Country Club, not only an invitation to the camaraderie of the weekend golf games and the Men's Taproom, but also the only place in town where they could go out to dinner on a

Saturday night with their friends without lugging liquor bottles in brown paper bags. In those days of dry counties, only the clubs could serve mixed drinks. They often drank too much on weekends and certainly they lived beyond their means.

"One of our problems from the beginning was that we always looked rich," Mallie said, "the way we lived in a big house and all—but we aren't and never were. My father bought the house we live in. He worked out some sort of a tax thing for Larry to pay him rent, then a few years ago my father turned it over to us rent-free. When we started going to Watch Hill with the boys for our summer vacation, Larry's parents gave us a house."

"What's Watch Hill?" Tom asked.

"A summer resort in Rhode Island," she said. "It's where Larry's family has had a place for generations. I fell in love with it the first summer he took me there. The cool, sunny climate. Swimming and tennis every day. The boys love it there to this day." A deep crease formed on Mallie's forehead. "It's also the place we got into trouble years ago."

"What do you mean, trouble?" As fast as they were shifting subjects, Tom was following her train of thought wherever it led.

Mallie told Tom about the Sunday morning she was cleaning up the living room and discovered one of Larry's old friend Louise's gold hoop earrings under the pillows of the couch. A group of friends had come back to the house after the Saturday night Yacht Club dance. Mallie had been tired from playing in a tennis tournament and had gone to bed earlier than usual. She had watched Louise—by then, her friend as well as Larry's—flirt with Larry at the dance, but she'd paid little attention. Lots of women flirted with Larry. He told her once that Louise's nickname in high school had been "Easy, squeezie, Weezie." That night, Mallie had seen them dancing together, both of Louise's arms around Larry's neck, The Four Tops record playing "Baby I Need Your Lovin,'" one of hers and Larry's favorite songs. Mallie knew she should have stayed up until everyone left, at least until Louise left. She would never know what really happened. She had thrown the earring in the trash and never mentioned it to Larry, or to anyone—up until now.

As Mallie finished telling Tom about the summer in Watch Hill, she saw him glance at his watch. Their time was up. He stood and opened both his arms to her. She rose from her chair and let him encircle her. For a second she wished she had not talked so much about the past. All those details about meeting Larry and those things about her art and Watch Hill and living in Memphis. Had any of that conversation been really meaningful? But Tom had encouraged her to talk about those things. Standing there in his office with his arms around her, Mallie hated for the session to end. She felt an affirmation that lifted her from the perplexities of her fractured, uncertain life with Larry. She wished a week could magically disappear so that Tuesday would come around and she could be with Tom again.

Chapter Nine

The following Tuesday could not come soon enough for Mallie. All week she had felt as if she were playing the role of a good wife, saying only what she thought she should say, asking only those questions she should ask of her husband. She hoped he had a good day at the office. Was he planning to go hunting over the weekend? Even her contact with the boys felt staged. She fixed meals, did laundry and drove carpools, but she felt detached from the deep connection with each of them that had been such a sustaining part of her life from the time they were born.

Walking into Tom's office, Mallie left the pretense behind. While he still had his arms around her in his way of greeting her, her emotions began spilling out. "Oh Tom, I just don't know how I can keep on doing this," she said.

He broke away and motioned for her to sit down. "Let's talk about it," he said. "Tell me."

"I feel as if I am living this phony life. I don't say anything I mean. He answers me in monosyllables. It all feels crazy." Mallie was shaking her head. She felt her hands clenching, as if something was about to explode inside of her. "The worst part is that I don't think I care anymore. About Larry, I mean."

"Mallie, this is a very difficult time for you, for both of you,"

Tom said. "But it's important that you try to stay focused on developing an understanding of who you are and what your life is really about, whether you are married to Larry or not. That's what you are doing here."

"But I feel so phony," she said. "I just want my life to be the way it was when we first got married."

"Life never stays the same, Mallie," he said. "What we have to do is the work to understand how we make decisions about what it is that is important to us. Then when life presents us with difficulties, we are better prepared to know how to make the changes we need to make."

Tom's voice was comforting to Mallie. Just being in the room with him was comforting. Still, she was not sure she understood what he meant. Changes? Changes in herself? Changes in her marriage? "How do I do that?" she asked.

"You said you wanted to go back to your early days with Larry. Let's talk about how you felt about yourself and your life with Larry after you began having children."

Mallie knew she could recall that time. She began talking as if she were reading from a diary. "In those days, Larry was hardly ever at home," she said. "We rarely talked on the phone. I was too exhausted to talk at night—and long distance was expensive. Our weekends were strained. He'd come home wanting to relax and have a home-cooked meal. I'd feel desperate to get a babysitter and get out of the house. We argued a lot."

"Did you make love?" the priest asked, lacing his fingers in his lap. "Besides the procreation times, I mean?"

Mallie lowered her eyes. It would be difficult to explain. Sex. How could she explain the truth about their sex life? "I thought about it all the time when he was away," she said quietly. "I used to have daydreams about being this beautiful, sexy, loving wife, waiting for Larry to come home and imagining that he would take me off to some magical place where we would make love all night.

For a time, I read Tom Robbins's books—*Roadside Attraction, Even Cowgirls Get the Blues*—do you know about those books?" she asked. The priest shook his head. "Really graphic, sensual books, unlike anything I had ever read," she said. "I could hardly wait for Larry to come home. But, more often than not, when we'd start to make love, I'd hear one of the boys cry and I'd have to jump out of bed. Or I'd start worrying about not putting in my diaphragm. Or—" Mallie felt tears forming. She shook her head. "It got really frustrating. You know—" Could she really tell Tom that sometimes she would lose the desire or Larry would lose an erection? "I began to worry about it all the time. I felt horrible. I thought our sex life was over, that I couldn't make him happy."

"Do you realize how normal that is?" Tom spoke softly.

Mallie shook her head again. "I didn't think it was normal at all. I thought there was something wrong with me—that I was a failure as a wife." As she spoke those words, her mind created the scene of her visit to Dr. Blagen before she was married. He was the gynecologist her mother had sent her to see for instruction. Knowing she was a virgin, the doctor had bluntly said, "So Mallie, do you want to ask questions or do you want me to just tell you?"

"Just tell me," she had said.

"It's really simple," Dr. Blagen looked at her over his half glasses and spoke as if he were the Delphic Oracle revealing the great secret of the universe. "It's the screw in the wheel that keeps the whole wagon going. If the sex is okay, honey, the wagon goes the whole distance. If it's not, the wheel comes off and the wagon falls in the ditch."

When Mallie heard herself tell Tom about Dr. Blagen's analysis of sex in marriage, she had the urge to laugh. "For years I had a mental picture of our wagon stuck in a ditch," she said. "I knew Dr. Blagen was serious, but it was so silly. I began to picture Larry and me wandering around the ditch wondering what to do next."

Tom smiled for a moment, then asked seriously, "Are you telling me that you thought it was purely what you perceived as a sexual failure that has caused all the problems in your marriage?"

She nodded. "I kept hoping it would change—go back to the way things were with us when we were first married—before I knew he was involved with someone else."

Tom listened without changing his expression. "Were there many occasions when you specifically knew about another woman?"

She nodded. "One of the worst nights was at a house party after a summer wedding in Clarksdale, Mississippi. Do you know the Delta?"

"Only by literary reference," Tom said. "Tennessee Williams's plays. Eudora Welty. I love Faulkner. Read all his books. Tell me about it."

Mallie and Larry had many friends in the Delta—Tunica, Clarksdale, and Greenville, Mississippi. From the memory vault of their various social visits—dove shoots, weddings or debut parties—she sketched out for Tom the grand lawns and gardens of the Delta, the opulence of their social events.

"That night in Clarksdale, the wedding began at eight to avoid the excessive heat of a July day," she said. "After a lot of champagne and dancing and a late supper on the lawn, Larry and I went to bed in an upstairs guestroom around two in the morning. I woke up at four and Larry was gone." She closed her eyes for a second. "I couldn't imagine where he was. In my nightgown, I crept down the stairs to find him lying on the floor next to our hostess, his pajamas hanging loose." She stopped and took a breath. "He didn't see me. I stood at the bottom of the stairs staring at them in disbelief then I slunk back up and sat on the landing, wide awake for at least an hour, trying to sort out how I felt. I couldn't decide if I was angrier at Larry—or at my hostess, who was, supposedly, a friend—or if was I angry at myself."

"Why would you have been angry at yourself?" Tom asked.

"Oh Tom, it was that same old thing. I always thought there was something I did—or didn't do—that caused Larry to get involved with other women."

Tom shook his head. "It's hard for me to believe."

"There were so many strange situations with other women. One time, years ago, I was on a business trip with Larry in New Orleans when I tripped on the edge of the sidewalk and broke my tibia in four places. I had to stay in the hotel for three days with my lower leg in a cast on a raised pillow. Larry spent the time shopping in the French Quarter. He brought me flowers and a pair of pale pink lace bikini panties. Then the strangest thing—he showed me another pair for his secretary Rosa." How ridiculous that situation sounded when she described it.

"He told you he was taking his secretary a pair of lace panties?" Tom could not disguise his skepticism.

"Yes, and if you could see Rosa, I mean, she's quite pretty in a candy box way, but she's definitely a bit overweight—not Larry's type at all." The idea of Rosa wearing those bikini panties under her prim navy blue suit had given Mallie a momentary smile, but at the same time she had not been able to stop wondering. Could there have been something going on between Larry and Rosa? But surely he wouldn't have shown Mallie the panties if anything had been going on with Rosa.

"Of course, the real question I should have asked was if he was not planning to give the panties to Rosa or to me, who did he buy them for?"

Then she told Tom about finding the letters.

"He left a packet of love letters in his open suitcase?" Tom leaned forward as if to challenge a completely implausible assertion. It was the first time since she brought up Julie's attempted suicide that he questioned her in mid-sentence. Since their first meeting in his study, Tom had listened to her stories with very few comments, at least not until she finished.

"With a ribbon around them," Mallie said. "I knew I shouldn't have read them. I just couldn't help it." She had lived with her mother's adage that "you get what you deserve if you read someone else's mail."

Mallie and Larry had gone on a week's trip to the beach in Destin, Florida, with her sister Anne and Anne's husband. The men had gone deep-sea fishing on the first morning, leaving the women to unpack and do the grocery shopping. The letters—a stack of six or seven—were under his folded polo shirts like a partially hidden golden egg waiting to be discovered on Easter morning.

"They were from women all over the world," she began. "One was from London. One from Bermuda. Another from Philadelphia, a woman named Georgia." Mallie's voice went flat, as if speaking about the letters was draining all the emotional air out of her. "The letter from Georgia asked if he'd gotten his divorce yet." She remembered how shaken she had been to see the word *divorce* actually written in reference to her—to her marriage. She had felt the finality of something already in legal process, something ugly and warped. The memory made her wince.

"What did you do with the letters?" Tom asked.

"I stopped reading them and put them back in his suitcase. I just sat there on the bed and waited for Larry to come home. I think I was in some sort of shock. Anne came in at one point and asked me what was wrong. I didn't want to tell her, Tom. I was afraid I would fall apart. Anne and I grew up together, only a little over two years apart—more than ten years older than our sister Kye. We were always so close, but after Anne got married and moved to Atlanta, we didn't see much of each other. I hadn't told her anything about what was going on with Larry and me. I said I had a headache and I needed to be alone for a while."

"She believed you?" Tom asked.

"I'm not sure she did, but she brought me an aspirin and left me alone."

"What happened when Larry came home?"

"The minute he walked in the door I could tell from his expression he knew something was wrong. He came over and tried to put his arms around me. I moved away from him—I was about to explode, but I pulled myself together and very quietly told him I'd found the letters—that I'd read them. It was so strange."

"What do you mean strange?"

"Well, he looked shocked at first then he closed his eyes and said he guessed he'd really wanted me to find them."

Tom raised a quizzical eyebrow and nodded for her to continue.

"I didn't say another word to him. I could hardly breathe. Finally he sank down on the bed, as if he were exhausted from carrying a heavy load and told me he needed to talk to me. I said I'd be willing to listen—but I was so upset I wasn't sure if I could actually hear anything he said. He began telling me that he'd been miserable for years at Malcolm Brothers. He said he'd felt demeaned, completely out of place—that he had no friends there. No one. He said he'd started talking to women on airplanes on business trips and creating stories to make friends with them. They began writing him letters. He wrote back. It all just got out of hand, he said. He hadn't cared about any of those women. They just made him feel good about himself."

Mallie shook her head. She remembered how nearly impossible it had been for her to equate whatever problems Larry was having at the company and his telling lies about their marriage to strange women on airplanes. "I said 'My God, Larry, why didn't you tell me any of this before?'"

"And what did he say?" Tom asked.

"He told me his confusion and difficulty had all been tied up with his working for my father. He said he'd known within months of moving to Memphis it had been a mistake, a bad decision to go to work for his father-in-law, but he knew how much I loved him—how much everyone in town respected him—so he thought he couldn't talk to me, or anyone in Memphis. It was easier to talk to strangers—women on airplanes and people in bars. With strangers he wasn't immediately categorized, even mocked, as "the boss's son-in-law" or "Yankee" or "preppie"—all the labels the men at the company had pinned on him. 'You can't imagine how humiliating it's been,' he said."

"Did you believe him?" Tom asked.

"I suppose I did," she said. "I knew there was some truth to what he said. Larry was born and raised in Rhode Island and had gone to prep school and college in the East—first to The Choate School and then Princeton. There was no doubt that moving to Memphis was a social and cultural shock. I knew enough girls from the East Coast at Sweet Briar to know that. But it seemed to please everyone, particularly Larry.

"The truth is I'd been so convinced through the years his interest in other women was because of me—that I was inadequate in some way. I wanted to believe it was because of my father or the company or Memphis—anything but me."

"Mallie, surely you know what an attractive woman you are," Tom said. He spoke with such conviction, a clear and unequivocal statement.

Beyond her control, Mallie's eyes filled with tears. Tom's encouragement, or whatever it was—was it just flattery?—was more than she could accept. What she had once seen in the mirror herself and all the positive things she had been told through the years by her friends—by Larry, too, during their first few years—had disappeared with her suspicions of his relationships with other women. She turned her eyes away.

Tom stood up and reached out for her, bringing her to her feet next to him. She did not move a muscle while he held her for several minutes.

"You are a beautiful, smart, lovely woman, Mallie," he said, his soft voice close to her ear. "An exceptional woman."

She kept her head down, her eyes closed. The warmth of his

words filled her whole body. She tried to think of him as her consoling counselor, but her heart leaped to imagine him as a loving man who cared about her. Still, she knew he wasn't just a man; he was a priest, a married priest with a wife and grown children. She knew all that, but she could not help what she felt.

"It's true, Mallie," he said. He took her face in his hands and forced her to look at him. "It's time for you to see yourself as you really are—as God intended for you to be."

She wanted to burst with happiness. In that moment, something inside of her clicked on, as if a light suddenly revealed all those things she ever dreamed about herself—a beautiful, smart, lovely woman—exceptional—everything Tom said she was and all she once believed, all that had been buried in the rubble of Larry's lies.

Each Tuesday afternoon their conversation became more intimate. It felt like psychic weight loss to release those secrets of her marriage that she had never been able to tell anyone. She felt freer and freer to tell Tom everything she had been hiding through the years. She could count on his response of compassion and support, renewing her belief in herself as a desirable woman. Each week when he greeted her in his study and each time he said goodbye, his hugs lasted longer and became more meaningful to her. She could think of nothing else for days.

One night she woke up from a dream in which she was making love to Tom. She was appalled at herself. Since 1960, in the sixteen years that she had been married to Larry, she had not allowed herself to consider touching—or being touched by—another man. And here she was dreaming about her counselor—an older, married Episcopal priest. *Oh God, no. All wrong,* she thought. She tried to push the lovemaking image out of her mind. But she could not stop smiling. However faint, she heard a new song. It was as if her senses had been dead and had come back to life.

Before the day following the sexual dream was over, Mallie began a fearful dialogue with herself. Should she tell Tom the way she felt about him, that she dreamed of making love to him? Suppose he sent her away—or recommended that she see another counselor. She tried to quiet her doubts. It was impossible. It would have been easier to coax a small child away from the candy canes on the Christmas tree. *Not now.* She would not tell Tom anything about her dream or her feelings for him. Whatever might happen down the line, she could not risk losing him in her life.

Chapter Ten

At the end of a Tuesday afternoon counseling session in mid-February, roughly six weeks after they began, Tom Matthews surprised Mallie by suggesting that it was time for her to have a joint session with Larry. She could not imagine being in the same room with the two of them. Her time alone with Tom had become so important to her that the idea of having Larry there felt like an invasion of privacy.

Mallie and Larry had been continuing their semblance of normal married life. None of their friends and family—with the exception of Mallie's sister Anne and her closest friend Jenny—knew that they had begun marriage counseling. She could never have confided in her mother. Joan Malcolm thought any form of therapy was for weak people, and besides, "Never hang your dirty linen out in public" was one of her strongest dictums.

In accordance with Tom's recommendations, Mallie and Larry were carrying out a loosely formed agreement that they would each make an effort to improve their relationship and hold their marriage together. When Larry was not away on a business trip, they would follow a routine of spending time in the evenings doing familiar family things. Larry shot baskets with the boys. Mallie helped with their homework. They would not criticize each other or bring up any of their problems of the past. No mention of the situation with Julie, nothing that would dredge up unpleasantness. Mallie waited for Larry to initiate sex and responded as best she could, her mind drifting further and further away from any hope—or even desire—to rekindle the excitement that had once brought her such pleasure. She tried not to dwell on any projection of Larry's true feelings for her.

Twice during that time, Larry had called to say that he would be late coming home from work—a departure from his old habit of never letting her know his plans—and once, in early February, on the threat of snow, he'd left the office to stake up the little pine trees they had planted in the front yard the summer before.

Mallie knew that Larry was trying hard to show a positive attitude, whether it came from any real desire to change or whether, like her, he was following Tom's instructions. At the same time she could not deny that some internal mechanism of hers had shifted. She continued to perform her given chores of the day, the boys' activities at school, planning meals for the family, her civic and cultural board meetings—the board of MIFA, the Memphis Inter-Faith Association, and The Memphis Art Academy—but all the while she was listening and moving to the rhythm of a new song, as if in her real life—in the life of her heart—she were somewhere else. Her daydreams went far beyond her daily life with Larry. In some undefined way, she was beginning a different life without him. Maybe someday, impossible as it seemed at the moment, her life would somehow include Tom Matthews.

With great reluctance, Mallie agreed to have a joint counseling session with Larry during her weekly scheduled appointment in Tom's study on the following Tuesday.

∽≈

Larry met her in the parking lot of St. Michael's. They greeted each other with a kiss on the cheek, no more intimate than two old friends entering a cocktail party.

Once inside Tom's study, the three of them sat down and formed a triangle: Tom behind his desk, Larry and Mallie side by side across from him. For about fifteen minutes, Tom urged both of them to express their feelings about their marriage, about each other. Mallie felt that she was being split in half, one half connected to her old life with Larry and the other half reaching out for a new life. The division left her speechless. She could not bear to look at Tom. Across the desk from her, his demeanor was far from the warm and loving Tom she had come to know when they were alone in his study. He looked closed, judgmental. She could not summon any of the trust she had developed with him. Larry, meanwhile, began mumbling about how he thought certain things about their marriage were better.

"What things do you mean?" Tom asked.

"Well, I don't know," Larry said. He shrugged his shoulders. "It just seems better."

"And how do you feel about the marriage, Mallie?" Tom asked her.

Mallie wanted to duck as if he had thrown a foreign object at her. The harsh tone of his voice was so different from his gentle probing into her stories when they met privately on Tuesdays. "I don't know," she said quietly, not looking at either of them. "I suppose I think things are better." She knew she was not telling the whole truth. Only the surface things were better. Mallie was no longer sure about anything—neither that she wanted to be married to Larry, nor that she wanted a divorce. All she thought she knew for sure was that she wanted to have her time alone with Tom Matthews—yet, at that moment, he seemed to be very much a stranger, perhaps even an adversary. He was not the same person who had been so sympathetic, so completely supportive of her during the past few weeks.

Without warning, as the answers to Tom's questions became more elusive and more inane, he stood up and announced: "I cannot seem to get either one of you to be truthful. Maybe you'd do better alone in this room without me." He looked sternly from one to the other, a sargeant addressing his callow recruits. "I suggest you stay here until you've said what you need to say to each other. This is your best opportunity." With those challenging words, he walked out the side door.

Mallie felt instantly abandoned. In spite of her confused emotions, she had maintained a certain confidence as long as Tom was in the room. Without him, she felt cut loose, adrift. Neither she nor Larry spoke.

Finally, she turned toward her husband and in a soft voice she said, "Do you love me, Larry?"

He looked away.

"No," he whispered, then quickly turning toward her, he added, "I mean, I don't know." He dropped his head into his hands, his elbows on his knees. "I don't know how I feel anymore."

Mallie held her breath, She could not move, could not look at Larry. She had not expected him to say no. Through all the years of lies, of doubt, of questioning herself, she had convinced herself that he still loved her—and there were many things she still loved about him. Like rewinding an old film, her mind raced through images of the good times with Larry, the way they loved the same music and danced together, the summer sunsets they shared in Watch Hill, the sailing trips, the nature walks, his surprise gifts to her on Christmas morning—so many things. The most important thing, of course, were the boys, their sons. How thrilled they had been at the birth of each one. But he had just told her he didn't love her. She felt something rip, as if a force greater than her will had reached into the depths of her life and torn up her marriage commitment. Mallie's mind went blank. She waited for him to say something else.

"I just don't want to be married to you anymore," he said, his eyes on the floor in front of him.

Larry's words sounded a death knell. At the same time, they

rang like the echo of a distant lifeboat. Mallie felt a strange sense of relief, as if she had been released from a lifetime obligation— her promise before God of faithfulness to Larry "until death do us part." In that moment she did not feel rejection or sadness or fear. Her mind jumped to a startling conclusion: the end of the marriage would be Larry's choice, his responsibility, not hers. She could imagine that her boys, her family and her friends would not blame her.

"I guess that's it," Mallie said with cool resignation, "if that's what you want." Maybe he intended to marry Julie. Whatever was in his mind for the future, the end of the marriage was Larry's decision. "Is that what you really want?" she said.

He nodded his consent, offering no more words.

Mallie stood up and in a voice she hardly recognized, she said, "Okay then. That's the way it is."

For a second their eyes met. Two blind people, looking at each other, unable to see.

"I'll go by the house and pick up a few things," Larry said. "When the boys get home, you can tell them I've gone out of town on a business trip. Whatever you want to tell them. We can deal with the rest later." His voice was a monotone recitation, as if he were speaking to someone at the office, giving instructions to be carried out by a subordinate.

They left Tom's study through the side door and got into their separate cars.

Chapter Eleven

Mallie spent most of the night fighting off waves of fear. The initial relief was gone. In its place was a kind of panic that she had never felt before. Her whole being was threatened. Whatever might happen in the future, the present—the prospect of being divorced—felt like a dark and remote planet, a place where she would have no idea who she was. She had been a daughter living at home with her sisters and her parents for twenty-one years. She had been a wife living with Larry and her boys for eighteen years. If she were not a married woman, who would she be? From the time Mallie was a child she had believed that she would grow up and be a wonderful wife; she would have only one marriage in her lifetime. She would be like her mother, who had disagreements with her father—there were plenty of nights when her mother screamed at her father and he screamed back, slamming doors before he drove around for hours alone in the car—but he always came home, and they stayed married.

She thought about her years with Larry. They never screamed at each other or slammed doors. They argued, disagreed on many things, and she sometimes criticized him about his spending habits. He bought expensive clothes for himself—Hong Kong shirts—and sometimes elaborate presents for her. As much as she liked his gifts, she knew he could not afford them. Once he came home with a vintage Mercedes sedan that he had bought from one of his hardware clients in Mississippi. The car spent more time racking up bills in the repair shop than being a source of pride sitting in their driveway. Mallie knew that Larry spent more money than his salary allowed. He had no doubt dipped into the small inheritance his grandfather had left him. Certainly she resented his constant traveling and the tension that had developed in recent years between Larry and her father. Thinking about all that, and, of course, the biggest anguish of all—the other women and the lies—Mallie had to admit she had been pretending that she loved Larry for years. Until her growing intimacy with Tom, she had forgotten how love felt: the desire to be in the other person's presence at all times and above all others—the comfort and joy of complete trust. She replayed Larry's admission in Tom's office that he did not love her. She relived the way Larry looked away from her when he said those words, the way he tried to take some of the sting back by saying he didn't really know how he felt, but that he didn't want to be married to her. Mallie shook her head. Of course he didn't love her. It wasn't possible that Larry could still love her and not want to be married to her. She wondered what might have happened if she had not been so quick to accept his decision, if she had tried to stop him from walking out the door. But she hadn't. The deed was done. It was over. The thought of what would happen now was terrifying. It made her want to pull the covers over her head and slip down into the dark, to disappear. No matter who took the blame, she could not imagine telling the boys, her friends, and her parents that she and Larry were getting a divorce. The word itself sounded like death. Finally, in sheer exhaustion, she fell asleep.

Just before dawn, as the pale first light came through the window beside her bed, Mallie opened her eyes and began to recall the dream that had awakened her. Slowly, slowly, the details came into focus.

She and Larry had been sailing on a small boat with friends in a familiar, but unnamed body of water. They were drinking cocktails and laughing while they were moored at the end of the day. She instinctively turned to look behind her and to her horror, she saw a tidal wave about to crash on top of the boat. She was too frightened to speak and warn the others. The wave hit and all of them were sent roiling in the dark sea water. She could not breathe and was certain that she was drowning. Suddenly she was aware that she had been tossed up on a distant, unfamiliar shore— alone but alive. The beach stretched for miles with nothing at either end and no one in sight. She looked around and saw a path winding up a steep cliff beyond the beach. She knew that was where she was supposed to go. Hand over hand, she climbed the rocky face and finally reached the top. Just ahead of her an old woman in a shroud was sitting on a rock, holding a baby in her arms. She walked over to the woman, who held up the baby to her. "Take this child," the woman said. "Care for her and you will be fine."

When Mallie held the child in her arms, she was filled with warmth and happiness.

For some reason Mallie could not immediately understand, she felt tears in her eyes as she recalled the dream. She was not sad. She knew the dream was positive and prophetic. It was meant as some sort of sign that she would live and she would be okay. She knew that. Why was she crying? She was anxious to talk to Tom about it. Tom. The question that she had asked herself over and over during the night came back to her. Did Tom know what would happen when he left her alone in the room with Larry? Was he aware that a "tidal wave" might hit her life? She would have to see him as soon as possible.

Chapter Twelve

The next morning, first thing, Mallie called Terry at St. Michael's. She was grateful that, through their conversations during her weekly visits to the chapel, she had begun to trust Terry. She even suspected Terry knew about her feelings for Tom. This was an emergency, she confided to Terry on the phone. She had to have an appointment with Tom as soon as possible. Terry assured her she would see to it that Tom found a place in his schedule at some point during the day. An hour later she called Mallie back to confirm that he would see her at three.

∽◆∾

The minute Mallie closed the door of Tom's study, she fell into his arms, burying her face in his chest. He stroked her hair. She was sure he knew what had happened. The thought fleetingly crossed her mind that he had planned for it to happen.

"Your life is not over, Mallie," he said. "Know that. Maybe it's just beginning."

She kept her eyes closed, trying to control her conflicting feelings. She was truly frightened about her future, but a part of her was relieved a decision had been made. She wanted to tell Tom about the dream—about the tidal wave—how terrified she had been that everything and everyone in her life would be gone and she would be dead. She wanted to tell him about the old woman and the baby—how happy and peaceful she felt when she held the child. But she could not speak. She could only feel his arms around her, hear his soothing voice consoling her.

"You're a beautiful, special, wonderful woman," he said, and, as if reading her mind, he added, "You're not to worry. Everything will be okay."

She put her face up next to his. Closing her eyes, aware of the warmth of his skin on hers, she felt another sweep of relief. The cold tension of the unknown that had gripped her with fear throughout the night disappeared. She felt total protection—as if nothing in the world could harm her—as long as Tom Matthews held her. She did not move from his arms. She breathed in his familiar, musty, aftershave scent, and felt the softness of his cheek next to hers. In a totally unexpected moment, her mouth found his mouth. The connection was electric, not a jarring shock, but a warm illumination that filled her whole body. Neither of them moved. Finally, she broke the connection and put her head into the space under his chin. "I love you," she whispered.

"I love you, too, Mallie," he said, softly. He patted her arm as he spoke. When she moved, her forehead touched the crisp, white, clerical collar around his neck. It felt like a stone wall jutting up between them. She backed away and moved to a chair next to him.

"I have something I must tell you, Tom," she said. Her heart was pounding against her rib cage. The fear gripping her chest was greater than all of the fear that she had experienced during the previous night. "It's something I haven't been able to tell you."

"Whatever it is—it's okay, Mallie." Tom Matthews reached out to hold her hand and to speak with a quiet authority. "You are not to worry."

"Tom," she said, "I don't care that Larry's gone. I know it's horrible. Shocking, maybe. I know that. But he doesn't love me. He said so."

In that moment she couldn't come right out and tell Tom that the real reason she didn't care about Larry leaving her was that she had fallen in love with him. It would sound so callous, proof that she had not taken her marriage commitment seriously. That was the last thing she wanted Tom to think about her—the last thing she had ever expected of herself. "I know it's strange, but I don't feel rejected," she said. She looked at him hoping she could read in his eyes that he understood.

Tom nodded, then surprised her with his answer. "Rejection is painful, Mallie. Even if you don't feel the pain at the moment, it's one of life's most hurtful and difficult human experiences. Do you still love him?"

It didn't take her a second to respond. "No," she said. "I don't think so. What it feels like is—the love is gone. The marriage feels dead."

"That feeling may be so," Tom said, as he sat back in his chair and let go of her hand. "But it's important for you to understand that love is more than a feeling; it's an act of will—a determination of the mind. At the same time, love has to be kept alive through actions and the honest expression of feelings." His voice was gentle, more consoling than advisory. "You've been married to Larry for nearly eighteen years and from what you've told me, you've been denying your true feelings for many of those years."

Mallie lowered her head, unable to look at Tom as she spoke. She knew she had to speak the truth to him. "What I really have to tell you *is* about my feelings," she said, "but it's not about my feelings for Larry or our marriage." She pushed a new wave of fear down in her throat.

"What is it?" he asked.

She swallowed and lifted her eyes toward him. "It's about you," she said. "I think about you all the time, Tom. I go to sleep thinking about you. I wake up thinking about you. I feel as if I am living just to be with you. I know it's wrong. I know." She stopped. "I'm so afraid you'll send me away—that you'll tell me I have to go to someone else."

Tom took both of her hands in his and spoke directly to her. "Mallie, there's nothing wrong with what you're feeling about me. It's perfectly natural in this situation. What you're feeling is all part of the healing process. This is a very difficult and painful time for you. More than you realize. You need not worry. I can handle this for both of us. You don't have to go anywhere else, to anyone else. I will always be here for you. I promise you." He tightened his grip on her hands and smiled at her.

She felt as if an invisible vise had let go of her body. She had risked everything by telling him of her love for him. All she heard in that moment was that she did not have to leave him and that he would always be there for her. *Thank God.* "I trust you, Tom," she said.

Inside, within seconds, she was bursting with confusion again. She had not allowed herself to imagine kissing another man in all her married life, but it had been years since she experienced the elation she felt from kissing Tom. She had begun to think that the sensual excitement she had once known with Larry was gone permanently from her life. She never imagined that she would fall in love with another man—certainly not a married Episcopal priest. She knew it made no sense, but it had happened. It was real. And when she told Tom she loved him, did he not say to her "I love you, too?" But then he said that her feelings were part of "the healing process." What did that mean? Nothing was clear. All her convictions of who she was, all her ideas of how life should be, everything impressed upon her from childhood were disappearing, vanishing, as if they never existed. Even the sensation of peace she had felt when she'd held the child in her powerful dream no longer mattered to her. Only one thing seemed real: the overriding determination in her mind that *nothing* was going to keep her from being with Tom Matthews. Nothing.

Chapter Thirteen

arry called and agreed to come home before dinner on Friday night to meet with the boys. They were accustomed to his being away during the week, so it would only become obvious that something in their lives had changed if he didn't come home for the weekend.

Larry was to be the spokesman. It was only fair, Mallie argued, that he should be the one to tell them about the separation. He was the one, after all, who had left home. Since Sammy was away at St. George's School in Newport, Rhode Island, he would have to be told by phone, or perhaps Larry would choose to go to Rhode Island himself. He could go to Providence on the same trip and tell his parents as well.

It was close to six when Larry came home. The four of them gathered in the library, Troy and David seated on the two-seater couch, Larry in his usual chair, and Mallie across from him next to the fireplace. It was the room where so many family events had taken place—the ritual opening of their Christmas stockings, the planning of their summer vacation in Watch Hill, the happy times of sharing special programs like the Olympic Games on television together.

Mallie had sat on that same couch with Larry, both of them glued to the television set throughout the entire weekend after President

Kennedy was shot in Dallas. In horror, late on that November Sunday morning in 1963, during a quiet, maternal moment with baby Sammy in her lap, they had witnessed Jack Ruby shoot Lee Harvey Oswald right in front of them. She had thought that nothing more dramatic than that event could possibly ever happen to her family.

Mallie closed her eyes, fighting the image of the news of their separation coming as a gun blast in her children's faces.

"What's going on, Mom?" Troy asked, looking at her with an earnest expression that Mallie recognized from her own childhood sense of responsibility. She was the oldest of her three sisters. Since Sammy was away to boarding school, Troy had taken over the position of the oldest boy. She felt his desire to say and do everything right.

For a second, she wanted to preempt Larry, to jump in and tell the boys that it had all been a mistake. There was nothing to talk about. Everything was fine. They could go outside and play with their friends. She kept her eyes on Larry, not answering Troy, forcing herself to wait for her husband to speak.

"We need to tell you both something," Larry said, his eyes nearly disappearing under his brow and his head tilted forward, as if he were hiding beneath a low rooftop in a storm. He was fidgeting with his hands, his left hand opening and closing into a fist. "Your mother and I are going to separate for a while." He stopped.

Troy looked again at Mallie. "Mom?"

Mallie raised her open hand toward her son, a signal to ask him to wait for his father to finish what he was saying. She closed her eyes.

"I'm going to live in an apartment near here—in Laurelwood," he continued, "and you'll stay here with your mother."

"Why?" David asked. "Did we do something wrong?" He sounded choked. His voice was even higher and thinner than usual.

Mallie wanted to reach out for him, hold him close to her. David was the sensitive one, the animal lover, the red-haired artist of the three boys. At eleven years old, he was the one who couldn't bear to watch when they buried Laddie, their lab before Bingo, who had been hit by a speeding car in front of their house on Walnut Grove Road.

"No, no," Larry said emphatically. "Neither of you did anything. It has nothing to do with you. This is a decision we've made."

Mallie wanted to correct him and say "a decision that you've made," but she knew that wouldn't be fair. She had agreed to the separation. She had thought she wanted the separation. At the moment, the idea felt like a betrayal of her children, of everything she held dear.

"Are you getting a divorce?" Troy asked. He was sitting up straight, looking from his father to his mother, directing his question to her. "Does Sammy know about this?"

"No, Sammy doesn't know anything about this yet," Mallie said, trying to keep control of her voice. "And we don't know what will happen, Troy."

She really didn't know what would happen in the future. That was the truth, as best she knew the truth at that moment. Mallie felt heartsick for each of her boys. A memory surfaced of the years she had spent as a child with her mother during the Second World War, when her father was stationed in the Pacific, her constant fear that her father would not come home and that they would no longer be a family.

"We don't know," Larry repeated. "For now we're going to be living separately. There are some things your mother and I have to work out. I want you to know that I'm leaving home, but I'm not leaving you. I want you to come over to my place whenever you like."

Larry sounded so very rational, almost mechanical. He spoke casually as if he were taking his old car out of the home garage and driving it to a new garage to fix it. The boys could come over to the new garage to be with him anytime. Mallie reminded herself that Larry was a charmer who had convinced her of untruths with his explanations for too many years. He was attempting to charm the boys.

"Is there anything we can do?" David said. Tears welled in his eyes.

Mallie could hardly bear to look at her son, at David's pained face. The plaintiveness in his voice and his tears dissolved all the optimistic thoughts she held for her own future—possibilities that she had envisioned only hours before. What she and Larry were doing was so selfish. How would she ever be able to forget David's tears? In that moment it didn't matter that she and Larry had been living separate lives under the same roof for years. It didn't matter that Larry had been consistently telling her lies. It certainly didn't matter that she had finally felt that maybe there was a better life for her without him. All she could see was the sadness in her son's face, the reality that his life, all three of her sons' lives, would never be the same. She felt an overwhelming accusation that somehow she had failed to keep the family together.

She got up from her rooted position in her chair and put her arms around David. "It's okay, sweetheart," she said. "It's okay. It's not your fault. I promise you it has nothing to do with you." She kissed him on the side of his face and looked back at Larry, hoping he would figure out some way to end the torture of dragging on the conversation.

"We'll talk again," Larry said. He stood up as if to say the session was over.

Troy took David's arm and they walked silently past their parents out of the library.

"You'll call Sammy tonight?" Mallie questioned Larry. She was sure that her oldest son would want to talk to her after his father called him, but she didn't want to be the one to break the news to him.

"I'll call him," Larry said. "Maybe not tonight, but I'll call him."

Mallie sat back on the couch and watched her husband go into their bedroom to pack his clothes. He was so particular and fastidious about his clothes. His suits, sports jackets, ties and tassel loafers all came from Brooks Brothers. He had found a shirt maker in Hong Kong, where he could order his shirts with a monogram on the sleeve at no extra charge. She wondered what he was deciding to take with him. In an unexpected flare-up of anger, she envisioned throwing what he left behind into a canvas bag and dumping it at Goodwill. That would serve Larry right. How could he have sat there so complacently and told the boys that "we have some things to work out?" That was another lie. There was nothing to work out. He was leaving because he didn't love her and didn't want to be married to her. He had another woman in his life named Julie. Maybe he intended to marry her. She, Mallie, his wife of almost eighteen years, no longer mattered to him. All those years, all those women. And she had stayed married to him, taken care of their family. The more she thought about it, the angrier she became. She had allowed herself to be a part of creating a marriage façade for years, and now she was allowing herself to be a part of creating a divorce façade—or at least, a sham separation.

From somewhere in the recesses of her consciousness, she remembered the conversation among the wives at Larry's tenth Princeton mini-reunion in New York City. Most of his Cottage Club fraternity brothers lived and worked in New York. Several of their wives worked in the city. At the time, Mallie had been very disturbed by the women's loud talk of bra burning, political activism, and male-bashing—it was against everything she had ever been taught by her mother or in school. None of her friends in Memphis talked about things like that. She had put the whole business completely out of her mind. Still, she had been haunted by the words of one of the brightest of the wives who worked as an editor at *The Atlantic Monthly*.

"Come on," the woman had said, accusing Mallie of living in the boondocks, "come out of the woodwork, Mallie. What do you mean you've never heard of Betty Freidan? You didn't read *The Feminine Mystique?* Good grief, when are you going to grow up and live in the twentieth century? This is the most important issue of our time. This is about becoming a person in your own right—about considering yourself to be someone of value."

Mallie sat on the couch, hearing the echo of those words as if for the first time. Once, her sense of self-worth had depended entirely on the approval of her parents and her friends. After she married Larry, her sense of self-worth depended on his approval of her as a woman and a wife. Because of Larry's other women, she had seen herself as inadequate, a failure. It had never occurred to her to envision who she was as a person in her own right, a person of value beyond her role as a wife and a mother. Tom had begun to change all that. By the time Larry walked out with a suitcase and a duffle bag, she had built up such a steam that she was ready to explode.

"Well," he said, calmly, "I guess we'll talk later."

"I guess we will," she said, her arms crossed tightly in front of her chest.

"Well, goodbye," he said. He came toward her as if he were going to kiss her goodbye.

"You're full of bullshit, Larry," she said and turned away.

Chapter Fourteen

Mallie could hardly wait for her Tuesday afternoon appointment with Tom Matthews. Throughout the weekend she mentally replayed the Friday afternoon scene with Larry and the boys in preparation for seeing him. She imagined telling him about Larry's farewell, his attempt to kiss her and her audacious reply. Surely the priest would be amused. Maybe he would praise her.

She marveled at herself. She had really told Larry he was "full of bullshit." Using the word *bullshit* was not her normal language. Since childhood her father had cautioned her about "the language of ladies"—how important it was not to use vulgar words, never mind the fact that she would not have known any vulgar words but for her father. He said "Goddammit" if the newspaper came late in the morning, or "Jesus Christ" if Muffin, her mother's beloved cocker spaniel, happened to walk in front of him, causing him to trip. "Fucking" was his descriptive adjective for anything seriously distasteful. "Crap" took care of most of his little daily annoyances. She had heard him many times behind closed doors in one of his temper fits calling her mother a "bitch." Growing up, there had been a great divide, creating much confusion in Mallie's mind, between her father's lessons of language and behavior and the example he set with his own.

∽

She was right about Tom's response. He grinned at her when she regaled him with the story. "You really told Larry he was full of bullshit?"

She nodded, blinking her eyes with delight. "Then I just turned away, not saying another word, and he left."

"Good for you," Tom said, then earnestly asked, "How were the boys? How did they respond to your telling them about the separation?"

"Sammy still doesn't know," Mallie said. "Larry promised me he would call him, but so far he hasn't done it. Troy was stoic—as usual. It was hard to tell about him. David was heartbreaking. He had tears in his eyes. It killed me to look at him."

Tom shook his head. "Divorce is toughest on kids," he said. "Initially there's no way for them to understand what's happening. You've been the center of their world—the two of you together. Most kids see their parents as one entity—as their protective authority, their compass in life."

"Is there anything I can do to help them?" Mallie asked.

"Several things. Try to keep their lives as routinely normal as possible," Tom said. "Kids hate change of any kind. But they do adjust fast. The most important thing to remember is not to try to influence them by telling stories about Larry and your life together. Answer any questions they ask as honestly as you can, but don't offer answers to questions they're not asking."

"But if I don't tell them the truth, how will they ever understand why this happened?"

"They'll each understand in his own time, in his own way," Tom said. "Children know certain things instinctively. Other things they'll sort out as they grow up—as they spend time separately with you and with Larry. The truth of your marriage in their minds won't be your truth or Larry's truth—it'll be their truth."

Mallie saw the sense in what he was saying, but it felt frustrating. She was angry with Larry and one part of her wanted the boys to be angry too. They didn't know about Julie and all the years of their father's affairs—and Tom was telling her that she wasn't supposed to tell them.

"And what about your parents?" Tom asked.

Mallie sank back into her chair remembering the phone conversation with her mother and father. She had called them in Vero Beach, Florida, where they spent several months every winter. She would rather have told them in person, but she knew she couldn't wait. The gossip around Memphis would reach them right away. As soon as a certain group of her friends knew about their separation— none of them did yet—the news would be all over town.

"My mother didn't say much really," Mallie told Tom. "I felt as if she went into shock. I was prepared for her to be furious at Larry. She's been angry with him since the first time he refused to go to her house for dinner on Wednesday nights. She used to go to her in-laws' house for dinner once a week, when they were still alive, and she expected us to do the same. Larry put his foot down one Wednesday about a year ago and refused to go."

"Why do you think he did that?" Tom asked.

"I didn't understand it at the time. I wasn't very sympathetic. I thought he was being selfish. Now I wonder if it was all part of his difficulty of working for my father. In the end my mother said she'd have to think about what I told her—about the separation—that she'd call me back or write to me."

"How about your father?" Tom said.

Mallie said she had not expected the despair in her father's voice. "'Oh my God,' he said. That was all he said at first. Then, as if I had told him I was terminally ill, he said, 'I don't believe it. I never thought something like this would happen to you. I feel like the shit's hit the fan.'" She shook her head. "It made me so sad, Tom. His voice sounded as if he were going to cry."

"What do you think your father was really feeling?" Tom asked.

Mallie had been pondering that question herself. Was he so upset by the idea of a divorce in the family? Or perhaps he was sympathetic to her humiliation over Larry leaving her. Maybe he was concerned about all the problems a divorce would cause because Larry worked at Malcolm Brothers. Or maybe it was something deeper, something personal. Maybe he felt responsible since he had been the one who had offered Larry a job and made it possible for him to move to Memphis.

"I'm not sure what my father was feeling," she said. "He was so anxious for Larry to come to work for him when we got married. For a long time it seemed to be mostly a happy situation—at least, I thought it was. They went duck hunting together and even played golf occasionally. In the beginning my father was complimentary of the job Larry was doing—he actually said he thought Larry was a master salesman. Then, something changed. I don't remember exactly when it happened, or any particular incident that caused it." Mallie took a deep breath, struggling with the recall. "I began to feel tension between them. It was horrible, Tom. When I sat in the living room with them, I felt as if I could hear the voices in their heads. I could hear Larry say, *You're too old. You drink too much. Why don't you retire and let me run the company?* Then I would hear my father say, *You're not the person I thought you were. You're not capable of running the company.*"

"Did you ever talk to Larry about that—about his true feelings for your father and his future with the company?"

"Not really—except for that time when I discovered the letters." She shook her head. "What could I say? I know my father's faults—his drinking and his temper tantrums—his ego. But I love him. And I admire him. The company's been very successful—all due to him. Since my grandfather's time, my father has tripled the size of the company, opened territories far beyond the southern states. He was a summa cum laude at Vanderbilt—did I tell you that?—then he went to the Wharton School of Business. Business people, all my father's friends, respect him, think he's brilliant." She stopped for a moment, considering what she was saying, what it all meant. "I guess I have to say that when I listen to Larry complain about the company, complain about my father and the employees—about how he doesn't fit in—doesn't have any friends there—I've sometimes wondered how competent he'd be if he were running the company himself."

"So you've had your own questions about Larry succeeding your father?"

She nodded. In spite of all that had happened, it still hurt her to think that she had ever doubted Larry's capabilities. She knew that her mother had always had reservations about Larry's intellect. The night before their wedding, Joan Malcolm had asked Mallie if she realized that she was smarter than Larry. Mallie had been shocked. She had not known what to say. She adored Larry and was excited about her wedding. She had not given any thought to whether she was more intelligent. Still, the question had planted a seed of doubt in her mind.

"When Larry first started working for Malcolm Brothers and he was sent all over the country to meet the salesforce, he was a big success. He won some sort of sales award his second year on the road. But it was tough for me. I hardly saw him during the week."

"I remember you telling me about those years," Tom said. "The constant travel and his low salary."

"I got used to it. I said something about it to my father once and he told me that he and my mother had lived that way for years. He said he made seventy dollars a week and learned the business by making sales calls out of town, all week long, every week. If he could do it, Larry could do it. I tried to keep my eye on how their life had turned out—all of us going to private schools and colleges, their trips to Europe, their beautiful houses in Memphis and Vero Beach—all those things I hoped Larry and I would have someday—and I figured we'd just have to endure the hard years to get there."

"And how are you feeling now, Mallie—about your own life—your future as a single woman?" It was a direct question that Tom had not raised before. She recognized that it was the same question her New York friends had been trying to get her to answer so many years ago. Did she believe in herself as a person?

She lowered her eyes, trying to hide her tears. They were not just tears for the loss of Larry. They were tears of confusion and loss of purpose. She had once had dreams of being an artist and she had abandoned them. Now her dreams of being a good wife, her dreams for her family were gone. She had little idea of who she was and no idea what it really meant to be "a person of value."

"I don't know," she said. "I don't know how I feel."

Tom reached over and took her hands in his. She thrust herself forward into his lap and tucked her head under his chin. He closed his arms around her. Within seconds, she felt transported, completely safe and loved. Once they began kissing, Mallie lost all interest in everything but Tom. As long as she was in his arms and felt his love for her, it didn't matter that her old dreams were gone—or that she had played her part in abandoning them. She no longer questioned who she was or how she planned to live in the future. In that moment, being with Tom was her only dream.

Chapter Fifteen

With the exception of Jenny Bolton, Mallie's and Larry's friends were shocked at the announcement of their separation. Cindy Morgan called Mallie when she heard the fast spreading news. "Ben and I just don't believe it," she said. "Mallie, tell me this isn't true."

Whenever a friend asked a direct question about what went wrong or if she thought the separation would end in divorce, Mallie chose not to elaborate. She said simply that it was Larry's decision to separate and she had no idea what would happen. Each time she said it, she felt torn. Her pride wanted her to publicly accuse Larry of years of infidelity and broken promises, but she could not bear to sound like a victim or be seen as a rejected woman in anyone's eyes. She wanted to hold her head up and say that yes, divorce was possible, even probable—and it was okay with her. Yet even as she acknowledged those thoughts, a deeper voice whimpered beneath the surface, a voice that begged for help—help to understand what was going on in her life, help to believe that she and her boys would really be okay.

Jenny, the one friend who had been in Mallie's confidence all along, was the only person she trusted to share her real feelings. Jenny had been through a divorce herself two years before. After nearly twenty-one years of marriage and five teenage children, Jenny was alert to the reality that a marriage could appear on the outside to end abruptly when the split was not so abrupt from the inside. In one of her discussions with Mallie, Jenny admitted that she had seen troubles brewing with Larry for years.

"I couldn't bring myself to tell you," she said. "Last summer when you drove the boys to Rhode Island to visit Larry's parents, I saw him several times out for dinner with some woman I didn't know. One night at Paulette's I spotted him in a back corner. He saw me. I know he did, but he looked right through me as if he didn't know me—as if I weren't there."

"My God, Jenny, why didn't you tell me?" Mallie said. She felt immediately resentful. Jenny had been keeping secrets from her.

"What would have been the point?" Jenny said. "I figured you'd seen Larry carry on for years—the way he danced at parties—his little trips 'outside' with women. You didn't seem to pay attention to all that. Also, I know how much it means to you to take the boys to Watch Hill."

Mallie was dismayed, hurt, that Jenny had known something about Larry's escapades when she was away and had not told her. The worst was Jenny's accusation that she had not paid attention to Larry's behavior through the years, as if she did not care that Larry was betraying her. That was so untrue. But she couldn't be angry with Jenny. She had watched the pain that Jenny had suffered over her own divorce.

Mallie had known Jenny's husband Webster all her life— his real name was Stuart, but he was so smart—a walking dictionary— that everyone had always called him Webster. He came home one day after work and told Jenny he wanted a divorce. Just like that. Five children in five years and a twenty-one-year marriage. Jenny told Mallie at the time that she felt like a tornado had hit her marriage and nothing was left standing.

As a result, Jenny had become involved with a Bible study

group that reached out and took her in. In that moment, according to Jenny, those women had been a life-support system. Mallie did not understand anything about it, but she accepted the fact that somehow the group and the religion had helped Jenny to survive.

Mallie recalled attending one of the Bible study meetings at Jenny's house. She went out of mild curiosity but mostly in support of her friend. Within minutes of the presentation, Mallie was completely turned off by their leader. The perfectly coiffed, well-dressed woman stood in front of the assembled group and very piously said, "God knows every hair on your head and He has a plan for every aspect of your life." The idea made Mallie feel creepy and spied on—God as a truant officer or someone sneaky peering in her windows. She tried not to let the woman's heavy eye makeup and her bright red lipstick bother her. What really irritated her was what she considered the woman's narrow and condescending biblical definition of a "woman's place." It sounded so patronizing. At one point, Mallie thought she was going to suffocate or break out in a cold sweat. She left the Bible study meeting that day without saying goodbye to anyone or even a thank you to Jenny. The remembrance of that day gave her the shudders.

"Mallie," Jenny said, interrupting her friend's thoughts of the Bible study group, "you need to move on from this situation with Larry. In two weeks I'm going to the Callaway Gardens Resort outside of Atlanta for a 'Creative Living Conference.' It's a weekend retreat put on by the Junior League of Atlanta and Faith at Work. I want you to go with me. I know it'll be helpful for you."

Mallie froze. The Junior League? She had resigned from the Junior League of Memphis several years before. Even though her mother had insisted she join the socially prominent women's organization when she was twenty, and she had learned a lot of skills from her volunteer work experience, she couldn't stand all the chatter at the meetings and the snobbishness of the members. The group had turned down membership to one of her friends who had a Jewish husband. It had infuriated her. And what was Faith at Work? The title sounded like a Holy Roller group.

"It may seem strange to you," Jenny said. "I know you didn't like the Bible study group at my house, but I promise you, you'll like the Faith at Work people. The Junior League's not really involved. They're just the sponsors of the conference—they put up the money for it. I went to one of their conferences in Gatlinburg last fall and loved it. Honestly, you can't imagine what it'll mean to you. I promise you."

Mallie shook her head. No way could she do that. "I don't think so, Jenny," she said. "That sort of thing is not for me."

"This is not just a Bible study group," Jenny said. "These are real people who talk about real life situations. They're concerned about the choices we make—how we learn to love and forgive each other—the idea of living a 'creative life.' It's about the quality of our relationships with each other as well as our relationship to God."

When Mallie was a child, she had believed in God as a kind, loving father—someone she couldn't see but a person she could trust to always be there and take care of her. She had lost that image of God along the way. Through the years, she had tried unsuccessfully to find it again—not God as a person necessarily, but God as a conviction of ultimate good. The closest she had come to any sort of "trust in God" was when she was with Tom Matthews. Those feelings did not last when she was out of his office for a few hours. How wonderful it would be if she could reignite a deeper sense of belief for herself. But she just couldn't imagine going to a Junior League–sponsored religious conference, no matter what Jenny said about it.

"Think about it, Mallie. There are four of us going together. You know them all. I'll make the reservation for you. It costs about three hundred dollars for everything—room, meals, workshops, and events. All you have to do is show up and go with us. It's been life saving for me. Truly."

Mallie heard the conviction in Jenny's voice. Jenny projected a new confidence that Mallie had never seen in her friend before. All through the years of her marriage, Jenny had appeared exhausted, broken down by the demands of her children and the expectations of her husband. Webster was a true scholar who had gone to Andover and Harvard. He had fallen in love with Jenny when he was at Harvard Business School and she was at Pine Manor Junior College in Boston. Early on in their marriage, he had teased her about being one of the pretty Pine Manor girls—"A ring by spring or your money back" was their reputation—but later, after the children were born, his teasing became criticism. He said she never bothered to read any of the books he gave her.

The reality was that she had neither the time nor the energy to read a book when she was driving carpools and cooking and doing laundry for five children. Once at a party within earshot of Mallie, Webster told someone that Jenny looked frumpy. It was true that she'd gained weight and she didn't wear makeup like most of their Memphis friends. She kept her hair so short that, except for haircuts, she never went to the beauty parlor. When they were in their mid-thirties, Jenny had begun to look years older than she was, and yet she was such a warm, caring person—everyone knew that—it seemed heartless that Webster had left her. But Mallie knew better than to judge what really went on in another person's marriage. Not even Jenny's marriage. Certainly no one knew all that had transpired in her marriage to Larry.

Mallie looked at Jenny. The taut sadness that used to dominate her face was gone. She had been devastated by her divorce from Webster—the first one of all their friends' marriages to break up. But in that moment Jenny looked different—lighter, happier. Something had happened to her that had changed her in the last year. Maybe it had been her experience at Faith at Work, as well as the Bible study group. As weird as it seemed to Mallie, maybe going to the conference with Jenny was something she should consider.

"I'll think about it," Mallie said.

"This could be a turning point in your life," Jenny said. "Let's talk tomorrow."

When Jenny was gone, Mallie kept weighing the idea. She liked the prospect of "living a creative life." Maybe it would mean she would find a way to go back to her painting. She thought about Jenny's happy demeanor, her positive approach to life. Mallie wanted to believe that she could have that same confidence in her future that Jenny seemed to have. She wondered what Tom Matthews would think about the idea. She imagined he would be pleased. Certainly from what Jenny had told her, the conference would be an opportunity to discover some spiritual connection that she had lost over the years. She was sure that Larry would keep the boys for the weekend. Other than the expense, she decided that she had little to lose.

The next day Mallie called Jenny to say that she would go with her to the Faith At Work conference on "Creative Living."

Chapter Sixteen

The lobby of Callaway Gardens, the fancy golf and convention resort about an hour outside of Atlanta, was burgeoning with people on the Friday afternoon of the Faith at Work conference. Men and women were greeting each other with bear hugs and squeals like students returning to college. Jenny's and Mallie's other traveling companions joined the camaraderie. Each one of them knew people from prior conferences. Mallie felt as out of place as a midwestern public high school girl arriving as a freshman at Sweet Briar College. She remembered the girl from Kansas who told her she felt like such an outsider when she arrived at Sweet Briar that she'd cried herself to sleep every night for a month. Mallie had tried to console the girl without fully understanding what it felt like to be an outsider. In Memphis, Mallie's identity had been clear. She was a Malcolm, the eldest daughter of Sam and Joan Malcolm. That identity had followed her to Sweet Briar in the company of relatives and friends who'd paved the way before her. As she stood by herself in the lobby of Callaway Gardens at a religious conference in rural Georgia, she knew precisely how the girl from Kansas had felt.

She wished she could pick up a phone and call Tom. She wanted to hear his comforting voice. She had, of course, told him that she was going to a Faith at Work conference; actually she had asked his advice about going. He had been supportive but told her that, as an Episcopal clergyman, he had never been to any sort of nondenominational Christian conference. He had known other ministers, Methodists and Presbyterians, who had been to religious conferences. Mostly he had heard good things about the experience. It couldn't hurt her, he had said.

"Mallie," Jenny called to her from the front desk where she was signing them both in. "Come over here. I want you to meet someone."

Mallie could see a small, stylishly dressed, older lady looking over at her and smiling. She could tell from Jenny's expression that the woman was someone important. The tiny woman wore high-heeled navy blue pumps and a navy blue short jacket with a frilly white blouse. Her silver hair was stiff with spray—a hairdo that she likely had set in place once a week at the hairdresser and protected with a hair net at night—just like her mother's, Joan Malcolm's, hair.

"This is Louise Mohr," Jenny said, as Mallie walked over to them. Jenny lifted her chin and announced the woman's name with admiration, really more with reverence, as if she were introducing a saint.

"Welcome, my dear," Louise Mohr said, putting both her hands on Mallie's shoulders, her eyes burning into Mallie's eyes like branding irons. "Now tell me, dear girl, are you a Junior Leaguer or a Christian?"

Mallie instantly felt short-circuited. She tried not to show her recoiling, horrified reaction. Louise Mohr's question implied everything that she had feared about coming to a Faith at Work conference. The woman was obviously one of those closed-minded, Bible study people. Mallie was furious with Jenny for convincing her that the people at the conference would be different. Louise Mohr had the same sanctimonious, smug attitude as the Bible study women Mallie had met at Jenny's house. Her question about whether Mallie was a Junior Leaguer or a Christian proved it. *Oh, dear God*, Mallie pleaded to herself. What could she say? She pulled herself up and took a step back. In a noncommittal voice she said, "Well, I recently resigned from one, and I'm working on the other." She felt a momentary satisfaction. Surely her response was clever enough to stand her ground without directly insulting the woman.

"My dear girl," Louise Mohr was quick to respond. "I do hope it was the Junior League you resigned from." She gave Mallie a pat on her shoulder and turned away to greet a long line of people waiting for her attention.

Mallie shot a look of despair at Jenny, then walked as fast as she could through the busy lobby and out the front door. She headed for a dormant rose garden that she had seen on the way in. She was not sure whether she would burst into tears or, perhaps, be violently sick to her stomach. In either case, she had to get out of there fast. Her body was heaving with regret for having come—and with fear of what would happen to her if she stayed. At the same time she knew there was no easy way out. She had no car. There was no public transportation. And she had already paid her money. The worst part was that Jenny and her other friends were counting on her staying with them. But Mallie couldn't bear the thought of ever seeing Louise Mohr again, or of meeting other people like her. In that moment, she wasn't even sure she was a Christian.

"Mallie, Mallie," Jenny called as she walked briskly toward her. "What is it? What happened?" Her voice was pleading and kind. She put her arms around her friend.

Mallie pushed Jenny away. "I can't do this," she said, shaking her head. "I'm not a Christian. I don't know what I am, Jenny—but I'm not like that woman. I don't want to be like her."

"Oh Mallie, Louise didn't mean anything to hurt you. Truly, she didn't."

"I don't care what she meant. I know what I feel. I don't know what I'm doing here. I shouldn't have come."

"Wait a little while, Mallie. You'll meet other people. You'll like them. I promise. Louise is a wonderful woman when you know her. She didn't mean anything by what she said—and besides, she's only one person here. There are so many others." Jenny patted Mallie's arm as she spoke. "Let's go to our room and have a glass of wine before dinner. Okay?"

Mallie felt like a four-year-old being coaxed into a noisy birthday party for some child she had never met. It wasn't that she was shy. She liked meeting new people. In most social situations, she made friends easily—in Memphis, at Sweet Briar, in Watch Hill in the summer. The problem was Faith at Work. The problem was *religion*. She felt so out of place—maybe even an imposter. But she knew she was trapped. She had committed herself. From childhood, the idea of commitment had been deeply embedded in Mallie's psyche. "Your word is your integrity," her father had instructed her. When she married Larry, she gave her word in front of God, her parents, and some three hundred people. If Larry had not released her from that commitment, she would never have separated from him. She knew she couldn't leave the Faith at Work conference. No matter how miserable she might be, she would have to go through with her commitment and stay at Callaway Gardens.

As Mallie walked back to her room with Jenny, she thought of her mother's parting words before putting her on the train for camp. At the time Mallie was eleven years old and fearful of going to a place away from home where she had never been and did not know anyone. Joan Malcolm had hugged her goodbye and said, "Chin up and smile. You can do it."

Mallie lifted her chin and reminded herself that the weekend would be over in two days. Maybe not with a smile on her face, but she could do it.

Chapter Seventeen

inner was held in one of the ballrooms of the vast Callaway Gardens Resort complex. Approximately thirty-five large round tables, each seating ten, were placed in a semicircle around a central platform with a podium and a microphone. Bright lights in the ceiling shone down on the colorful fresh flowers in the center of a sea of white tablecloths. Lines formed at each end of a long buffet table, laden with hot chafing dishes of barbequed chicken breasts, mixed vegetables and rice. A large ice sculpture of a fish surrounded by a mass of fruits and flowers rose from the center. It occurred to Mallie that the fish carried some sort of Christian symbolism, but she wasn't sure what it was. The only reference to fish that she remembered from her childhood was the baked fish that the family were required to serve on Friday nights. After they finished filling their plates, Jenny led her to a nearby table and introduced her to several couples who were already seated there.

A man whom Jenny had obviously chosen ahead of time as Mallie's dinner companion pulled out a chair and reached for her hand. "Hi Mallie," he said, "I'm Alan Fremont. Welcome to our table."

He had a wonderful smile that seemed to span his whole face, dark curly hair, a few wisps covering his collar in the back, and long dark eyelashes. Handsome, Mallie thought—nice.

"That's my wife, Paige, across the table," Alan said, pointing to a shorter, blonde, vivacious woman who was in animated conversation with the person next to her. Paige Fremont looked up and waved to Mallie, as if she could hear Alan's voice, even when she was in the midst of another conversation. "Hi Mallie," she said. "Don't let my husband talk your ear off." She winked at Alan.

"Look who's talking whose ear off," he said, smiling.

His wife laughed, the way one does at a spouse's familiar teasing remark.

Mallie put her plate down on the table and settled into the chair. The routine was familiar. Since young adulthood, and particularly since her marriage, she had been seated at formal dinner tables after a cocktail hour, often meeting her dinner partner as they sat down. The accepted social protocol for married couples in her world was to separate husband and wife and introduce each one to someone new, preferably of the opposite sex. The idea was to stimulate provocative conversation throughout dinner. She had been carefully taught by her mother that it was her responsibility to make the effort to lead the conversation, bring the other person out. Mallie had watched Joan Malcolm hold her dinner partners in rapt attention. "What you want is for someone to fall a little bit in love with you," her mother said.

Mallie wondered if Alan Fremont would fall a little bit in love with her—or if she would have to talk to him about religion, and he would discover right away that she was not a true Christian and that would be the end of the conversation.

"So, you're from Memphis?" he said. "An old friend of Jenny's?"

"Yes," Mallie said, "we've been friends for years."

"I first met Jenny when I was in college," Alan said. He grinned, a sign of remembering happy times. "She was dating my roommate at the University of Virginia. Did you know her then?"

"I didn't know her until after she married Webster—I mean Stuart—and moved to Memphis. We took family skiing trips together when our children were little. Actually, his family was close to mine when I was growing up. His mother was a sort of grandmother to me after my grandmother died."

Alan smiled. "How nice for you to have had a surrogate grandmother. It's such a special relationship for a child. My grandmother died when I was ten. I miss her to this day."

Mallie pictured Aunt Lolly, Webster's mother—not her real aunt, much less her grandmother. Old family friends in the South were often referred to as Aunts and Uncles. Aunt Lolly took her to buy the white shoe skates that she wanted so desperately when she was twelve. Most of the other girls in her class had them, but Joan Malcolm said that shoe skates were too expensive and Mallie's feet were growing too fast to warrant buying them. Aunt Lolly let her pick out exactly the skates she wanted and gave them to her for an early Christmas present.

She also took Mallie and her sister Anne to see the movie *The Song of Bernadette*. For a time after she saw the movie, Mallie dreamed of being chosen by the Virgin Mary—like Bernadette in Lourdes. She talked Anne into helping her dig a hole in the back yard that they filled daily with water, hoping that the Blessed Mother would come to visit. When six months went by and there was no sign of the Holy Mother, Mallie gave up the idea. She wondered what Alan would think of her folly.

"Did you ever see the movie, *The Song of Bernadette?*" she asked, totally out of context in the conversation about their grandmothers.

Alan's eyes lit up. "I remember it well," he said. "I fell in love with Jennifer Jones in that movie." He leaned closer to Mallie. "I was raised in the Roman Catholic Church, and after I saw that movie, I was convinced that the Virgin Mary would come to tell me I was meant to be a priest. Thank God, she didn't come, but it took years before I got over it."

"I was a Catholic child, too," Malle said. In her head, she heard the faint, tinkling sound of communion bells and her body tightened, as if she were being watched. "I know exactly what you mean. The day before our first communion, Sister Margaret—our home room teacher—told us if we were meant to be a priest or a nun, God would tell us while we were kneeling at the altar."

She realized that she was excitedly telling Alan a story that she had never repeated to anyone. It had been one of her childhood secrets with God. "I remember closing my eyes under that stiff white veil in my white organdy dress—feeling slightly faint from no breakfast—and praying so hard: 'Please, God, please don't tell me I'm supposed to be a nun. I want to be married and have children. I don't want to be like Sister Margaret.'"

Alan laughed. "You being a nun in those days would have been a terrible waste," he said. "Thank God neither of us was called to the church."

The more they talked, the more Mallie felt that she had known Alan for years. He was easy to be with. They were sharing stories about many aspects of their lives and found they had much in common.

As the Brown Betty dessert was being passed, the room darkened and a spotlight shone on the center of the platform. Mallie could see that a small group of people seated behind a podium with a round Faith At Work plaque across the front of the lectern. The colorful calligraphic logo reminded her of the cover of the old, elaborately illustrated *Bullfinch's Mythology* that she had loved as a child.

"Welcome, everyone!" A tall man in an open shirt and a dark jacket lifted his arms as he spoke. "I'm Bruce Larson," he said, leaning into the microphone. "I particularly want to welcome each one of you newcomers to Faith at Work. I want you to know how happy we are to have you among us tonight. We hope the experience of this conference will bring you the joy and peace many of us have come to expect from being together."

Mallie settled back into her chair, a little more relaxed from her dinner conversation with Alan. She liked Bruce Larson right away. She felt no phoniness about him. She decided she would try to be open to hearing whatever the speakers had to say.

"Before I introduce all the good folks up here," Bruce Larson said, turning to acknowledge the group seated behind him on the platform, "let's begin by singing together our opening song, 'Amazing Grace.'"

Alan reached over to the center of the table and picked up the Faith at Work songbook that Mallie had not even noticed was there. He handed it to her, already opened to the correct page. "I know this one by heart," he said.

Mallie knew it too, at least the words of the first verse. *Amazing grace, how sweet the sound, that saved a wretch like me . . .*

When the song ended, Bruce Larson began introducing the workshop leaders, including a handsome man named Keith Miller. Mallie thought he looked like Burt Lancaster in the movie *From Here to Eternity*. His abundant crop of brown wavy hair was appealing to her. Keith Miller stood and gave a brief nod and a wave to the crowd, followed by a burst of applause from the audience.

Bruce Larson then introduced a short, balding man named Dave Stoner. Such a contrast. Dave Stoner looked like an aging cheerleader with his crew cut hair, his shortened pants and white socks. None of the people on the platform looked the way Mallie had expected Christian workshop leaders to look. Except for Louise Mohr, they were all younger men and appeared to be full of athletic energy.

The last person Bruce Larson introduced was Louise Mohr. Mallie felt her heart begin to race and a rigidity take hold of her body when he said the woman's name. It was the same dread that she had felt as a child about Sister Margaret, the tight-lipped, Catholic nun who ruled her second-grade class by fear of the paddle.

"Hello friends," Louise Mohr said in a velvety voice, very different from the clipped tone that she had used with Mallie in the lobby. She picked up the microphone from the lectern and walked with it to the edge of the stage.

"I've just returned from a week's vacation in the Caribbean," she said, holding up a large fluted conch shell in her other hand. "As I collected beautiful shells all along the beach, I began to think of each one as a gift—like Anne Morrow Lindbergh's *Gift from the Sea*. Each one was more beautiful than the last. I thought to myself, 'If God created a home as lovely as this for tiny little sea creatures, imagine the home he has created for us—his beloved children—in heaven.'"

Mallie shuddered. She sensed the onset of the God-talk that she had been afraid all along was coming.

"You'd never have guessed it, but Louise was once a nightclub singer," Alan whispered in Mallie's ear. "Wait till you hear her sing."

Mallie crossed her arms, trying to protect herself from the dread she felt was overtaking her. She heard her mother's voice, "Chin up. You can do it." She would force herself to just sit there and smile. She could tune Louise Mohr out.

"God has given all of us gifts to share with each other on this earth," Louise said. "I want to share mine with you tonight." Without a piano or guitar or any instrumental background, she lifted her head and began singing the popular song "People."

Mallie was prepared to cringe, or at the very least, to unfavorably compare her to Barbra Streisand. To her surprise Louise Mohr soared through the notes as if she had taught Barbra to sing. The words, *"People who need people are the luckiest people in the world,"* took on a different meaning for Mallie. She had always thought the song was corny, overly sentimental, and that needy people were weak people. As much as she loved her sisters and her friends, she had never thought of herself as someone who "needed" anyone—although, as a child, she had certainly needed her wonderful, loving nurse Bernice. But since her separation from Larry, her perspective on so many things had changed. Over the past few months she had discovered that she definitely needed people. Certainly, she needed Tom Matthews. Whatever fear or pain she was experiencing in the chaos of her life was always dispelled in Tom's presence. She felt *lucky* when she was with him, just as the words of the song suggested. She knew she needed her friend Jenny—and she had no doubt that Jenny had set her up for a positive dinner experience with Alan Fremont. There was something about Alan that night that made her feel lucky to be with him, even though she had just met him. Her pleasure at being with Alan was not based in an attraction to him. She felt safe with him. In spite of all her fears about going to a religious conference, where she had nothing in common with anyone, she had discovered a real person who had much of her same background and faced the same life questions.

Chapter Eighteen

When Louise Mohr finished singing, she took a deep bow. The applause nearly brought the walls down. Even Mallie had to admit that the song had touched her.

"Thank you," Louise said, rising and placing her hands over her heart. "Thank you all so much. Now it's time for us to choose a partner and begin our evening's work together."

Mallie panicked. Choose a partner? The evening's work? Before she could sort out the possibilities, Alan turned to her and said, "Would you be my partner for tonight? I think we have a lot to talk about. That okay with you?"

"I'd like that," Mallie said, relieved.

As the lights went on, many people around the room were standing up and stretching, some hugging their dinner partners. Alan smiled and gave Mallie a quick, easy hug. "This should be fun," he said. "Let's find a quiet spot."

He led her to an uncrowded corner of the room where he pulled up two chairs across from each other with a small table in between. Slowly the overhead lights dimmed and the noise level in room lowered to hushed, conversational tones.

Alan pulled out a notebook and glanced at the first page. "The one specific question we're supposed to discuss tonight is,

'What would you most like to leave behind when you leave this conference?'"

"I have no idea," Mallie said, taken by surprise. "I hadn't thought about leaving anything behind."

"Would you like to know what I want to leave behind?" Alan asked. He put his notebook on the table.

"Yes," she said. Listening to him would give her time to think about the possibilities for herself.

"I want to leave my job behind."

"What do you do?" Mallie asked. She instantly thought of Larry. Leaving his job would certainly have been something Larry would have said. "Why do you want to leave your job?"

"I've been a mortgage banker ever since I got out of the University of Virginia," he said. "I'm a vice president of the Barnett Bank in Jacksonville. I'm bored to death with it."

"What would you want to do instead?" Mallie asked.

"I've been offered a job as assistant publisher of the *Florida Times Union*," he said. "It's what I've always wanted. I've been a writer at heart—first as a child, then all through college. Writing has been the way I feel free and at the same time connected to myself, to what's really important to me. I love the idea of being in publishing—but it's a major salary cut, and it's a role I'm not familiar with."

Mallie thought of her own life. She was a wife and a mother, a daughter, a sister and a friend. She was a board member of MIFA and the Art Academy. It wasn't that she was bored—she wasn't—but it was always as if something were missing in her life. She thought back to her joyful moments as a child. That joy mostly occurred when she was alone drawing pictures. She could create a world that was completely hers, where no one told her what to do or how it should be done. Ideas popped into her head like stars in the night sky. She could draw a pink horse if she wanted, or purple apples. She loved the smell of crayons and the feeling in her hand when she was drawing—a clear line between her mind and her body and the paper. All through school she felt most alive in her art classes. She understood what Alan said about the freedom he felt from his writing. Drawing and painting gave her that sense of freedom. He had also said that his writing connected him to himself. She had never thought about her art as a connection to herself. Her connection to herself had been tied to her marriage and her family. Now it looked as if all that were about to change. There would be no Larry. Her boys were growing up. As if she were about to walk into a dark room, she could not see where to take the next step.

"I think we're in the same situation—sort of," she said. "Although I don't really know what I want—how I'd go about changing my life." She stopped and sighed. "I think what I'd most like to leave behind is my fear of the unknown."

"Then we're definitely on the same wavelength, Mallie. We'll keep that goal in mind for both of us throughout the weekend."

Alan put his coffee cup down on the little table beside them. "Let's talk about your Catholic childhood, So much of our faith as an adult is founded in our childhood experiences. Were both of your parents Catholic?"

"No, no," Mallie said. "My mother's an agnostic, influenced by her intellectual father who never set foot in a church. Her mother, my Montell grandmother, never went to church either. My grandmother was sort of an heiress who apparently lost most of her money in the Crash of 1929. According to my mother's stories, my grandmother tried to bury the resentment of losing her money by going to parties and running committees. Nothing churchy at all. It was my father's family who were the devout Catholics. My Malcolm grandparents were the ones who took me to church."

Mallie recalled the consistent, happy experience of being with her grandparents on Sunday mornings. She loved the service, even though she never understood a word of the Latin Mass. She could still hear the priest's melodic voice: *Dominus vobiscum*. And the response: *Et cum spiritu tuo.* She loved the statue of the Virgin Mary holding the baby Jesus. Sometimes Mallie felt as if she were the baby in Mary's arms. At the end of the Mass, she could hardly wait to put her nickel in the metal slot and light one of the little red glass candles. She always knelt and made a wish. Nannie Malcolm told her she was really sending a prayer to God but she could call it a wish if she liked. There was something magical about the service that made Mallie feel loved and protected.

"My grandparents were the ones who took me to church, too," Alan said. "And did you go to Catholic school? I seem to remember you did—at least, you told me about your First Communion."

"Only in the second grade," Mallie said, "the year my father went away to the war. We lived with my grandparents and I walked to Immaculate Conception Catholic School. It was not a happy experience."

Mallie told Alan that her homeroom teacher had terrified her. Sister Margaret looked like a gigantic black duck with her big chest and her beaky face peering out from under her black hood. She had small eyes, a wide nose, a protruding upper lip and a hairy chin. It gave Mallie a chill to remember seeing her waddling up and down the aisles in her flat black lace-up men's shoes. The worst part was Sister Margaret's lectures about sin. She said sin was something evil that got into your body like a worm and had to be beaten out. Every day at two o'clock she chose a boy or girl who had committed the worst sin that day. In front of the whole class, Sister Margaret paddled the child until he or she cried. Mallie had been so filled with the fear of committing a sin that she hardly spoke the entire year.

"That would explain a lot about doubting the love of God, don't you think?" Alan said, shaking his head. "What a difference in the nuns today. They don't even wear habits and some of them wear makeup. They've become human."

Mallie found that hard to believe. "Do you know any?" she asked.

"I do," Alan said. "I went to a Cenacle retreat last year run by nuns. They were a far cry from the stern 'black ducks' that you and I knew as children. Talking to one of the Cenacle nuns was when I first got the idea of quitting my job. She said God would want me to do what I was created to do."

The conversation continued for about an hour. Mallie was startled—and disappointed—when the bell rang for the small group sessions to end. The experience of being with Alan had given her a new perspective on the idea of "Creative Living."

Chapter Nineteen

The following morning, sitting in the back of the lecture hall in a long row of metal chairs, Mallie began to fantasize about the speaker, Keith Miller. Right away she recognized something about him that reminded her of Tom Matthews. Maybe it was as simple as being an attractive, masculine man in a clerical collar. It was certainly not his hair—Tom's hair was polar-bear white and neatly combed. Besides Keith Miller's almost teenage mop of unruly brown hair, which she had noticed the night before, he had bushy sideburns. It was certainly not his voice—Tom spoke in a highly educated, unaccented, carefully modulated tone. Keith Miller was assuredly a Texan—an effusive, expansive, southern-talking Texan. It wasn't their religious disciplines. Church of Christ or Baptist, or whatever denomination Keith Miller was, his loose, self-referencing style could not have been more different from the Episcopal formality of Tom Matthews.

Mallie recalled the times she had listened to Tom's sermons at St. Michael's on Sunday mornings. Rarely did he mention anything personal. Sermons are for preaching the Gospel, he told her. Also she knew how much he revered the poetry and the tradition in the King James Bible. And there was Keith Miller speaking about his personal life, rejecting the King James Bible and quoting passages from his own book: "*We do not realize how unreal our language and 'in' expressions are . . . and to the uninitiated they seem pious or phony. Very few couples I know fight or make love in King James English. The men and women with whom I counsel have problems, anxieties, and doubts, which don't have a religious sound. And in my own life—when I scream silently at night in my aloneness and frustration—I do not do it in the language of the liturgy, or systematic theology.*"

Those words rang so true to Mallie. She believed him. She had never met Keith Miller, but as she watched him on the stage and listened to him talk about himself and his beliefs and his relationships, she felt oddly attracted to him. There was something powerful in her mind about a handsome, compelling man who spoke about God and the Bible in real life language. She thought of Tom Matthews. For months she had been living in the aura of her attraction to Tom. Now she found herself drawn to Keith Miller. How was it possible that she—still a married woman—could sit there in a lecture about what it means to be a Christian in the world today, and think about the sexual appeal of two married ministers?

When the lecture was over she ran back to her room for her rain jacket and was late for lunch. In the large crowd of people, all arriving at the same time, she couldn't spot any of her Memphis friends. Where was Jenny? They had agreed to meet at noon in the dining room, but Jenny was not there. Panic set in. She couldn't find anyone she knew. Where were Alan and Paige Fremont? She felt abandoned by everyone. It occurred to her to return to her room and order room service for lunch. No, she couldn't do that. She had not come all the way to the conference to be alone. She tried to push away the fear. The comfort of her time with Alan Fremont the night before seemed lost in the sea of strangers.

Mallie made herself walk over to the buffet table and begin filling a plate: tuna salad, a cup of vegetable soup, two small pieces of French bread. She looked around for an empty place at a table. Like a deer seeking safety through a hole in the woods, she dove through a group of people into the first empty chair she saw between a pleasant-looking man and a woman.

"Hi there," the man said to her without rising from his seat. He introduced himself, as did the woman on the other side. "Where're you from?" He peered down at her nametag. "Mallie? That's your name? That's really an unusual name."

She hadn't been asked about her name since Terry questioned her the first time she went to Tom's office. "My real name is Valeria," she said. "Mallie comes from Malcolm, my maiden name. My married name is Mallie Vose."

She took a bite of her tuna salad hoping he wouldn't ask where her husband was. She tried to envision Larry at a Faith at Work conference. A silly exercise. She knew he would never have agreed to come. He actually had very little interest in religion and never went to church with her. He would no doubt be shocked if he knew she was there. She had not told him where she was going for the weekend, even though he was keeping the boys while she was away. She had given him her sister Anne's number in case of emergency.

"I'm from Memphis, Tennessee," she said, answering his first question. "Where are you from?"

"Knoxville," he said. "The other end of the state."

She didn't know anyone in Knoxville to play the do-you-know game. "Oh," she said. "It's beautiful and mountainous there, I'm told."

She was feeling disoriented; some of the old apprehension that she felt on arrival was creeping back. Where were all her friends? She kept looking around the room. Finally she spotted Jenny at a table on the far side, but it was too late to pick up her plate and walk over there. She knew it would be rude to the people at the table where she was seated. Still, right away, she felt more comfortable just knowing that Jenny was in the room.

"Yes," the man said quietly, "East Tennessee is beautiful." He offered nothing more.

"Is this your first Faith at Work Conference?" Mallie asked. Surely that would provoke a conversation so she would not have to sit there in silence.

The man turned to look at her and began to talk. "This is our third conference in two years. I'm here with my wife and a group of friends," he said. "We lost our youngest child three years ago. She was on her tricycle and was hit by an Asplundh truck in front of our house. He never saw her." The man spoke as if he were telling a story he had told a thousand times, each time convincing himself of the truth of it.

Mallie was stunned. She could not imagine anything in life more horrifying or painful than losing a child. And an Asplundh truck in front of his house. Dear God! She could see the huge orange behemoth with its black lettering on the side, lumbering down the street. Why hadn't the child seen it? Or heard it? Why hadn't the driver seen the child? The thought was unspeakable. Still, she felt that she had to say something. "Oh, I'm so sorry," she said, "so, so sorry." It sounded hollow.

"She's with the Lord," the man said quietly. "That's my comfort. She's with him."

Mallie reached over and touched his arm. "I admire your courage," she said.

"Thank you," he said. Then, as calmly as if he had changed channels on a television set, he said, "So, what workshop are you going to this afternoon?"

Before she even thought about the best way to respond to his question, she blurted out: "Well, *unfortunately*, I'm going to Dave Stoner's workshop on 'marriage and divorce'."

The man didn't flinch or change his expression. He asked simply, "Why'd you choose to go to that one?"

Mallie took a deep breath. This was going to be her second experience in two days of revealing herself to a total stranger. She might not have had the courage if he had not told her about losing his child. "Because I'm separated from my husband and I may end up divorced." There. It was the truth and she had said it aloud. She tried to prepare herself for his critical judgment in case he was not as empathetic and kind as Alan Fremont had been the night before. He might even be one of those Christians who did not believe in divorce.

The man smiled at her—an understanding, not a mocking smile—and said, "Well, then, Mallie Vose, if that's the case, I'd say *fortunately* you are going to Dave Stoner's workshop on 'marriage and divorce'."

What a twist of thinking! A cool stream ran through the heated knots in her body, releasing the grip of negative thoughts. She sighed and looked at him in admiration. "Thank you," she said. "You're absolutely right. Thank you for that."

They continued eating and chatting easily about Louise Mohr's singing the night before and the books that had been written by different workshop leaders. Mallie admitted that she had never heard of any of the leaders before, certainly had never read any of their books.

"Keith Miller's *The Taste of New Wine* is one of my favorites," the man said. "And *The Becomers*. He's really a good writer. Really honest about life and himself."

Mallie recalled her thoughts about Keith Miller as he stood on the platform talking about *The Becomers* in the morning workshop. She was embarrassed that she had been analyzing his beautiful hair, his handsome face, and the way he spoke so intimately into the microphone, rather than listening to the message of his words. Maybe she would buy one of his books and read it after she got home.

"He's recently separated from his wife. Did you know that?" the man asked.

Mallie shook her head. She couldn't imagine that anyone who had written a Christian book and was a workshop leader at Faith at Work would be separated from his wife.

"And Dave Stoner's been recently divorced," he said. "They say it's has been a horribly painful time for both of them."

Mallie tried to keep her expression calm with a million thoughts raging through her head. Separation and divorce. Keith Miller and Dave Stoner. Painful times for both of them. Neither of them had perfect lives, as she had been taught to believe that Christians had perfect lives. Nor had the man sitting next to her who had lost a child. She thought of Tom and his wife and their three children. He told her his wife had been diagnosed with multiple sclerosis years before, but that she was mostly in remission. Obviously he didn't have a perfect life either. It seemed that being a Christian was no protection against human difficulties.

Chapter Twenty

For Mallie, Dave Stoner's workshop on marriage and divorce that afternoon was full of helpful information, some aspects resonant with what she had been learning in her counseling sessions, some completely new. Initially, Dave spoke of the "death of a marriage." Ever since she first heard that concept from Tom, she had taken it to heart. It had become a mantra against the assault of guilt that she felt for breaking her commitment "until death do us part." But underneath the idea, she still had her doubts. Dave Stoner's lecture was another step toward liberation.

"When a marriage is dead," he said, "when the love is dead—the commitment is dead. Love, after all, is the core of commitment."

"What is love?" he asked the assembled group. Then, without waiting for an answer, he wrote his definition in big block letters on a blackboard.

A DEFINITION OF LOVE:

I WISH FOR YOU GOOD AND NOT BAD.
I WILL BE THERE FOR YOU.
I WILL NOT RUN AWAY.
I WILL BE WHAT YOU NEED ME TO BE—
WITHIN THE LIMITS OF MY VALUE SYSTEM.

Mallie studied the words. Right away, the ideas appealed to her, although the last two lines were puzzling. What did he mean by "I will be what you need me to be—within the limits of my value system'?"

"Everyone's value system is not the same," Dave Stoner explained. "Suppose someone wants you to physically or psychologically abuse him or her in some way. If you see that as harmful, then it is not within your value system. You must trust yourself in that case. Your value system is between you and God. You need to honor that trust."

Mallie wondered if she had gone against her own value system through the years of denying Larry's affairs with other women. Perhaps she had been lying to herself that she was being loving to him by protecting him—and her family. Maybe she had not really been *what he needed her to be* —maybe, however misguided, she had been protecting herself and her marriage. And what about the idea of *running away*? She knew she had run away—if not physically, certainly emotionally. She knew also that there had been times when she had wished for Larry *bad and not good*. She was angry with him. According to Dave Stoner's definition, she had obviously not been *loving* to Larry. But neither had he been *loving* toward her. Larry had unquestionably run away from her, from their marriage. She thought about Tom Matthews. Could she follow those criteria for loving him? Yes, she believed that she could easily do all of those things for him. She smiled, remembering that Tom had said that he "would always be there" for her.

"Love exists in relationship," Dave Stoner went on to say. "If there's no relationship, there can be no love. Love starts with your relationship to yourself. To use the First Commandment as a guide—to love God with all your heart and with all your mind—it begins with the belief that God exists in the deepest part of you. That means that your first relationship responsibility is to yourself. You must love yourself if you are ever to love anyone else."

He went on to explain that in his own life—and therefore, in his marriage—he had not really understood that loving God meant loving himself. He and his wife went through many years together—raising a family and going to church every Sunday—without being honest and loving within each of their own hearts. When trouble came, that habit, that outward expression of love, did not sustain them. He did not specify the trouble, but he spoke to his rapt audience with passion and conviction. "We must have an honest, loving, personal relationship to whatever it is that we think of as God within us, and we need to apply those same values in our relationship with each other—in both marriage and in divorce."

In the question and answer period of Dave Stoner's lecture, someone asked about a parent's responsibility to children in a divorce. He began by suggesting that both parents needed to support their children in learning to live with only one parent at home, no matter what the relationship was to the other parent.

"Answer all their questions as honestly as you can," he said. "Don't offer any information they're not ready to hear. It won't help them, and it'll only end up hurting you in the long run." That was similar to what Tom had told Mallie when she and Larry separated.

He ended his lecture by saying: "Love is not only the core of a good marriage, it is also the core of a good divorce."

Mallie left the room with much to think about.

At the farewell dinner that night, Bruce Larson addressed the theme of the conference, the core idea of "Creative Living." It seemed a perfect echo of Dave Stoner's workshop message—and exactly what Mallie knew she needed to hear.

"The essence of God is the Creative Spirit," he said, "always present, constantly renewable, an underground spring that is eternal. It exists in the deepest part of our being—as well as in the core of everything that lives and breathes. In order to know that spring, we must break the chains of our childhood fears, the negative barriers that are lodged in our minds. That is our most difficult task as Christians—as spiritual human beings. All of our poets and painters instinctively know that spring, that connection to the Creative Spirit, whether or not they call it God. They hold and nurture that relationship to the eternal. And so must we."

By the end of the weekend, Mallie's mind was exploding with ideas. She could almost laugh at the dubious, skittish person who had arrived at the front desk and met Louise Mohr on Friday afternoon. With a new enthusiasm, she sang the songs of praise along with the group at their final dinner. She didn't go so far as to walk up to the stage when there was a call for new Christians to come forward and give themselves to Jesus. There was something about the drama of all that staged business that still bothered her.

At the end she hugged all her new friends goodbye—Alan and Paige, some of the people in her workshops, even a brief hug with Keith Miller. Besides carrying a signed copy of his book *A Taste of New Wine*, she left with a stack of "relational religion" paperback books to read. She was determined to go home with a new understanding of the Creative Spirit in her heart. She could hardly wait to share her new beliefs with Tom Matthews.

Chapter Twenty-one

For the first ten minutes of her weekly appointment with Tom, Mallie spilled out her stories of her Faith at Work experience— the opening night with Alan Fremont, the lecture by Keith Miller and the workshop with Dave Stoner, the idea of God as Creative Spirit, the prospect of believing in herself because that Creative Spirit was the deepest part of herself. She even told him about the man that she met at lunch, whose name she had forgotten, who had lost a child and turned her thinking around about attending the workshop on divorce.

Tom listened patiently, then said, "What you had, Mallie, was a mountaintop experience. It's a great place to reach, but it's a hard place to maintain."

"Are you saying it won't last?" It was discouraging to imagine losing all the positive things she had gathered from the weekend, deflating the buoyancy that had so lifted her spirits.

"No, not that you will lose it," he said. "I'm saying it will change over time. It's like stretching a knitted sweater out of shape. It never goes back to its original size. What you heard there—what you learned—was all good information and much of it has lasting value. But getting all that spiritual insight at once is so powerful— you can't hold onto it in exactly that way."

Mallie sat back in her chair. She knew he was right. She had already betrayed her own private Faith at Work vow to give up her fear of the unknown and be patient and honest with everyone in her life. All the way home in the car her mind went back and forth between happy positive thoughts and anguish over her financial situation. Before she had been home an hour, she had lost her temper at Larry. He had brought the boys home after seven thirty on Sunday when he had assured her he would be there by five. She hardly let him explain that the game on television ran overtime and the boys asked to stay until the end. She had also lied to her mother in her Monday morning long distance conversation.

"I guess I've already come down," she said with a shrug. "I blew up at Larry and I lied to my mother this morning. I told her I'd gone to Nashville to stay with an old friend from camp. She would never have understood about Faith at Work."

"Sometimes you have to fudge the truth a little to protect yourself—or someone else," Tom said. "That's not really lying, not in any sinful sense. Sin, after all, is not something you do—or don't do. It's a state of separation from God."

It didn't occur to Mallie at the time that Tom might "fudge the truth a little" to protect himself. Nor did she want to pursue the definition of sin as separation from God. She didn't want to talk about sin or God. All she was interested in at that moment was getting through the talk stage of her appointment. With a part of her still floating in the euphoria of her experience at Faith at Work, she felt even more passionate toward Tom.

Within seconds, she reached for him and the two of them fell onto the couch. When he kissed her, she wanted to burrow inside of him. Too soon—at least in her mind—he lifted her away from him, reminding her that their time was up. It always came too soon for her. He kissed her one last time and assured her he loved her and he would be thinking of her all week between their appointments.

Mallie drove away from St. Michael's on a high note. She felt nothing but the positive things in her life. Faith at Work had given her a new perspective on religion as a Creative Spirit and on surviving her future without Larry. Tom had given her reassurance that he loved her.

Quite suddenly, as if a foreign body had invaded her consciousness, she began to experience clear images of some of her most cherished memories with Larry. The timing seemed absurd. Her whole being had been filled with Tom and suddenly she was face to face with Larry—the Larry that she had once loved—along with an entire scrapbook of their life together. As if her experience with Tom had opened the door to the place in her brain where she stored happiness, she was blinded by pictures of the past, joyful times with Larry that had been all but crushed under the weight of suspicion and anger and fear.

For the first time she saw the possibility that all the places and people she had loved and shared with Larry for eighteen years would change dramatically if they were divorced. Christmas mornings with the boys, the joy of standing beside her husband and watching their sons' eyes widen when Larry lowered the sheets covering the entrance to the living room, their rush toward the lit Christmas tree and all their presents stacked in piles. Family hikes with Bingo on Sunday afternoons in Shelby Forest. Boating trips on Pickwick Lake—Larry teaching each of the boys to waterski. Their summers in Watch Hill. Until that moment it had not occurred to Mallie that she would lose Watch Hill. Of course, she would. The place belonged to Larry's family. It had been Vose territory for generations. And she would lose Edie, her dear mother-in-law. In her mind's eye, she could see the tiny, trim woman with her cap of curly, silver-streaked hair that framed a face dominated by enormous light brown eyes. Mallie always thought Edie resembled a small, lovable, furry animal, bubbling with chatter and infectious laughter. On the day that she met Edie, her future mother-in-law had asked her to call her by her first name. "I always knew Larry would marry someone I would love," she said. Hearing the echo of her mother-in-law's voice, Mallie felt a searing pain in her chest. And what about her father-in-law? She thought of the tall, taciturn, professorial lawyer, an overseer at Harvard whom she had once called Mr. Vose. How she loved both of her in-laws! After the boys were born, she had learned to call her father-in-law Poppy. Through the years, she had watched him patiently teaching his grandsons to fly-fish. She listened to him give brilliant toasts at family events and speak quietly to her about politics and world affairs. Certain pronouncements he made were etched in her mind. "Civilization is a race between ignorance and education," he once said.

In all Mallie's years of knowing her in-laws, neither one of them had ever criticized her and often praised her for being a good mother. She even felt that, on occasion, they would take her side over Larry's. The thought that she would never be with either of her in-laws, close to them again, saddened her. Her summers in Watch Hill had opened a new world of family experiences that she could not bear to think of losing.

As if God himself had spoken to her, she felt the full force of Tom's pronouncement of "sin as separation." She had never thought of herself as a sinful person. But if sin were separation and sin caused pain, she was surely sinful. She was separated from Larry, separated from her marriage—separated from everything that she had valued and tried to protect. She was alone in the world. She pulled over on the side of the road and buried her face in her hands.

Chapter Twenty-two

"Mallie, where've you been? I've been calling you all day with no answer." Jenny's usual soft, comforting voice was sharp with breathless urgency.

"Today was my April board meeting at the Art Academy. Why? What's the matter?"

"Hold on, my friend—you've got a shock coming," Jenny said.

Mallie's back stiffened, her jaw tightened. "What is it?" She knew whatever was coming must have something to do with Larry. Jenny had promised her that she would not keep any information about Larry a secret from her ever again.

"I had a call this morning from a friend of mine who works at Continental Travel Agency downtown. She knows you and Larry are separated—and that you and I are friends. She said she thought I should tell you that Larry came in yesterday and booked a trip for two to some fancy resort hotel in St. Bart's. They're going to the Caribbean next week."

Mallie was stupefied. Somehow she managed to thank Jenny for the call and said she had to think about it, that she would get back with her later.

In spite of her three month separation from Larry, Mallie felt blindsided. Never mind all her musings about the possibility of divorce, she still lived in the limbo of indecision. She had not yet met with a lawyer, and as far as she knew, neither had Larry. Even after the Faith at Work conference and all the positive feedback about new beginnings, she had not been able to fully see herself as a divorced woman. When Larry left home, he said it was "to get my life together, to try to work things out." He had made that statement in front of her and the boys. A week later, Sammy had called Mallie from St. George's School and told her that his dad had assured him on the phone that he would probably not get a divorce. The whole idea of Larry going to the Caribbean with another woman—no doubt that woman named Julie—felt like a final betrayal to Mallie. She wondered if Tom Matthews knew about the trip. She knew that Larry was still counseling with him on Thursdays—and recently Terry had told her that Tom had also started counseling sessions with Julie. The more Mallie thought about Larry's jaunt to the Caribbean, the angrier she grew. Larry obviously had no intention of "working things out." If he planned to take Julie to St. Bart's, that would prove his real intentions. It would make their separation a sham. Maybe it was not true. Somehow she would have to see Larry herself. She had to know the truth.

Before she could make any serious plans to try to find Larry, she had to fix dinner for the boys. It was a school night and she always tried to have dinner for them promptly at six. Fortunately, she had stopped at the Krystal for burgers and french fries on her way home, so dinner was ready made.

It was an unusually hot day in late April, hot enough to close the windows and turn on the air conditioning. For several minutes, as she set the table and put the meal together, Mallie began mentally putting together a plan. First of all, she would have to change her clothes. She had on her pale pink linen suit, one of her best board meeting outfits. She would take a shower and change into a sleeveless cotton sundress, something comfortable and casual. Once the boys were settled into doing their homework, she would drive over to Larry's apartment. Maybe he would not be at home. The more frightening thought was that he would be at home. She could not imagine exactly what she would say to him. She would have to trust that the right words would come to her.

∽◌

A little after eight, Mallie turned the key in her Plymouth station wagon. She knew where Larry's apartment was located in Laurelwood. She had dropped off and picked up the boys there several times in the past few months, but she had not been inside. Her car radio was tuned to a rock station, the one she listened to when she drove carpools. She turned it off. She drove in silence, her mind filling the void with a cacophony of conflicting, threatening possibilities. There was a chance that Larry would lie about the trip and she would have to confront him with the facts. There was also a possibility that he would readily admit he had planned it. He might even say that he was taking Julie with him. If he admitted it, that would break their impasse. How ridiculous, Mallie thought, there was no impasse. There never was any hope of "working it out." She had to question the real reason why she was going to his apartment and not just calling him on the telephone and telling him it was over. She wanted to see his face when she told him she knew about the trip.

There were no lights on in Larry's apartment—at least, from what she could see in the windows—but his light gray Audi was in the driveway. She banged once on the brass doorknocker. Moments later, just before she banged it again, a light flashed on the porch. The door opened and Larry stood in front of her in his pale blue Brooks Brothers cotton pajamas and bare feet.

"Mallie." He spoke her name as if he were identifying a long lost friend in an unexpected place.

She stood speechless. She never expected to find him in pajamas. They looked at each other for several seconds.

"Do you want to come in?" He ran his fingers through his tousled hair and then added, "I've had a really tough week. I thought I'd go to bed early. I was reading." He did not say: *Why are you here?* or *Is anything wrong?*—just a simple, semi-cordial invitation to come in to his apartment—and a feeble attempt at explaining his attire.

"Larry, you know why I'm here," Mallie said, as she came through the door.

"No," he said. "I haven't the slightest idea." He looked genuinely puzzled. "Want to sit down?"

"Well," she said, standing next to the door that automatically closed behind her, "I suppose you thought I'd never find out about your little trip to St. Bart's."

Larry's body tensed under his lightweight cotton pajamas. His expression did not change. He sat down in the closest living room chair and said nothing.

"I suppose you're taking Julie with you," Mallie said. There was no point in leaving it up to him to speak the truth.

"Maybe I am," he said. "I need to get away for a few days."

Mallie felt a furor beyond anything that she had previously experienced. She wanted to bellow out like her father, *Goddammit Larry! How could you do this?* But instead, she said, "You know what this means."

"What?" He looked like a child, holding some loose change he had taken from his mother's purse, denying he had taken it. He had no idea how the silver coins came to be in his hand.

"It means that this separation time is over. It's a lie."

Larry said nothing.

"Say something, Larry," she said. "What were you thinking? *You need to get away?* How could you do this?"

"I'm sorry, Mallie," he said, his voice low. He did not look at her. "What else can I say? I'm sorry."

There was no denial, no explanation, no fight.

Mallie realized she hardly knew the person sitting across the room. The man she married, the handsome, always well-dressed, well-spoken, life of the party—the person everyone thought had the greatest potential in business and in life—the father of her boys, her friend and her lover—was a stranger in cotton pajamas and bare feet. He appeared to be uninterested in defending himself or his behavior, except to say, "I'm sorry."

Despite her underlying lack of confidence in who she was or how her future might unfold without Larry, Mallie knew that the separation was over. She would call a lawyer. She would file for divorce.

Chapter Twenty-three

When the news was out that Mallie and Larry were definitely getting a divorce, Cindy Morgan called her to say, "Don't you worry for a second, Mallie, honey, you'll be married again within a year." Cindy was not the only one of Mallie's friends to assure her that the right man would appear for her in no time. Every time someone said those words, Mallie felt a seismic shift, a disconnect from her friends. She knew she was on a different path. Where that path was leading she had no idea. She couldn't explain those thoughts to Cindy or even to herself. She just knew that her most pressing concern was not finding another husband. She needed to find herself. She needed to find a way to make her life meaningful and to figure out how to believe in herself without being "a wife." She needed to talk to Tom Matthews.

⌒⌒⌒

On Tuesday afternoon, Tom agreed with Mallie that before ever thinking of another man in her life, she needed to think about making a good life by herself. His specific concern followed her explanation that there would not be enough alimony to allow her any choices beyond paying the most basic expenses for herself and the boys.

"I will obviously need a job," Mallie said. But even as she said it, she realized that no one would hire her without any real work experience—the volunteer jobs and board positions she held would not account for much. She only had three years of college. Thinking about the possibilities of a job was as remote and abstract as preparing for a possible earthquake within the New Madrid fault—Memphis was sitting on that fault—or making a plan for her old age. The idea sounded right and logical, something she should do, but she had no clue as to how it might work or what form it would take.

To make the financial matters more complicated, Mallie explained to Tom, Larry had apparently taken out a mortgage on their house. For a number of years, maybe as many as ten or twelve, Mallie's father had been the owner of their house and Larry had paid rent to him. When the tax advantage presented itself, her father had deeded the house over to both of them. She had no recollection of ever signing the paper that Larry's lawyer produced to prove that she must have known about the mortgage.

Other than her frustrating attempts through the years to make her allowance from Larry last a whole month, she had little knowledge of their true financial picture. She never understood what happened to all of his salary. Only once did she look at one of his bank statements and was shocked at a large overdraft notice. Larry had an explanation and assured her it had been taken care of. She never looked at another statement or asked again.

In all their years of marriage, she had known nothing about taxes or insurance and had no money in her own name. No credit card. It was obvious, even to her naïve understanding of their monetary situation, that Larry's salary would be problematic to divide for each of them to live apart. They had difficulty enough staying within its boundaries together.

Larry's financial offer to her included sole ownership of the house—assuming the mortgage payments, of course—and all its contents. The idea was intended to disturb the boys' lives as little as possible. Larry would give her an amount of monthly alimony that would allow her to pay basic expenses as best she and her lawyer could calculate them. He would pay for the boys' education—except for the St. George's tuition for Sammy, which Larry's parents supplied—and all of their medical expenses. There would be nothing else to share with her.

Before Tom could ask any further questions or make comments, she said, "Another possibility might be to sell the house, pay off the mortgage, buy something much smaller—live more simply—and go back to school. I've always wanted to go back to art school. Maybe get my master's degree."

Tom got a quizzical look on his face. "Really?" he said. "What a wonderful idea. I know we've talked about your time studying art in Italy—how much you loved it. Going to art school is a grand idea."

Mallie remembered feeling embarrassed at Tom's suggestion that she was an artist. She revered artists as the truly gifted people of the world. When she was growing up, she secretly believed that she might be a great artist someday—like her Aunt Valeria—but she had given the idea up and willingly chosen a family instead. When she had questioned her ability, Tom had assured her that "Once an artist, always an artist."

As if it were only yesterday, she saw herself immersed in her daily life at the Villa Mercedes in Florence. She felt both the simplicity and complexity of her time there. Visions and sounds floated through her mind: the view of the red rooftops and the Duomo from the expansive property on the hilltop of Bellesguardo, the bustle of the city below, the roar of Vespas, the clacking of streetcars. She felt the regal presence of the ancient stone sculptures calming every busy piazza. She recalled the studio where she touched the wet paper with a wet brush and watched the color spread out, taking on a life of its own. She closed her eyes to feel the recurrent sense of magic that had taken over her life for all of those months.

Except for desperately missing Larry in the beginning, Mallie's life in Florence had been perfect. It was the only time she could ever remember that she had no thoughts of anyone but herself, her surroundings and her art.

"I guess I always wanted to believe I would go back to my own art someday," she said. "I talked about it a little when I was at Faith at Work. Maybe the right time has come."

Tom smiled. "I can't think of a better time," he said, "or anything better to do with your time."

Mallie assured him that she would think seriously about it.

She was becoming anxious. Too much talk. The routine they had established during the months of counseling sessions was to spend about half the time talking, usually twenty minutes or so, at the beginning, enough time to run through all the issues that she often felt had been exploding inside her during the week, and then, after he managed to diffuse them—as he always did—they would spend the remainder of the hour on the couch embracing. All she wanted at the moment was for Tom to hold her. It was what she dreamed about all week.

Often, during the endless nights at home alone, unable to wait for Tuesday, she composed long letters to Tom. She wrote paragraphs—occasionally lines of poetry—devoted to her romantic thoughts about him. In one letter she told him of a blissful early morning dream that the two of them were sea otters, rolling and tumbling in the cool Pacific waters. She found it easier to pour out her feelings on paper rather than speak the words to him face to face. Occasionally she slipped the papers in a sealed envelope under his door before the chapel opened for the day.

Mallie reached over to put her face against his. He took off his glasses and pulled her toward him. She floated into his lap and drew in the smell of his skin and the softness of his mouth the way she thought some people might inhale cigarettes, pulling the stimulant down deep into her body. Nothing else mattered in those moments of intimacy. She would readily have taken off every stitch of clothing and given herself to Tom. She knew that was not going to happen. Early on he had firmly advised her of his limitations. As much as he would like to make love to her, he said, *under the circumstances*, he could not—would not—ever—let that happen. In spite of his pronouncement, spoken with such earnestness, she felt a new level of desire for him—and of being desired by him. The way he kissed her—the urgency, the tenderness—made her believe with all her heart that Tom wanted to make love to her, but that, as a married man, he was taking the only moral stand he could. However contrary to every thing she had criticized about Larry's behavior, she did not allow herself to question her own moral stand.

Chapter Twenty-four

For the remainder of the week following her Tuesday afternoon in Tom Matthews's study, Mallie relived and rethought every moment. Alone in the car, as if she were in a psychology class, she analyzed his every word and gesture. Over and over she heard him say that he could not make love to her "under the circumstances." That statement was hard to rationalize. She could admit and understand that he was a married man—and a priest—and her counselor—but his embraces were so loving, and so romantic. And yet it all seemed so contradictory. How could she make sense of it? The connecting hinge always came back to the fact that whenever she said she loved him, he told her that he loved her, too.

What she knew for certain was that when she was in his arms, she felt that she was once again a desirable, seductive woman. She would give anything, anything on earth, to know that she would someday make love to him and be with him—really with him—all the time. Surely *the circumstances* could change. She knew ministers who were divorced and remarried. The men who spoke at Faith at Work, for instance. Keith Miller and Dave Stoner were both divorced, and she had recently heard that Dave was remarried. But Tom was a highly respected Episcopal priest in Memphis.

He was known for his integrity, as well as his intelligence. Occasionally, when he held Bible study classes at the cathedral, many of the most important businessmen and lawyers in Memphis came to hear him. He had counseled countless couples and individuals, all of whom, she imagined, admired him. And furthermore, he would never leave a wife with multiple sclerosis—or his three children. Mallie felt guilty for even imagining that he would do such a thing. She, of all women, who had suffered for so many years with the pain of doubt over the "other women" in her husband's life—how could she have even thought of Tom betraying his family? He had often told her how much he loved his son and his twin girls, how he had gone to his son's graduation from the Indiana University and been so proud of his magna cum laude degree. The boy was now in his second year of Emory Law School. The girls were seniors at Memphis State University, one in psychology and the other a math whiz. Lauren, the math whiz, would be the one, he told her, who would, if anyone could, help him to get his papers organized. Tom had written pages of his doctoral research material in longhand on yellow legal pads, then hunted-and-pecked his writing on a typewriter. He had ten years' worth of notes stuffed into drawers of his desk.

A history buff all his adult life, Tom had been working on completing his doctoral thesis about Andrew Jackson's place in American history. Besides his fascination with Jackson's military record and the political issues of his presidency, Tom was moved by the untimely death of his "illegitimate" wife, Rachel.

As a result of their discussions, Mallie had spent time in the public library looking up further information about Rachel Jackson. She discovered the pitiful details of Rachel's demise in a dress store in Nashville, trying on ball gowns for her husband's presidential inauguration. Rachel was said to have overheard two women talking loudly in the dressing room next to her, disparaging her for marrying Andrew Jackson without obtaining a divorce from her first husband. It was apparently of no concern to them that Rachel's first husband had abandoned her. The women called her a whore. "Imagine having that harlot in the White House!" one of them said. Poor Rachel fainted in the dressing room and never quite recovered. She died before the inauguration and, therefore, never spent a night in the White House.

Mallie became consumed with the cruel criticism of Rachel Jackson. Somehow the thought reminded her of her own life. She imagined that if her friends in Memphis knew of her love for Tom, they might accuse her of being a harlot like Rachel. After all, Tom was a married man, and she was still married to Larry. But no one knew. It was her secret.

The one aspect of her life that superseded her secret life with Tom Matthews was her concern for her boys. Each of their lives had begun to show specific signs of stress. The nurse at St. George's School had called the night before to inform her that Sammy had been in the infirmary with a low-grade fever for nearly a week. He complained of a headache, but there was no identifiable cause. The nurse would continue to watch him, she said, and she would keep Mallie informed. Troy, the most outgoing and gregarious child, had stopped wanting to bring friends home and only wanted to spend time at the barn with the horses. David shut himself in his room and drew pictures that he mostly ripped into little pieces. The disruption in her boys' lives that Mallie so feared as a result of divorce was coming to pass. She so wanted to find a way to help them. Surely, eventually, they would understand and they would be okay.

She turned up the radio full blast in the car. "*Bye, bye, Miss American Pie—Drove my Chevy to the levee and the levee was dry.*" She swayed her shoulders to the lilt of Don McLean's voice. "*This'll be the day that I die.*" The strange words didn't matter. She wasn't really listening to the words anyway. She was alive in the sensuous beat of the music, the stirring she felt from her secret connection to Tom Matthews. Mallie knew that she was driving out Poplar Avenue on her way to the barn to pick up Troy—her adored second son—and yet, she felt as if she were speeding to the edge of the earth where she would willingly careen out of her old life into the arms of a new life with the man she loved.

Chapter Twenty-five

B y the beginning of August in 1977, Mallie was sweltering in the high humidity and relentless ninety-five-degree heat of Memphis. It was the first summer she had not driven the boys to Watch Hill in fifteen years. She longed for the cool ocean breeze and the summer life. It further annoyed her that Larry was flying the boys up there to visit his parents for two weeks without her. Not that she necessarily wanted to be there with him, but the thought of the boys and Edie and her friends all together in her adopted summer place—at least, through the years she had come to believe that it was also hers—made her steam with envy. To add to her irritation, Tom, too, was planning to go away on vacation with his wife and children for a week.

When Jenny offered to take Mallie along to visit her sister Elizabeth in the English countryside, Mallie was thrilled. She had not been to England since she was an art student in Italy in 1959, and then only to London for a few days before school began.

Besides paying her own airfare—she could manage that from the remainder of the Christmas gift from her parents—Mallie would have few expenses. They would stay at Jenny's sister Elizabeth's house in West Sussex on the southeast coast of England. Mallie had known Elizabeth and her husband Ian from the years when they'd visited Jenny and Webster for the Memphis Cotton Carnival week. She and Larry and all their friends had cavorted through the social festivities with them. She had always liked Elizabeth and Ian.

Jenny's plan for Mallie included a weekend retreat entitled *Summons to Life: The Search for Identity Through the Spiritual* at St. James Church in the nearby town of Arundel. The title of the retreat was taken from a book written by Martin Israel, an Anglican priest well-known throughout the British Isles. Mallie had never heard of Martin Israel, but that didn't matter to her. She trusted Jenny to include her in a worthwhile, perhaps even uplifting, experience. Jenny's insistence that she go to Callaway Gardens for Faith at Work had proved to be uplifting—although Tom had been right about the impossibility of sustaining the mountaintop aspect of the conference. She knew that she had been spiritually stretched in ways that would never allow her to return to her pre-Faith-at-Work shape—but she had long since come down to earth.

Perhaps the retreat at St. James Church would rekindle the transcendent feelings that she had experienced at Faith at Work. At the very least, she would not be left at home alone for two weeks. Also, the prospect of cool, damp English mornings and the smell of blooming garden roses gave her something to look forward to.

Telling Tom goodbye was difficult. She could not imagine being without his presence in her life for two full weeks. While he was away and she was in England, she couldn't even write to him and sneak the letters under the door of St. Michael's. She would keep a journal, a way to share the retreat at St. James when they both returned. Surely, whatever she might learn from studying a book subtitled *The Search for Identity Through the Spiritual* would offer something meaningful she could share with Tom. Certainly the concept was something she believed she needed—and wanted—for herself.

"I hope you have a wonderful trip, Mallie," Tom said, holding her shoulders and forcing her to take her burrowed face away from his chest and look at him. "I'll be thinking of you and praying for you."

"Praying for you" sounded so cold and detached to Mallie after they had been kissing on the couch—prior to his lifting her to her feet—so completely lacking in the intimacy she had been feeling. Still, she reminded herself that he often said he would pray for her when it was time for the session to end. She rationalized that it was just his way, his ministerial, priestly way, of protecting her when they were apart.

"I'll pray for you, too," she said, applying the moment in the Episcopal service when the priest says, "The Lord be with you" and the congregation responds, "And also with you." After all, he would be traveling, too.

He gave her a small white leather *Book of Common Prayer* to take with her. Inside was an inscription that read: "For Mallie, in Christ's love, Tom." She would treasure it, read it on the airplane, treat it as if a part of him were going with her. "Oh Tom," she said, "it's so thoughtful of you."

He hugged her once again and found her mouth one last time. "Tom," she whispered, as he pulled away from her. "I don't want to go. I don't want to leave you."

"It's all okay, Mallie." His voice was soft. He took her face in his hands, his gray-blue eyes holding her as if they were physically connected. "I'll be here when you get back. Go to England and have a wonderful time."

⁓

Somewhere over the Atlantic Ocean during the long night flight, the captain interrupted the darkened cabin with an announcement: "Sorry to wake you folks, but I think you'll want to see the phenomenon of the Northern Lights—the Aurora Borealis—off the left side of the airplane. It's a bit unusual this time of year, but on all my flights over, I've never seen them any more spectacular."

Mallie roused from her curled-up sleep and lifted the tight little shade next to her window seat. The sight was startling: Niagara Falls in the sky. Waves of white light pouring down from the high heavens, covering the area as far as she could see on both sides of her window. Electric, alive, the shimmering white curtain illuminated the night sky. She felt as if she were the tiniest speck of life, an absolutely inconsequential observer, and yet, here she was, in a front-row seat, watching a show of nature more amazing, more beautiful, than anything she had ever seen. It had to be a good omen, a gift to her from God. She wondered if she could ever paint what she was seeing. No, she could not paint motion. Always she had painted something static: a landscape, a figure patiently holding a pose, or a still life with inanimate fruits and objects. In that moment, the animation, the movement, the light, was what excited her. Surely that was what inspired contemporary artists—Jackson Pollock and de Kooning, for instance. She had been to the Museum of Modern Art and admired their work but had never understood it. She had recently seen the movie about the artist Paul Jenkins, a visual lesson on how he poured paint directly onto the canvas. She was fascinated with the fluidity of the paint as it flowed out of a bucket, but once it was down—like the swirls of paint on Pollock's canvases—it looked like a mass of meaningless color to her, sometimes beautiful but without meaning. Did the Aurora Borealis have meaning? She was totally captivated by its visual energy. She felt as if she were part of it. That was meaning enough.

Suddenly she wanted to share the Aurora Borealis with someone she loved. She wished she could share it with Tom. It was too extraordinary, too exciting for her to keep to herself. She thought of her youngest son, David. She wished she could share the phenomenon with her artist son, her nature lover, David. For a fleeting second, she closed her eyes and pictured him with his brothers and his father at the beach in Watch Hill. Larry, drinking beer and cavorting on the beach, Sammy and Troy racing their friends to the float, their strong legs propelling them through the cool blue water, David collecting bucket-loads of sea treasures. She missed her boys. She wondered if they ever gave her a thought. She opened her eyes. The white light was still there, sweeping over the dark sky. The colorful projection of her family experience in Watch Hill faded into a sepia landscape, a portrait of the past.

She lightly poked Jenny on the shoulder. "You've got to see this," she whispered and pushed herself back in the seat for Jenny to lean over her toward the window. More asleep than Mallie had been when the captain spoke, Jenny blinked as if blinded by strobe lights. The two of them, their heads pressed close together against the window, watched silently until Jenny had finally had enough and pulled back into her middle seat, closing her eyes again. Mallie kept a vigil until the vibrant, crystalline light faded into the soft pink hue of dawn.

Chapter Twenty-six

Driving in England proved to be too difficult for Mallie. She had volunteered to be the first to take the wheel out of Gatwick Airport and had promptly blown out a tire, edging too close to a curb on a roundabout. Their rented black Humber Hawk sat wounded on the side of the road while they waited for the rental company to send someone to change the tire.

The accident was not surprising, given Mallie's sleepless night on the airplane. Still, she felt a pang of inadequacy for her inability to drive properly on the left side of the road. Jenny was her usual understanding, forgiving self, reassuring Mallie that she could easily have done the same thing. It would take time to acclimate to the English way.

Jenny's sister Elizabeth Carlisle lived in an eighteenth-century brick manor house, surrounded by flower gardens and a sweep of lawn down to the distant shoreline. On first glance, there was a peace about the place that Mallie imagined existed only in old monasteries or convents.

When the massive wooden front doors opened, a small herd of corgis, long, low-to-the-ground, fox-like dogs with no tails and erect ears, and two Jack Russell terriers, short and wiry, bolted out of the house, encircling the newcomers with ardent sniffings and noisy greetings.

"I do hope you like doggies," Elizabeth said with the slight British accent she had cultivated from living in England for so many years.

Mallie recognized the tall, silver-haired, tweedy figure in the doorway, although Elizabeth looked much older than she had remembered and nothing like Jenny. The sisters had grown up in Louisville, Kentucky, and Elizabeth had married Lord Ian Carlisle, the eldest son of their father's distant cousin, the Earl of Carlisle. Ian had come to Louisville for Elizabeth's debut party in 1950, and that was that. A match made in heaven, Jenny said—unlike her ill-fated match with Webster. The British tabloids reported the wedding as "English Royalty Marries American Whiskey Heiress." The headline had been accurate, though somewhat tacky, according to Jenny. She and Elizabeth were certainly "whiskey heiresses," thanks to their grandfather's Kentucky bourbon distillery, and Ian was due to inherit his father's title as a large English landowner although neither carried a large cash reserve. The girls' inheritance from their family's whiskey business, a fact that Jenny had tried to keep more or less under wraps in Memphis, had made both of them independently wealthy women from the age of twenty-one.

"I love dogs!" Mallie said, dropping her bag and reaching to scratch behind the ears of the closest corgi.

Jenny rushed up the stone stairway and threw her arms around Elizabeth. Mallie was instantly envious of the closeness of the sisters. She loved her two sisters but rarely had the opportunity to spend time with them. She had not seen Anne or her younger sister Kye in months. Neither Anne nor her husband was fond of Larry, particularly after Mallie called Anne to tell her about what was going on in her marriage and why she had been so upset on their weekend trip in Florida—the whole story of her discovery of the letters. As geographically close as Atlanta was to Memphis, they did not exchange visits, only Christmas presents, and occasionally telephone calls—usually when someone in the family was ill or got married or died. Anne did send Mallie a large bouquet of flowers after Mallie told her about her separation from Larry. "Because you're you," the note on the flowers said, "with love, Anne."

Her sister Kye, on the other hand, adored Larry and found it hard to believe that Mallie was divorcing him, cutting him out of the family. Born exactly nine months after Mallie's father returned from the Second World War, Kye had been twelve years old and a junior bridesmaid at the time of her wedding to Larry. He had always brought her presents when he came to court Mallie, mostly boxes of chocolate. Kye had graduated from Briarcliff Junior College several years before and had taken a job as an intern with *Mademoiselle* in New York. She was the only one of the sisters to take flight from their father's house and live the independent life of a young professional in the big city. Mallie had tried to explain her separation to Kye without painting Larry red with horns and a tail, but she could tell that her younger sister was refusing to see Larry as anything but a prince. Mallie realized that Kye couldn't possibly know anything about marriage and children and living in Memphis—about betrayal. Someday when her sister had a family of her own she would understand, Mallie hoped, and maybe they could be friends again.

"Come, come," Elizabeth said, gesturing to Mallie, then shooing the dogs back into the house. "Leave your things. Jacob will bring them up later." She put out her hand. "Welcome to Sarabande House."

The entrance hall in Sarabande House was larger than Mallie's living and dining rooms combined. A grand, highly polished, dark wood stairway began in the middle, then rose toward the rear and split at a landing before going up on either side to the second floor. The ceilings were at least fourteen feet high. Open doorways revealed a parlor on one side and a dining room on the other, both highly formal rectangular rooms. Besides the eighteenth-century polished furniture, Mallie could see a pale, worn, Aubusson rug and a double marble fireplace in the parlor. The house was exactly as she had imagined an English country house would be.

She watched Elizabeth sprint up the stairs in her thick-soled, brown suede shoes and cable-stitched knee socks. Mallie had not worn knee socks since Sweet Briar, and then only on walks in the winter. She looked down at her shiny, black leather Pappagallos with their little heels and felt very American and very urban.

"This will be your room, Mallie," Elizabeth said, striding into a sunny, yellow room with twin beds, plumped up by down comforters. Windows on two sides looked out onto the gardens, one with a lovely round pool in the center, a small bronze sculpture of Pan spouting water in the center. Roses were everywhere.

"What do you call that beautiful red rose?" Mallie asked Elizabeth. She pointed to the brilliant red floribunda blooms highlighting the border gardens on both sides of the pool.

"That's called Sarabande," she said. "It blooms from June until November. Actually, the house got its name from that particular rose."

At dinner that night Elizabeth and Ian anchored both ends of the grand table, with Mallie and Jenny seated on either side. Mallie speculated about whether their dinner parties would seat sixteen or eighteen. She thought she might need a megaphone to be heard without raising her voice. Old lacey linen mats and napkins with heavy English silverware further contrasted her daily use of plastic mats and stainless steel. Her mealtime life with the boys in Memphis had become both casual and rushed. The English scene reminded her of her childhood: the formality of the setting, the servants, the timelessness of the meal. She couldn't remember a single experience of sitting down to a beautifully set table for dinner with Larry and the boys.

"I love Memphis," Ian said, a broad, brown-tinged, toothy grin on his jowly face. "Haven't been there in years, sorry to say."

Mallie instantly recognized the reference to Jenny's divorce from Webster. She remembered their experiences during Carnival week many years ago.

Like Mardi Gras in New Orleans, the Memphis Cotton Carnival was a citywide celebration of Memphis on the Mississippi as the cotton capital of the world. Taking Egyptian names from the original Memphis on the Nile, the secret societies were named after Egyptian royalty. Osiris, Ra Met, Memphi. The groups took over hotel ballrooms that served as party headquarters in downtown Memphis for the week. Mallie and Larry had once belonged to Osiris and her parents had belonged to Memphi. Members could refill their glasses before walking from party to party or watching the parades on Main Street. Besides the elaborate floats, every small town high school band from Eastern Arkansas, Northern Mississippi, and Western Tennessee participated with lively brass-heavy music and baton twirlers.

Mallie never got to know the Carlisles well during their visits to Memphis—the Osiris crowd drank heavily and often stayed up dancing until late hours. On the last night of Carnival, they all wore elaborate costumes and the men wore masks. The anonymity of the costumes and the masks gave permission to drink even more. Much of it was a blur.

She did remember seeing Ian in a rabbit costume at the Mad Hatter's Party one Sunday afternoon at the Polo Club—the final social event of the Cotton Carnival week. By four in the afternoon, when the traditional "men's leg contest" began, everyone was giddy with gin and tonics or rum and orange juice or champagne cocktails. Mallie remembered seeing Ian tuck his baggy white pants up above his bony knees and, with the long cottony ears flopping over his shoulders, do an English jig. The thought of the dignified, somewhat paunchy, balding Ian, looking like Old King Cole at the end of the table, having behaved with such abandon, made her smile.

"Do they still have the Cotton Carnival?" Ian asked, as if wondering out loud whether his memories were real and if it were still possible to have that degree of fun.

"I wouldn't know," Jenny said quickly. "No one I know cares anymore."

Mallie nodded agreement. She had not thought of Cotton Carnival in years. "Actually, it's all changed now," she said. "Since the death of Martin Luther King, Memphis is a different place today."

"What a pity," Ian said. "It was such jolly good fun."

Mallie kept her thoughts to herself. She knew it would have been inappropriate to mention that the institutionalized segregation that existed in those days was not "jolly good fun" for everyone. It was fun for some—certainly her group of friends—and a perpetuation of inequality and subjugation for others. It mortified her that, at the time, she had been as blind as the rest of her crowd to what was going on around them in the black community in Memphis. Thank God, the old way of a "white Carnival parade" and a "black Carnival parade" that had once been a part of the Cotton Carnival was gone forever.

When dinner was finished, Elizabeth ushered the three of them into the parlor. "You must forgive me," she said. "I have to shut the doggies in the dining room for a bit. We've got a slight problem tonight." She then scurried the two Jack Russells into the dining room and closed the doors.

Within seconds, scratching, barking, ripping sounds emanated from behind the doors. Mallie looked at Jenny who shrugged in disbelief. It seemed to go on for many minutes, becoming wilder and louder. Mallie thought of the long dark green velvet curtains hanging from the double windows, pooling on the floor. Were the little doggies ripping up the curtains?

"What are they doing?" she asked.

"We have to do this every now and again," Elizabeth said. "These old houses are prone to the invasion of horrid little creatures. The

Jack Russells are our best ratters. They'll get them." Mallie shuddered at the thought of the benign and friendly little doggies turning into voracious killers.

Presently, all was quiet. When Elizabeth opened the doors, the Jack Russells rushed toward her, still panting from their successful activity. "Good doggies," she said as she bent down and praised the wiry little hunters. After surveying the positive results behind the curtains in the dining room, she closed the doors again and walked calmly into the parlor. "Sorry for the intrusion," she said. "Will you have coffee or tea?"

Chapter Twenty-seven

On Saturday morning Elizabeth gave Jenny driving directions to St. James Church in the nearby town of Arundel. She explained that for over a hundred years the Carlisle family had been contributing members of St. James— the church had been founded in the fourteenth century—but she and Ian had long since stopped attending services. Still, she had a fondness for the place and admired the current vicar.

"I think you'll like Father Jonathan," she told Mallie and Jenny. "Actually I believe they refer to him as Father Jon these days. He sat in the hospital with me while Ian was having his gallbladder removed a few years ago. Such good company. Very well-read and he loves the theater. I'm told he and his wife take in paying guests at the vicarage to support their London theater jaunts."

Mallie instantly thought of Tom. Tom loved theater, too. He had attended all the plays at the Front Street Theater, the resident professional company in Memphis, before it closed for lack of funds. Maybe Father Jon would remind her of Tom. It had been over a week since she had seen him, the longest period away from him in nine months. Looking out the car window as they drove toward Arundel, she felt an ache of loneliness. She would try to put Tom out of her mind and concentrate on the picture book landscape of the English countryside.

A semi-walled city, a Disney creation, Arundel centered around a medieval Camelot castle with flags and turrets and a cathedral with huge stained glass windows and a rising bell tower. Weathered gray stone buildings and narrow streets, people on bicycles or briskly walking, dogs of all shapes and sizes. Mallie wanted to get out of the car and poke around. Everywhere she saw places and scenes that she wanted to draw: colorful pub signs, inns, flower shops, butcher shops, bakeries and greengrocers with their wares displayed out front. She could see herself standing in any number of spots with her pad and her colored pencils.

St. James was on the other side of Arundel, smaller than the cathedral, but still imposing with its ancient stone façade. According to Elizabeth, the church was a relative newcomer compared to nearby St. Andrew's by the Ford, an eleventh-century building without electricity, lit entirely by candles. Mallie instantly imagined the contrast with tiny, modern St. Michael's Chapel in Memphis. Within seconds she could travel the many miles, as well as the many years, between her student experiences at the American Church in Florence, St. Michael's Chapel in Memphis, and St. James in Arundel. The American Church and St. Michael's had both appeared in her life at exactly the time she needed them. She hoped St. James would prove to be of such timely spiritual value as well.

As they entered the side door from the parking lot of St. James, a short, stout woman came bustling toward them with a nametag pinned to her blouse. "Welcome," she said, offering both her hands to Mallie and Jenny. "You must be the Americans. I'm Jane Brady. I'm a member of the vestry. We're so very delighted to have you here with us."

Unlike the sophisticated, snappily dressed Louise Mohr that Mallie remembered from her arrival at the Faith at Work conference, Jane Brady wore no makeup, with a simple white blouse and gray cardigan over her gray knitted skirt. With her clipped accent and her bird's nest hair, she appeared to Mallie straight out of a Miss Marple novel.

"Come, come," Jane Brady beckoned, taking quick steps ahead of them. "We must get you coffee and a sweet before we start."

Mallie and Jenny followed her into a baronial, paneled reception room. Immediately Mallie spotted Father Jonathan. She was sure it had to be him. Very tall, with thinning gray hair and a large paunchy build, the priest was distinctive in his long black robe with a yellowed ivory cross hanging from his neck. His shiny black shoes reminded her of her first patent leather pumps. He seemed to be in rapt conversation with another man, perhaps sharing a confidence, Mallie thought. It occurred to her that she had never seen Tom in conversation with another man.

Tea and coffee were being served at a lace covered round table in the center of the room. The surrounding group, mostly middle-aged and older women, stopped refilling their cups and choosing between the offerings of scones and muffins just long enough for Jane Brady to introduce the newcomers.

"These are the Americans," she said, obviously proud of the visitors coming all the way to her church in Arundel. "This is Jenny—she's Elizabeth Carlisle's sister, you might remember—and this is her friend Mallie Vose."

Shortly, a tinny bell rang and the various small groups in the room broke away from their conversations and found seats in the semi-circular rows facing the lectern. Jane led her new friends to seats that had been saved for them in the third row. Father Jonathan took his place at the lectern.

He looked from one person to another in silence for a few seconds. "Before we actually begin our work together," he said, "I would like to quote from the book we will be studying: A *Summons to Life: The Search for Identity Through the Spiritual*. Here are Martin Israel's own words from the Prologue: 'In the mad rush for security and peace, there is too often an escape from the person to an outer world of authority, where responsibility may be laid at the door of someone else. Yet there can be no peace that does not come from the depths of our own being, no security that does not arise from the love within, and no knowledge that does not proclaim the unity of the person in the greater community of creation.'" He closed the book and put it down on the lectern.

"It is that message from the text we will be considering," he continued, "through today's meditations, group sessions, individual conferences—if you should choose to have a conference with me—and tomorrow's worship services. I look forward to knowing and sharing this time with each of you."

He seemed to shift gears, becoming more informal, leaning over the lectern. "Before I tell you a bit more about Martin Israel, I want to introduce myself. I'm Father Jonathan Parrish, but you're welcome to call me Father Jon. I'd like for each of you to stand and introduce yourself—just give us a brief description of the reason you've come to St. James for this retreat."

Mallie's heart immediately began thumping against her chest. She hated the thought of standing up and speaking in front of a group, particularly a group of church people. She always felt transparent in front of a group, as if they could read her mind. She feared that they would instantly know that she had her doubts about being a good Christian and that she was going through a divorce. She had come to Arundel and to St. James because Jenny had invited her to come and she wanted to get away from the heat of Memphis. But she also had to admit that there was a part of her in search of a new life: to find her identity as a new person "through the spiritual."

She had been moved by the opening quotation from Martin Israel's book: the idea of peace coming from the depths of one's own being. As vague as the idea felt to her, she knew it was the truth. That truth was what she wanted for herself. She decided that she would not waste time second-guessing Father Jon and the people of St. James. She would trust them in the same way that she had learned to trust the people at Faith at Work.

Most of the people in the large room seemed to know each other. One by one each person stood and gave a brief statement of introduction. The women and a few men had come from all over England—the Lake District to London to Brighton. "I've read Dr. Israel's book and believe it to be most provocative," one woman said. "I'd like to know more."

"I'm a surgeon at the City of London Hospital," a man said. "I've known Dr. Israel as a colleague and I admire him. I want to know more about his views of the spiritual life."

When the introductions reached Mallie and Jenny's row, Jenny stood up first. "I'm Jenny Bolton from the United States, my sister Elizabeth Carlisle lives in Arundel. I'm here visiting her and to study *Summons to Life*. My priest at home discovered the book on a trip to London last summer and recommended it to me. I'm very happy to be here." She smiled and sat down.

Mallie took a deep breath. With determination, she stood and looked directly at Father Jon, as if imploring him, as well as everyone else in the room, to hear her—to help her. "I'm Mallie Vose from Memphis, Tennessee. I've come here with my friend Jenny. I don't know anything about Martin Israel, but I admire the subtitle of the book: *The Search for Identity Through the Spiritual*. I'm searching. That's what I'm here for."

Father Jon smiled and thanked her for her introduction. Jenny patted her knee and whispered that she had said exactly the right thing. Mallie turned her attention to the remainder of the people, relieved that she had spoken from her heart and had, apparently, not made a fool of herself.

"Thanks to you all," Father Jon said after the last person spoke. "We have a good beginning. Now, before we attempt to study the chapters of the book, I would like to tell you a bit about Martin Israel. I had the distinct pleasure of being one of his teachers in seminary. Of all my students through the years, he was the most brilliant and the most spiritually gifted.

"He was born in Johannesburg, South Africa, to rather wealthy Jewish parents. His early years introduced him to the inequities of the races in South Africa and taught him about the loving spirituality of the black people as their only path to rising above their most difficult plight. Martin's parents recognized his intellectual genius as a boy and sent him to England for schooling. He never returned to South Africa. He became a medical doctor—and later, he had a Christian conversion. Eventually, he became an Anglican priest. That is the simple version. But, as all of us in this room can attest, living life to the fullest, balancing the sacred and the secular, is never quite so simple."

Mallie listened intently as if Father Jon were speaking directly and solely to her. She thought of her childhood and the inequities, as Father Jon put it, of the black people in her life in Memphis. Her nurse Bernice often came home from her day off exhausted because she had to climb the stairs of the fire escape on the outside of the Malco Theater to see a movie. No "colored" person, as black people were called in Memphis in those days, was allowed in the theater with white people. She remembered the segregated "white" and "colored" drinking fountains as well as "white" and "colored" restrooms. She had been unaware until years later that Bernice could not enter a department store in downtown Memphis without the company of a white person. Without her and Anne at her side, Bernice would have been required to sit in the back of the bus. Mallie had always known that something was wrong, but unlike Martin Israel, she had accepted the reality of the racial divide and continued to live with it. It made sense to her that no real spiritual life—no belief in a loving God—could exist with racial inequality. Fortunately through the years, particularly after the death of Martin Luther King, there had been many changes in Memphis. It seemed sad to her that Martin Israel had never returned to South Africa to try to change life there.

"Here are the words of Martin Israel," Father Jon continued. "'True life is liberation from the bondage of matter to the mutual communion of all creatures in God, Who is our home. When we know ourselves we begin to live with meaning and purpose. The world expands, and our hearts respond in joyful radiance. This is the life abundant, which alone is worth having.'"

That phrase "life abundant" bothered Mallie. She had always associated the word "abundant" with a picture of a cornucopia, an object filling the center of an expansive Thanksgiving table, brimming over with gourds and vegetables and pomegranates. That image made a cornucopia "matter." Martin Israel had also referred to "the bondage of matter." It was difficult for Mallie to envision an abundant life of the spirit. Perhaps it was a cornucopia of good feelings. Maybe it was what she felt when she fell in love with Larry, or in that moment when each of her boys were born. Maybe life abundant could mean all of her experience with Tom Matthews. Perhaps it could also have something to do with the thrill she felt when she watched a blank piece of paper or a canvas come to life with one of her paintings.

She decided that she would sign up for a private conference with Father Jon to discuss the idea. The conferences were entirely voluntary, she understood, and only a few could be scheduled during the two day period. She had come all the way to England; she might as well take advantage of the opportunity to talk to Father Jon.

At the first break of the morning session, she found Jane Brady, who showed her where to sign up. She took one of the last remaining spaces on Saturday afternoon for a private conference.

Chapter Twenty-eight

The second half of the morning was spent in silent meditation, some individuals with their eyes closed, others quietly reading portions of the Martin Israel book.

Lunch was served picnic-style in the walled garden outside the reception hall. Mallie loved the warm sun on her face, so different from the oppressive, enervating heat of an August day in Memphis. The manicured border garden, like Elizabeth's garden, was at its height. Rows of hollyhocks, with their soft pink and white blooms, nestling in green leafy pockets along the spiky stems, stood tall against the old gray stones of the church walls. In front of them, roses, mixed with other varieties of annuals and perennials, created a mass of texture and color. Again, Mallie felt the desire to paint what she saw. There was something that struck her as "abundant" about the church garden. Surely a garden was not merely "matter."

At four o'clock, she entered Father Jon's small office. It was very different from Tom Matthews's expansive, messy study with its fraying rug, rumpled couch and books everywhere. Father Jon's Spartan quarters had only two straight back chairs and a small, uncluttered desk on a bare wood floor.

"Come in," he said. He stood up behind his desk, greeted her and pointed to the chairs in front of his desk. "Do have a seat, my dear."

Mallie thanked him. She looked at his face, the becoming English ruddiness in his cheeks, his midnight-blue eyes, small and very deep set, with white, brushy eyebrows nearly covering his forehead above them. He had a kindly, grandfatherly demeanor. His black robe and cross further reminded her of Father Peter, a Catholic priest she had loved as a child.

"I liked the way you introduced yourself," Father Jon said, sitting back in his chair. He folded his hands, crossing his fingers on his lap. "In truth, we're all searchers."

Mallie was pleased with his compliment. "Elizabeth says you like to go to the theater in London," she said.

Father Jon sat up, tilting his head, a childlike delight in his eyes. "Oh yes, I do! My wife and I go to a matinee every other Wednesday." He leaned toward her. "Do you like theater?"

"Jenny and I will be in London next week and are planning to go on Tuesday night to see *The Threepenny Opera* at the Prince of Wales Theatre," she said. "I go to a theater in Memphis where I live, but I haven't been to the London theatre since I was a student in the fifties. I remember seeing a wonderful musical called *Salad Days*. Did you ever see that?"

"Of course, I saw *Salad Days*. It was classic British whimsy. How delightful that you saw *Salad Days*." He beamed and sang a bar from the musical: "*It's easy to sing a simple song, if you sing it after me.*"

"Oh yes, I remember that one." Mallie smiled in recognition. "I loved it."

Father Jon sat back in his chair; his expression became serious. "Now, tell me, how did you like this morning's session?"

"I liked it very much," Mallie said, "but I have a question. Would you talk to me about the idea of 'life abundant,' I don't think I understand—I mean, what does Martin Israel mean by that?"

"I'll tell you what I think he means. It's not a concept to be defined. It's a joyful way of living, something to be experienced—as love is experienced—something beyond definition."

"And 'the bondage of matter'? Does that mean a dependency on material things?"

"We're all dependent on elements of material things, my dear," the priest said. "We're human. Matter is part of our civilization and our survival. It only becomes bondage when we worship matter—and when we see ourselves as sole creators—as separate from God as the Creator of matter."

Mallie had a vision of the Aurora Borealis in the night sky—the awesome beauty of it and her exhilarating experience of feeling connected to it. Perhaps that was the mutual communion that Martin Israel spoke of. She thought about her feelings of communion in a garden.

"Is a garden considered 'matter' created by man?" she asked.

"I see a garden as one of man's greatest collaborations with God." Father Jon said. "There are glorious fields of wildflowers in meadows all over England that have nary a whit's assistance from man, but God never grew a rose bush in a garden without a man to dig the hole."

Mallie liked that idea. "Sometimes when I'm painting—or, when I used to paint—something happens that feels as if it came from somewhere beyond me—beyond what I know. I don't know how I did something to create exactly what I wanted. It just seemed to happen. When it happens, I feel overcome with gratitude, a sense of utter joy about it."

Father Jon nodded his approval. "When you're in touch with your creative self, you're reaching into the deepest part of yourself—your spiritual connection to God. That's where true joy comes from. That's the experience of 'life abundant.'"

Yes, yes, Mallie thought. That made sense. She remembered hearing Bruce Larson say nearly the same thing at Faith at Work. As if she had to travel on many roads to discover truth, she felt that her path to St. James was adding to her life experience and bringing her a deeper understanding.

"And what about love?" Mallie asked. For an instant, in her mind's eye, she saw Tom's face. "Is experiencing the love of another person the same thing?" She suddenly wanted to tell Father Jon about Tom, about the new love in her life—about the loss of love in her marriage.

"Love is many things," the priest said. "Martin Israel says that 'love is the keystone of the arch that joins the soul to God.'"

Mallie felt deflated. She was not thinking about her soul—or God's love. That was different. "I'm talking about loving a real person," she said.

As if he read her mind, Father Jon said, "Loving another person is also loving God—and at the same time, it's loving yourself."

"But suppose the other person doesn't love you the way you love him." She couldn't believe that she was questioning Tom's love in front of Father Jon.

"Love is the most powerful force—the greatest gift—on this earth," he said. "It is also our finest teacher."

He opened *Summons to Life* to a particular page: "Here's what Martin Israel says: 'Until you give yourself, and suffer betrayal if need be, you cannot know what the soul is and what of yourself can never be lost. A fool in love is also a fool for God. Whatever is lost is repaid by increased self-knowledge.'"

Mallie's heart felt weighted with fearful images. Her father. As a child she had so adored her father. Yet, she carried the horrendous memories of being betrayed by her father. His smile one minute, his terrifying rage at her the next. Larry. Loving, generous, handsome Larry—then the strange phone calls, the letters, the lies. Larry, too, had betrayed her. She thought of Tom. She loved him. Surely he would not betray her. The idea of losing Tom—or of his betraying her—was unbearably painful. Martin Israel's words echoed in her head. Surely she was not just a fool in love with Tom, a fool learning about herself.

"Love is never lost," Father Jon said. "It is sometimes obscured by our behavior—or someone else's behavior—but it's never lost."

His words were fatherly, warm and comforting to her. In halting sentences, she told the priest about her divorce, her sadness at losing her family center. She told him about Tom. Not everything about her relationship with Tom. She told him that she was in counseling with an Episcopal priest, and that she loved him—she was certain that he loved her. She watched his face as she spoke, waiting for any sign of his negative judgment.

"You have been blessed by all of your experience," he said. "In all that you have suffered, you have also been blessed."

Mallie left Father Jon's office both gratified and puzzled. She was not sure how to interpret his meaning about being blessed by all of her suffering. Maybe after she and Jenny attended the Sunday service, the whole picture would become clearer.

Chapter Twenty-nine

E lizabeth met Mallie and Jenny at the front door of Sarabande House when they returned from Arundel. No wide smile this time. No doggies circling her feet.

"Mallie, you've had a call from the States," Elizabeth said. "You are to call your sister Anne right away." She handed Mallie a piece of paper with an unfamiliar Memphis telephone number written on it.

What was Anne doing in Memphis? She lived in Atlanta. Mallie knew, instantly, that something was seriously wrong at home. Her children? Oh God, please, surely nothing had happened to one of the boys. No, the call was from Memphis. The boys were in Watch Hill with Larry.

"Come." Elizabeth took her arm, walking her toward the paneled library. "Let me show you the telephone. You'll have the privacy of Ian's study."

What time was it in Memphis? Six hours earlier. About noon. Mallie sat in the dark green leather captain's chair at Ian's desk and dialed the number on the piece of paper. It also had an extension number.

"Methodist Hospital," the voice of a switchboard operator said.

Mallie's heart sank. Something serious had happened.

"Extension 614," she said promptly, trying to stay composed.

Anne picked up the receiver on the second ring. "Hello." Her voice was unusually subdued.

"Anne, it's me. What's happened?"

"Oh, Mallie," she said, immediately recognizing her sister's voice. "It's Daddy. He's had a stroke. Late yesterday afternoon. He's still in intensive care. I'm here with Mom."

The connection was clear and direct. Anne's voice could have come from across the room, its shocking message provoking a thousand questions in Mallie's mind. Before she could sort them out to speak, her mind went blank. She felt as if her electricity had suddenly gone out and her wits disappeared in the dark. She waited for Anne to say something else.

"Mallie, I think you should come home as soon as possible," Anne said. "I've called Kye too. She's on her way here from New York."

Mallie murmured into the phone that, of course, she would come home. "What does it mean?" she finally asked.

"The doctors don't know," Anne said. "It happened while Mom was at the country club playing bridge yesterday. No one else was in the house. She came home and found him. He's been unconscious ever since."

Mallie could tell that her mother was nearby, and that it was difficult for Anne to say too much.

"I'll get there as quickly as I can," Mallie said. Her mind began racing through the mechanics of getting from West Sussex to Memphis—changing tickets, finding a ride to the airport, being sure she had enough cash. "Take care of Mom," she said.

"Wait," Anne said, "Mom wants to talk to you."

Mallie braced herself for her mother's voice.

"Mallie? Is that you? Are you coming home?" Joan Malcolm sounded small and almost soft, so unlike her—so different from the woman with the rigid spine who took charge of everything. She was also the woman who had always put her father's needs above everyone else's. "I hate for you to ruin your trip, dear."

"I'll get home as soon as I can, Mom," Mallie said. She could only imagine the fear that her mother must be feeling. Her husband—Mallie's father—was her mother's whole life. Surely her father wouldn't die. But a stroke! She knew it was possible that he could die or that he could be left severely paralyzed. How would her mother cope with that? She could cope with anything. She always had.

Joan Malcolm said a quiet "thank you" and handed the telephone back to Anne. Mallie assured Anne one last time that she would make arrangements and be there as soon as possible.

When she hung up the telephone, she slumped forward onto Ian's desk with her head on her hands, unable to move, the reality of the situation encircling her like a vise. Her father might be dying or paralyzed. She could not imagine life without her father. Life would not be the same for her. Not for her family. Not for Malcolm Brothers. What would it mean for Larry? For his job? And, of course, her trip to England was over. She had so wanted to go back for the Sunday services at St. James, the last day of the retreat. And she would miss the London theatre entirely. She thought of Tom. She wasn't certain when he was getting back to Memphis from his vacation. It had been a week already since she had seen him. She had thought when she left that he would be there when she returned, but perhaps her early return would mean that she would be at home alone—without the boys or Tom. Of all the people in her life, in that moment, she wished that she could be with Tom.

Jenny came into the library and put her arms around Mallie. "I'm so sorry. So, so sorry," she said. The extent of the problem, even without the details, was obvious.

Ian called a friend at British Airways and arranged for Mallie to exchange her return ticket for a flight to Memphis through Atlanta the following morning. He offered to drive her to the Gatwick airport at dawn.

Chapter Thirty

Dozing intermittently on the airplane, Mallie tried to imagine her father in the Methodist Hospital, tubes and bleeping machines, doctors using their skills and technology to save him. She willed him to live—at least, until she could get there. All of her childhood fears of him as the unpredictable giant—sometimes panda, sometimes ogre—gave way to her adult experience of loving him, respecting him as a person, enjoying his company and counting on him as her father to always be there. The thought that she might not see him again was unbearable.

Hospitals in Memphis had played a poignant role in Mallie's life. Her memories of the Methodist Hospital came from giving birth to all three of her boys. The Baptist Hospital, the largest hospital in Memphis, was where Nannie Malcolm, her favorite grandmother, died of emphysema. She never passed John Gaston Hospital, the city's charity hospital, without feeling a pang of loss, of longing for her beloved nurse Bernice.

Mallie and Bernice had lived in the same room from right after Mallie was born until she was ten. Besides her sister Anne, Bernice had been Mallie's constant and caring companion throughout her childhood—the one she turned to for solace when her father scared her, the one she turned to for answers to questions too embarrassing to ask her mother. Bernice was the one who showed her how to use a Kotex. She explained the meaning of the word shit—the word Mallie had heard the older girls at school giggling about. "It means what happens when you go to the bathroom and it is not a word for you to ever use," Bernice said. She taught Mallie about her heroes, Joe Louis and Lena Horne. And about cancer. Mallie remembered the horror she felt when she unexpectedly caught Bernice in her room before she had finished dressing. A jagged black scar ran across her bare chest into her armpit as if she had been cut by a barbed wire fence. Later when Bernice was in the John Gaston Hospital, Mallie had not been allowed to see her— no visitors under the age of fifteen. Several times she and Anne had waited in the car while their mother went in to see Bernice.

Mallie recalled the day in June when her mother phoned to tell her that they were transferring Bernice from John Gaston to the Home for the Incurables, a hospital out in the county. She said that if Mallie and Anne wanted to see Bernice, Mallie could take the Morris Minor on the back roads over to Summer Avenue, and the ambulance would stop for a few minutes at the corner of Mendenhall Road. Her mother had an engagement that she could not change, or she would come home to take them. Normally, Mallie's learner's permit would not authorize her to drive alone at fourteen, but her mother had given her permission.

The Morris Minor had once belonged to a business acquaintance of her father's. It had been a gift, more a toy than a real car. The tiny maroon convertible, made in England, had a stick shift and a thirty-mile-an-hour governor on it. Mallie's father thought it would serve the purpose of teaching her—and, eventually, Anne and Kye—how to drive safely. She had been driving by herself, up and down their street, since she was twelve. Taking the car to the corner of Mendenhall road to see Bernice would not feel unnatural to her.

The ambulance was already in the driveway of an abandoned Texaco station on the corner when Mallie drove up. She could see the driver was leaning against the ambulance door smoking a cigarette. Mallie parked the Morris Minor and took Anne's hand in hers as they walked over to the ambulance. Mallie was both excited and fearful of seeing Bernice. Images of the scar on Bernice's breast surfaced making her feel nauseated. Still, nothing would stop her from wanting to be with her beloved nurse.

The driver stamped out his cigarette on the cracked concrete. "Miss Bernice is waiting for you," he said without emotion. He opened the ambulance door and motioned for the girls to step up. "Watch your head," he warned. "One at a time."

As if entering a cave, Mallie bent over and took small steps toward the back, where she could see a figure lying on a gurney, covered tightly in a thin woolen blanket. Her initial shock was Bernice's small, brown, shaved head on the white pillow, her hollowed cheeks and the dark streaks across the top of her right forehead. Mallie got down on her knees and buried her face in Bernice's blanket, determined not to cry.

In a weak voice she heard Bernice speak to her. "You musn't worry about me, Mallie," she said. "I'm all right." Mallie lifted her head and looked into Bernice's eyes, her soft brown eyes. She felt Bernice take her hand out from under the blankets and touch her face, the warmth of her long graceful fingers assuring Mallie that she was really Bernice, not just a skeleton of the person she had known and trusted so completely for her entire life. "I'm all right," she said again. "The Lord's taking care of me." She smiled—a smile so familiar that, for a second, Mallie forgot why she was there, that Bernice was on her way to a place called the Home for the Incurables. "I love you, Bernice," Mallie whispered. "I love you so much." She buried her face again. She couldn't control her tears.

"Time for your sister now," the ambulance driver called to her.

Mallie kissed Bernice's hand, patted her blanket one last time and crawled out the door. Neither she nor her sister could speak when they returned to the car. She was not sure how she drove the

Morris Minor home, barely able to see the road in front of her. She knew that she would never see Bernice again.

Those painful images came back as she stared out the window of the airplane at endless blue sky over the Atlantic. It had been twenty-six years since the summer day when she knelt in the ambulance to tell Bernice goodbye. It felt like yesterday. She held on to Father Jon's words—"love is never lost." Her love for Bernice was certainly not lost. Still, she knew she was going home to face the possibility that her father was dying. Maybe she could see him to tell him she loved him before he was gone.

Chapter Thirty-one

Mallie walked into the Methodist Hospital in Memphis around five o'clock in the afternoon, eleven o'clock London time. She asked the woman at the front desk for directions to the waiting room for the Intensive Care Unit.

Anne stood up to greet her. "Oh, Mallie. I'm so glad to see you," she said, putting her arms around her sister. They stood in silence for a few minutes, tacitly acknowledging their shared history, a deep and abiding link that had often seemed diminished by distance and the demands of their own husbands and children.

"Mom's in with Daddy. Kye's with her," Anne said, before Mallie had time to ask about her mother.

Anne looked weary: her blond hair, usually perfectly curled and bouncy, was pulled back in a stringy ponytail, her flowered cotton skirt full of wrinkles.

"How is he?" Mallie pushed her suitcase into a corner behind their chairs. "Any change?" It had been nearly twenty-four hours since she and Anne had spoken.

"He survived the first twenty-four hours—nearly thirty-six, actually," Anne said. "That's crucial. But he's still not regained consciousness. They don't seem to know whether if he lives—and that's a big question—there will be brain damage, or if he'll be paralyzed."

"What's the doctor telling you?"

"Nothing optimistic today. We don't even know which doctor is really in charge. It's not like having dear old Dr. Prentiss who would sit and talk to us."

"What brought this on, do you suppose?"

"He's had terrible high blood pressure for years. You knew that."

Mallie nodded. But lots of people have high blood pressure. She had never been particularly worried about her father's health. He always seemed so strong. But she also knew that he smoked Camels, at least two packs a day, and had drunk too much most of his adult life.

"Have you been here the whole time?" Mallie asked.

"No, the three of us went home last night, but none of us slept. We came back around six thirty this morning."

Mallie knew that getting up so early in the morning would have been nearly impossible for her mother, who was not a morning person. She stayed up late reading and often slept until ten or eleven. For a time, years ago, when she had live-in help, she had her breakfast served to her on a tray in bed.

"How's Mom? She sounded so sort of strange, not herself, on the phone."

"Hard to tell," Anne said. "You know Mom. She's got that steel thing." Anne shrugged her shoulders, as if exasperated. "Sometimes I want to shake her. She's got to be terrified and she won't talk about it. Nothing. We sat across from each other in the cafeteria for lunch, and she never said a word."

That sounded just like her mother, Mallie thought.

"God, Mallie, you must be exhausted," Anne said. She ushered her sister toward the plastic bucket seats beside the only window in the ICU Family Waiting Room.

"Beyond exhaustion," Mallie said. "Feels like the trip was a dream, a figment of my imagination." Snippets of the dream came back to her. "You want to hear about it?"

Anne nodded. "Of course."

Mallie briefly sketched the highlights of Elizabeth's house in West Sussex and the "doggies." She knew that her sister had always loved dogs. Anne raised Springer Spaniels at one time. There was no point in telling her about her experience at St. James. It would take too long to explain, she was too tired, and she wasn't sure Anne would be interested anyway. The experience at St. James was, first of all, hers. After this crisis with her father was over, she would take her time reading *Summons to Life: The Search for Identity Through the Spiritual* and decide for herself what it meant to her. But without reading a single page of the book, she knew from her time with Father Jon that Martin Israel was an extraordinary writer—an extraordinary priest—and she could hardly wait to discuss his ideas and her day at St. James with Tom Matthews.

"Jenny and I had planned to go to the theater in London next week," Mallie said. "'The Threepenny Opera.' Looks like we might be writing our own opera right here in this hospital."

Anne abruptly stood up. "Here comes Mom."

Walking into the family waiting room, Joan Malcolm did not look like the mother Mallie remembered from only a week ago. Her shoulders, normally as straight and rigid as a hotel coat hanger, were bent forward and loose. Kye's arm was around her, both of them walking slowly, methodically. Mallie stood and went toward them. Her mother looked up to see her oldest daughter. In an instant her downward expression became animated.

"You're here," she said. "Thank God." She reached out for Mallie.

Kye let go, and as Mallie held her mother, she watched her two younger sisters exchange a silent message. She wondered how they really felt about the obviously touching moment between her and her mother—or if there were some old sibling jealousy rising toward her. It wasn't just that Mallie was the oldest child. She knew that. It was also that she was the only one who lived in Memphis and had spent inordinately more time with both of her parents than either of her sisters. The closeness to her mother was inevitable.

"They asked us to leave," Kye said to Anne in a tremulous voice. "Daddy's taken a turn."

"He's not going to make it," Joan Malcolm said, as if no one, not even the doctors, knew her husband the way she did. "I know it."

"You don't know it, Mom," Mallie quickly corrected her mother. She walked with her over to a chair and both of them collapsed. "You've told me all my life to think positively. Now you have to think positively." Even as she said it, she didn't believe it. She knew her mother was psychic. Her mother would know.

Joan Malcolm sighed and said nothing. She was true to form, true to the mother that all three of the girls knew best. When she knew something and pronounced her knowing, that was the end of the subject. Victorian, intelligent, stubborn—clairvoyant—all of those things. There was nothing more for them to ask or to say to their mother.

Mallie desperately wanted to see her father. She walked to the doors of the intensive care unit. When she found a nurse, she asked if it were possible to see Sam Malcolm. She had just arrived from England, she added, hoping that would give her an advantage.

The nurse went down the hallway and returned quickly. "I'm so sorry," she said. "I'm afraid it's not possible at this time."

"What does that mean?" Mallie asked.

"His signs are not good. The doctor's with him now."

Her tone was kind but firm, starched like her white uniform, Mallie thought.

"It's best you wait outside—at least, for now."

Mallie walked slowly back to the waiting room. Kye jumped up and embraced her. Mallie realized that in her concern for her mother, she had not even spoken to Kye. She adored her youngest sister, had loved her since she had been brought home from the hospital when Mallie was ten years old. Kye had been her live baby doll to dress up and push around the block in a baby carriage. They had lost touch when Kye was away at college and Mallie was occupied with Larry and raising the boys. As a working girl in New York, Kye looked so chic in her very short skirt and high heels. Mallie realized that she hardly knew her.

"Oh, Kye," she said, "What's going on in there? What do you think?"

Kye seemed unable to speak. She held Mallie tight like a frightened child, all her New York sophistication out the window. Mallie wanted to console her, but the fear began creeping over her too. She closed her eyes and continued to hold her younger sister.

"Mrs. Malcolm?"

Mallie heard a strong male voice behind her. She broke away from Kye to see a doctor, dressed in green, his mask hanging down below his chin, walking toward her mother.

"I am Mrs. Malcolm," her mother said. She did not stand. She sat upright in her plastic seat, waiting for the doctor to approach her. Anne stood next to her mother.

"I need to speak with you," the young doctor said. He sat down beside her.

From where she stood with Kye, Mallie could only see her mother out of the corner of her eye. She dared not move. She could hear the doctor's voice, low but firm. "Mrs. Malcolm, I'm sorry to tell you that we've lost him." He hesitated when she did not change her expression. As if, perhaps, she did not understand what he was saying, he leaned toward her and very quietly said again: "Mr. Malcolm has passed away."

"Yes," Joan Malcolm said, "I know."

Chapter Thirty-two

Through the night, Mallie watched the illuminated numbers on the clock next to her bed. Not since before her boys were born had she ever spent a night completely alone in her house. She had recurring visions of her mother alone in her bed after nearly forty-two years of marriage to her father. Maybe her mother could shed tears when no one was around to see her. At least, her mother had Anne and Kye sleeping down the hall in her guestroom. They would be there for her in the morning. No one would be in Mallie's house, not even dear old Bingo, who was boarding in the kennel.

With the additional problem of the six-hour time change from England to Memphis, Mallie was not able to sleep. She continually forced her eyes shut, trying to evoke happy memories of her father. All she could picture in her mind's eye was the image of him in the hospital bed after he had been pronounced dead and the family had been allowed to see him.

She had hardly been able to look at him when she walked behind her mother into the windowless room, and yet she could not take her eyes off him. He was covered to his neck in a white sheet, his head on a white pillow, all the tubes gone, his eyes closed as if he were asleep—a lifeless statue of her father in a hospital bed. He did look peaceful, not a wrinkle in his face. She could not cry.

Her body felt stony cold as if she had become a statue too. She pressed against her mother. The four of them stood touching each other next to her father's bed while her Mother began softly saying the twenty-third psalm. Mallie had been surprised, knowing that her mother was not religious and probably did not believe in life after death. She was not absolutely sure what her mother believed, but she and her sisters followed her lead and said the words along with her. "I shall fear no evil, for thou art with me." When they finished, Joan Malcolm stepped toward the top of the bed and leaned over to kiss her husband goodbye. Each of the sisters followed and kissed his forehead. Only after Mallie's lips touched her father's cold, bloodless skin did the implication of his death become real. He was not there.

In her bed that night, in the dark of her room, the reality that he was gone finally came through to her and allowed her to cry. Her father was dead. Not just *passed away*, as the doctor had said, a term that sounded to her as if he might be down the street or out of town and he might come back someday. He was dead, gone from her life forever. She heard her father's voice from those special times when he held her shoulders with his large, freckled hands and told her how proud he was of her, what a good mother she was turning out to be. Her father had a way of making her feel important and loved— and he was gone. He was only sixty-six years old. Too young. Why couldn't it have been someone else's father? She needed her father. She was going through a divorce and he had supported her—told her not to worry, that he would take care of her and the boys. Now he was gone. Larry was gone. She was a forty-year-old woman alone in the world. She tried to envision herself in Tom's study at St. Michael's. His study was her place to be safe and loved. He would always be there for her, Tom had said. She desperately wanted to be with him, to be held by him. Surely he must have returned from his vacation. She would call St. Michael's in the morning and leave a message on his answering machine.

There was so much to do, Mallie thought, as she turned her attention toward the day ahead. She would not bother to unpack. As soon as it was light, she would take a bath and dress in something cool. It would be a hot August day in Memphis. Her first job was to call Larry. She should have called the night before, but she didn't have the strength to tell the boys about their grandfather. They adored Sam Malcolm. He had taken them duck hunting every winter since they were old enough to hold a gun, and he had promised them that someday he would take them to Africa and shoot a rhinoceros. All promises were off.

They would have to come home for the funeral, cutting their time in Watch Hill short. She could not imagine how Larry would feel. He had loved her father too, at least before things went sour at Malcolm Brothers. Perhaps her father's death would change everything for Larry. Maybe he would be promoted—or maybe he would be fired. Maybe he would choose to leave the company. Maybe he would leave Memphis—go back to Providence or somewhere in the East where most of his friends still lived. No, he would never leave the boys. Totally spent from crying and speculating on the unknown and frightening future, Mallie fell asleep until the alarm roused her at eight.

∽

Mallie's refrigerator was empty except for the orange juice and a small carton of cream that she had bought on the way back from the hospital. She made coffee and took the mug out on her terrace. The grass was brown from the intense southern sun and lack of rain. Her flowers, so profuse and colorful in the early summer were dry, faded sticks, standing bent and broken, or lying dead on the ground. She had not been away a full week and yet the whole back yard looked like an abandoned battlefield. Her garden had suffered a summer of neglect. She would have to start a routine of watering in the late afternoon and deadheading a patch of the withered flowers every day. As if it had not been her responsibility to maintain all along, she knew that when the divorce was final, the house and the garden would be solely hers to care for. She checked her watch. Nine o'clock. It was time to go to her mother's and put her mind to the funeral arrangements.

Chapter Thirty-three

"The phone's for you," Kye said in a soft voice, nodding to Mallie. She stood in the doorway to the sunroom in their mother's house. Mallie and Anne were meeting with the Reverend Carl Menefee from Holy Trinity—their mother's choice for their father's funeral. "It's someone named Terry from St. Michael's Chapel."

"Thanks, Kye," Mallie said, jumping up and closing her *Book of Common Prayer* in her lap. "Excuse me, Father Menefee, I'll be right back."

It was mid-afternoon. Mallie and her sisters had spent the morning taking turns calling various relatives and friends who needed to be informed of their father's death, all those they had not called the night before.

Mallie had recovered, more or less, from the trauma of calling Watch Hill and giving the news to Larry and her boys. Larry had tried to be consoling. "I'm so sorry, Mallie," he said. "I'll do anything you need me to do to help." He told her that he would make the arrangements and bring the boys home as soon as possible. David had immediately burst into tears when he heard his mother's voice. Ever her sensitive, youngest child, he needed his mother. She wished she could have been there to hold him.

∞

"Hi, Terry," Mallie said, nearly breathless, as she walked into the kitchen and picked up the receiver. "I'm so glad you called back."

"Sorry to have taken so long," Terry said. "I got your message this morning—I'm so sorry about your father. I finally reached Tom to tell him. He got home late last night from his vacation and wasn't planning to come into the office today."

Mallie's heart sank. She had counted on seeing him before the day was over. "He's not coming in at all?"

"Actually, they're painting the front steps of the chapel this afternoon—I'm leaving the building now. Tom said to tell you he wants to see you, if you'd call him—I'll give you the number—he'll meet you at a convenient place late this afternoon."

Mallie felt a sweep of relief. Thank God. She remembered Father Jon telling her—enigmatically, she had thought at the time—that she had been blessed by Tom. This was certainly a blessing. She wrote Tom's number down and thanked Terry again. Before going back to the sunroom where she and Anne were planning the service for her father, she took a deep breath and dialed the number.

"Tom," she said, speaking his name with a sweep of relief. As if the call had reached heaven and she was speaking directly to God, she could not say another word.

"I'm sorry about your father, Mallie," Tom said, filling the void. "I know what this means to you."

Mallie felt a surge of emotion, the relief that Tom was there for her.

"Would you like to get together this afternoon?" he asked.

"Yes," she said. "Yes."

To see him—be with him—would mean everything in the world to her. She ran through options of where they might meet. She didn't want him to come to her mother's house. She certainly couldn't imagine meeting in a public place, a restaurant, or even a park bench. She thought of her empty house. She dreaded going back there alone.

"Tom, is there any chance you would come to my house? The boys are still away."

"Of course," he said. "It must have been terrible for you to come into your house alone last night."

She felt gratified and thankful for him. He understood her so well; he always said exactly what she needed to hear. "I could be home around five thirty," she said. "Would that suit you?"

He confirmed that he would be there at five thirty.

Mallie felt a leap of exhilaration. It was nearly three o'clock. Two and a half hours until she would see him. Her heart began to race. The thought of Tom Matthews in her house—he had never been there before—felt strange and thrilling. She had often daydreamed of having him in her house, being a part of her life. She hung up the phone and walked with a sprightly step back to the sunroom.

"We think that the Gospel reading from John 14 would be the best," Anne said.

"Which one is that?" Mallie asked. Relieved that she would be with Tom later, she brought her full attention to the planning of the service.

"It begins here," Father Menefee said, holding his Bible up for Mallie to see. "'Let not your hearts be troubled.'"

"And then the part about 'in my father's house there are many mansions,'" Anne added.

"Oh, yes, of course. It's definitely the right one for Daddy." Mallie nodded her approval. "Did you decide on an Old Testament lesson?"

"Anne likes Ecclesiastes," the priest said. "Is that okay with you?"

Mallie thought back to her last conversation with her father about religion. The ardent, forced Catholicism of his childhood had all but obliterated his interest in any form of the church. Whereas Mallie had loved going to Mass on Sundays with her grandparents, her father had grown up with priests dominating his family dinners and requiring attendance at Mass every day. One of the brothers in his Catholic high school had been sadistic. Her father, along with his friends, had been routinely beaten with a rod. Factoring all his negative religious experiences, along with his academic awakenings in college, he had become an agnostic. "I believe there's a God—or some sort of divine order, somewhere, somehow—but he or it is not in the church, at least not for me," her father had said.

She thought of the Ecclesiastes verse: "For everything there is a season, for every activity under heaven, its time." Yes, she thought, Ecclesiastes was the right lesson to speak for her father—for her, too, and her whole family. She wanted the boys to hear those words: "a time to be born and a time to die, a time to weep and a time to laugh." Surely that was what a funeral was for—to honor the person who died and to console the family with timeless words and music. They had already chosen "Oh God, Our Help in Ages Past" as the opening hymn. Mallie loved the line: "A thousand ages in thy sight are like an evening gone."

Anne agreed to go immediately to the printer to work out the program. Father Menefee asked if the sisters would like to pray with him before he left them. The three of them moved their chairs closer together and held hands, their heads bowed. Mallie tried to concentrate on his prayer of comfort for each of them, but her mind was removed, already skipping through all the possibilities of what might happen with Tom in her house later.

More flowers and platters of food were arriving as Father Menefee left the house. "Give my love to your mother," he said, putting on his white straw hat at a slight angle. "And tell her that I would be happy to see her at any time she would like to see me."

Mallie was aware that her mother hardly knew the Reverend Carl Menefee. She never attended services at Holy Trinity, unless it was Christmas or Easter or the boys were somehow involved through Holy Trinity School. Her mother had no affiliation with a church in Memphis and her father wanted nothing to do with the Catholic Church. Holy Trinity had become Mallie's church connection for the whole family. It was ironic that since she had been going to St. Michael's Chapel on Sundays, she had stopped attending any services at Holy Trinity herself.

From the time Mallie walked into her mother's house that morning, the telephone and the doorbell had continued to ring. Someone—a friend of her mother's, a friend of hers or her sisters'—was always there to answer the phone or the front door and to take the food to the refrigerator, or place the flowers around the house.

All the tabletops in the living room were already covered with various sizes of vases. The dining room table, filled with silver trays of cold cuts, cheeses and crackers, stuffed eggs, fruit and nuts, looked as if a wedding buffet had been planned. One efficient friend had placed a white leather book, opened like a guestbook, next to the front door for friends to sign. Another notebook was kept in the kitchen to record the names of those sending flowers or food with a full description of each offering. Joan Malcolm or someone in the family would be responsible to write thank-you notes later.

Except for her meeting with Anne and Father Menefee in the quiet of the sunroom with the doors closed, Mallie felt as if she and her family were observers—or maybe props—on the stage of a theatrical production. In Memphis, a funeral for a member of an old, ruling family was a theatrical production. Along with their genuine grieving in most cases, friends had an opportunity to prove their connections and their societal solidarity through their participation in events surrounding funerals.

When Anne's husband arrived from Atlanta, he went straight to the liquor store to stock the bar with bottles of gin, scotch, vodka and Jack Daniels. Kye went to Seessel's—her mother's preferred grocery store where she had always had a charge account—to buy tonic, soda water and soft drinks.

Joan Malcolm, impeccably dressed, as she always was, remained secluded in her room for most of the day. It was apparent, however, that the show revolved around her. "Is Joan okay?" "Would Joan like lunch, do you think?" "Where do you think Joan would like these flowers to go?" "Should we wait for Joan to set up the bar?"

Whenever Joan appeared, her friends were reverential to her—telling her that she looked so well, or that she should get some rest, or have some lunch, or sit down and put her feet up. Occasionally they squeezed her hands without words.

Mallie looked at her watch. Four thirty-five. It was time for her to go home and wait for Tom. She felt a flutter in her stomach. She wanted to take a shower, change her clothes. What should she wear? She walked quickly through the house looking for Anne and Kye to tell them that she would be back later, that she had something she had to do at home. Both of them were occupied with other people and decisions about the ever-more-crowded refrigerator—whether to chill the wine in a large bucket with ice cubes. Neither of her sisters seemed concerned that she was leaving. Mallie had a momentary thought of the Emily Dickinson poem about death called "A bustle in the house."

Chapter Thirty-four

Through the open blinds on the windows in her living room, Mallie watched Tom's dark green Chevy sedan rush up the driveway. Relief poured over her. She had been standing there rigidly poised for twenty minutes after their appointed meeting hour had passed—waiting, stifling sweeps of dread that he would not show up. Possibly he had changed his mind about coming to her house. He would have his reasons. He would sound very apologetic when he finally called her on the phone. Perhaps he would tell her that he thought it best to wait a day and have her come to meet with him in his study at St. Michael's.

But Mallie had jumped too quickly to a conclusion. As he shut the car door behind him, her mind let go of all the negative presumptions. She felt the tension in her body release. It was only five minutes to six. She smiled as she reminded herself that he was always late, always rushing to his next appointment, but he always came. She walked to the front door to greet him.

Without saying a word, Tom put his arms around Mallie and held her in the open doorway. She wanted to burst with happiness. Even as she felt the hard, starched, white collar band pressing against her forehead—usually a reminder of the barrier between them—she reveled in the pleasure of his embrace. With her face in his neck, she breathed in the scent of his skin. She knew that smell, so unlike Larry's athletic, masculine odor that had once intrigued her. Tom's smell was comforting, like baby oil, and at the same time, provocative, sensuous, like musk. She wanted time to stop. She wanted to stay in that position forever.

"Mallie, Mallie." Tom repeated her name so softly, so sympathetically. "Such a shock for you. I'm truly sorry." He loosened his arms from holding her and tried to take one of her hands. "Had your father been ill?"

"No, not really," Mallie said, wanting to resist his release, but taking his hand. "He had very high blood pressure, and, I suppose, a lot of stress lately. I know he had been drinking more than usual." She remembered how devastated her father had sounded on the phone when she told him about her separation from Larry. She had been surprised at his reaction, knowing that her father had become disillusioned, angry at times, with Larry—probably more than he allowed her to know. "It's just so hard to believe he is really gone," she said.

"Your father will never be gone from you, Mallie," Tom said.

She recognized his Episcopal priestly stance, his words of comfort that the spirit never dies. As if they both knew the time had come to move from the front door, they turned and started into the house. Mallie let go of his hand.

"Can I get you something to drink?" she asked.

"A drink of water would be fine," he said.

He followed her through the short side entrance hall into the kitchen. "What a lovely home," he said. He walked past her to look out the window at the back yard. Mallie cringed at the vision of her brown grass and dead flowers.

"Ice?" she asked.

"Just plain," he said.

She fixed two glasses of water and walked ahead of him into the library. It seemed both natural and strange that Tom was in her house. She had never been with him anywhere other than in his study at St. Michael's. Mallie's heart raced with ideas. She tried to imagine what sort of house he lived in, and in the same breath, she tried to calculate how long he might stay with her. Maybe he would spend the night. No, no, that was a ridiculous thought. That was too much to hope for, but her whole body felt alive with the possibility. She sat down in the corner of the sofa. To her disappointment, he sat on a chair across from the sofa, rather than next to her.

"Have you made plans for the funeral yet?" Tom sipped his water as he spoke.

"It's day after tomorrow at Holy Trinity," she said. "Eleven o'clock. Anne and I met with Father Menefee this afternoon." It occurred to Mallie to ask Tom to be a part of the service along with the Reverend Carl Menefee, but she knew that was not the right thing to do.

"Is there anything I can do to help?" he asked. The tone of his voice was earnest, caring, his expression one of deep concern for her.

Suddenly Mallie felt overcome with desire for Tom. Everything flew out of her mind—her father, his death, the funeral, her children—everything. She reached her arms out to him. "Oh Tom, I have so needed to be with you."

He rose and went over to her on the sofa. In a second his mouth melded with hers, his tongue, his breath became intertwined with hers. She thought she would lose consciousness, dissolve into him. He put his face next to hers, skin on skin, and wrapped his arms tightly around her. "I love you," she said, her eyes closed. "I love you too, Mallie," he said quietly. He tried to pull away as he said the words. She held her face next to his. In a desperate voice she said, "Please, please Tom. I need you." In an abrupt, definitive move, he released her, shaking his head and attempting to stand. "I can't, Mallie," he said, his voice a pleading declaration. "You must understand. I can't."

As if the moment that she had rehearsed a million times in her mind had arrived, Mallie sat up and jerked off her blouse. She wore no bra. Her pink nipples were high and rigid. "I want you, Tom," she said.

Tom's head fell forward, the flush in his face drained to white. "Oh no, Mallie. Oh God, no—I'm so sorry. You must understand." He kept shaking his head.

"I don't understand," she said, feeling sick with confusion.

He stood up in front of her. "I have to go, Mallie." He bowed his head and closed his eyes. "Know that I love you, Mallie—just know that. But I have to go." He turned and fled from the living room.

Within seconds Mallie heard the side door slam shut and the sound of Tom's Chevy engine start up. She could not move. In her mind's eye she trailed the car down her driveway and away from her house—away from her. She crumpled into a ball on the sofa, holding her scrunched-up blouse to her chest, feeling utter despair. Frustration. Confusion. Fear. The timing had been wrong. She feared that she had ruined everything with Tom. She fought the recurrent accusation against herself that she had consciously planned to take off her blouse—although she knew she had not worn a bra on purpose, hoping that he might touch her breasts and the surprise might excite him. She had never done anything so brazen in her whole life. She tried to deny that she had made an overt plan to seduce him. But in her heart, she knew that was exactly what she had done—and the worst part of it all was that she had failed. She had once again been rejected.

Chapter Thirty-five

Dinner at Joan Malcolm's was always a sit-down formal affair. Even with the funeral of her husband pending, the evening meal was served as usual. Amelia, her mother's daily housekeeper, had stayed on to help out with the cooking and serving. Mallie's Aunt Peggy, her mother's sister from Chicago, and her husband Pete were there, along with several cousins and two of her mother's childhood friends who had flown in from other places.

Mallie had outwardly recovered from her reckless debacle with Tom. She kept herself busy going back and forth to the kitchen, finding it difficult to make light conversation at the table with the group. Internally she kept returning to what she knew she had done. Over and over she played out the scene in her living room, trying to stop herself at the last second before taking off her blouse. She felt as if she were existing on two levels, one part of herself completely detached from the reality of all that was going on around her in her mother's house.

"Are you okay, Mallie?" Anne whispered the question next to her sister's ear while they walked together, carrying empty soup bowls from the first course back to the kitchen.

"Fine," Mallie said, not looking at Anne, handing two bowls to Amelia. There was no way she could tell Anne about Tom.

"I'm worried about you. You keep so much inside—and you've got to be still exhausted from your trip home from England."

"I'm okay, Anne. Thanks. Not to worry." Mallie pushed through the swinging door to the dining room.

Aunt Peggy was telling a story about her father. "You remember that old Stutz Bearcat Sam used to drive when he was at Vanderbilt?"

Joan Malcolm smiled. "Do I!" she said. "I thought that was the jazziest car I had ever seen. Sam even wore his raccoon coat when he drove it to Chicago to ask me to marry him."

"Well, you weren't aware of this, Joan," Peggy said, "but he was so scared you might say no, he drove that car over to my house and had two martinis before he came to see you."

Everyone at the table laughed. Mallie's parents' generation always responded to drinking stories with laughter. Maybe it had something to do with living through the Prohibition years. All their stories about bathtub gin, sneaking into speakeasys without their parents knowing. They loved to tell tales of a teenage boy's first "harmless" encounter with too many beers, a young man making a blunder in front of his girlfriend's father while discovering stingers as an after-dinner drink, or an older man still trying to be the life of the party with his off-color jokes or by wearing a wastebasket on his head. Anyone doing or saying something ridiculous while drunk was always a joke and always forgiven. Martinis—straight up, or with olives, or tiny white onions—Gibsons, they were called—were a particularly good source for amusing stories. Her father had once called martinis "infuriators"—an appropriate term for his own behavior. According to him, nothing short of murder—or failure to pay a gambling debt—could be held against a good man when he was drunk.

Mallie pushed the ancient, fearful memories of her father's drinking out of her mind. At that moment they no longer had any hold over her. He would have loved the dinner table conversation

Alice Bingham Gorman

about drinking and about him. Maybe he—or his spirit—was listening.

Mallie had never been certain of what happened to a person after death. Somehow the spirit lived on, she was sure of that. But "the resurrection of the body" seemed impossible to her. It was one thing for Jesus Christ—whether or not he was really *the only true son of God*, he was surely the most godly person who ever lived. But she couldn't imagine any place—even heaven—full of all the resurrected bodies of regular people who had died. She repeated the words in the Nicene Creed whenever she attended an Episcopal service with communion, but the idea of the resurrection of the body was one among several tenets of the church that she had to gloss over. Like myths, she had once read, they were both true and not true at the same time.

When she had questioned Tom about his belief on the subject, he said that the "body" in resurrection meant the essence of being, not the actual physical body. It was more the idea that we would know one another in death the way we would know a loved one in life if we were deaf and blind. We would sense that person's *essence of being*. Mallie had liked his explanation. She had never been able to accept the prospect of nothingness after death. A person's spirit—his essence—leaving his body and living on as a form of energy, as a part of all living things forever and ever, felt more likely. Surely her father's spirit lived on somehow, somewhere. Maybe he was present at that moment in the dining room.

Tom. She closed her eyes reliving the afternoon's scene with Tom. She knew that she had lost control and gone too far. Now he was gone. She could not bear to think that he was gone forever. She would call him—or maybe she should wait for him to call her. She looked at her watch. Eight thirty. She had to be home by ten. Larry was bringing the boys home from the airport. At least she would not be at home alone overnight again.

"Would anyone like coffee?" Amelia asked.

183

The three sisters cleared the table after dessert, while Amelia made coffee to be served in the living room. The group was still telling Sam Malcolm stories, laughing to the point of tears, as only family and close friends can laugh in the height of their grief. Mallie regretted that she was so preoccupied with thoughts of Tom Matthews that she could not even hear the stories. If her father's spirit were alive and observing her, she hoped that he would understand and forgive her.

Chapter Thirty-six

B reakfast with the boys the next morning brought a sense of normalcy back into Mallie's world. Her emotional life had been turned upside down by her father's death and by her impulsive behavior with Tom Matthews. The future seemed even more unpredictable and frightening than before she went to England. But here she was in her own kitchen on Walnut Grove Road, cooking the boys' favorite food: silver-dollar blueberry pancakes with melted butter and maple syrup, a breakfast treat she had made a thousand times before.

As she watched her sons silently devouring the little round pancakes, she was comforted by their appearance, each one true to form: David's rumpled red hair, seemingly always in need of a haircut; Troy's buttoned-down neatness, his alligator shirt and khaki shorts; Sammy, still in his pajamas, always the last one up and the last one dressed. How gratified she had been when she kissed them all goodnight and David told her that their experience in Watch Hill had not been the same without her.

Breaking the silence and looking straight at his mother, Troy raised the question each of the boys was thinking. Why did their grandfather Poppy have to die?

"I don't know why anyone has to die, Troy," Mallie said. As

she said it, she had an instant vision of the way she had felt when Bernice died. Just like Troy, she'd wanted to know why. Her mother told her at the time that Bernice was in heaven with God. At fourteen, the idea had been helpful to Mallie. That very day, she went to Immaculate Conception Church and lit a candle for Bernice, envisioning her without scars and happy in heaven.

"As much as we will miss him, we shouldn't worry about Poppy," Mallie said. "He's with God in heaven."

"I don't believe in heaven," Sammy said, barely looking up from his pancakes.

Mallie was shocked. All of the boys had gone to Sunday school and studied the Bible from first grade. Something must have happened to Sammy at St. George's, an Episcopal school where she was told the students went to chapel every day. She sat down at the table. "What do you mean you don't believe in heaven?" she said.

"I thought about it on the airplane coming home yesterday," Sammy said. "We were up in the sky and all I could see were some clouds and more sky. No sign of heaven. And besides, in my science class we've been studying planets and galaxies. Mr. Waters says the galaxies go on forever. A man walked on the moon. It's silly. There's just no heaven up there."

Logic, she thought. Sammy had always been a questioning, intelligent child. He was becoming a logical young adult. Her own concept of heaven had changed through the years. No longer could she envision God as a kind grandfatherly figure making decisions about bringing a person home to heaven. She would have to be more real with her son.

"Suppose heaven is not a place you can see, as it's pictured in the Bible, but it exists in some spiritual way that we can't see?" Mallie said.

"Well, it's not in the sky. That's for sure," Sammy said. "Are there any more pancakes?"

"I agree with Sammy," Troy said. "I don't think Poppy would like all that white robe stuff anyway. I'd like to think he's off on some hunting trip somewhere with Old Parker. You remember that old dog he loved so much that died a few years ago?"

"I believe in heaven," David said. He had been listening to the conversation without saying anything. "I looked at the sky outside the airplane, too, and I saw heaven."

Mallie had gone back to the stove turning a new batch of pancakes and marveling at her sons. Thinkers, all of them, but so very different. David's words of faith touched her.

"Maybe heaven is different for each of us," she said. "The point is it's there—somewhere—and wherever it is, your grandfather is there."

That seemed to be enough about heaven. Troy was grabbing the syrup from David who protested that he was not finished with it. Sammy took his plate to the sink.

After breakfast, while she was getting dressed, the phone rang. She picked it up on the table next to her bed.

"Mallie?"

She froze, instantly recognizing Tom's voice. "Tom?" She closed her eyes and sat down on her bed.

"I'm calling to check on you. I hope you had a good rest last night." He sounded like his old self, as if the scene on her couch had never happened. "Also, I want to be sure I've got the time right for the funeral."

Her heart was beating so loudly against her chest that she could barely hear him. "Eleven o'clock," she said, "at Holy Trinity." She took a deep breath. "Tom." Her voice saying his name was timorous. She couldn't speak further.

"Mallie, I want you to listen to me. You're not to worry," he said. His tone was calm and assuring, the same tone she remembered from when she first knew him. "Be with your family. Do not worry about what happened yesterday. I love you—I always will.

When the funeral is over, and you've had some time, we'll get together. I'll call you."

She did not know whether to feel relief or frustration or anger. She could not immediately decipher what he was saying. *Be with your family. Not to worry about yesterday.* How was it possible for her not to worry? Surely what happened yesterday afternoon was important enough to address immediately and directly. And yet, she was fearful of addressing it herself. She had convinced herself that he would never want to see her again. Now she would have to put the whole incident out of her mind and wait until after the funeral, possibly until after all her relatives had gone home. At least, he had said "I'll call you." He would not have said that if he never intended to see her again. She kept hearing his voice say, "I love you—I always will." The comfort she initially felt when he said those words was fading into questions of what he meant by "love." She sank down on her bed and felt hot sticky tears running over her face. It was a hopeless situation. She had tried to be somewhat real with Sammy and the boys about heaven. She needed to be real with herself about Tom. She knew there was no heaven perched up in the sky waiting for all the good people to pass through the Pearly Gates. Neither was there a way for her to have a real love relationship with a married priest.

Chapter Thirty-seven

Nearly everyone that Mallie had ever known in Memphis came to her father's funeral. All the men at Malcolm Brothers, some of whom she had grown up thinking were part of her family and had always called "Uncle," were there with their wives. Her family's multi-generational social friends filled the church, along with her father's golfing buddies, his old school friends, and his political and civic friends. Sam Malcolm had been a behind-the-scenes force in conservative Democratic politics and had served on boards from the Red Cross to the Chamber of Commerce. There was not an empty pew when the Father Menefee read the opening sentences from the back of the church. "I am Resurrection and I am Life, says the Lord."

She held David's hand through most of the service, trying to concentrate on the hymns and prayers, the lovely psalms—trying to keep herself from looking around the church for Tom. He had said he would be there. She knew also that Larry was there, somewhere, not up front with the family. Wherever he was seated, she hoped her mother would not see him. Joan Malcolm was angry and unforgiving about Larry. In a way that would be difficult to explain to her mother, she wished that Larry could be standing in the pew with her and the boys. After all, they were still married. The divorce would not go to court for another three months. She wondered how it would feel to be permanently, legally disconnected from her children's father. She suspected that she would feel a residual connection to Larry—if only because of her children—for the rest of her life. Maybe it was the same connection that she would always feel to her father. They were both gone from her daily routine and her future, but they were ingrained in her past, participants in the most important times of her life.

"Our Father, who art in heaven." The entire church resounded with the Lord's Prayer in unison. With her eyes closed, her head bowed, Mallie heard the words as never before. "And forgive us our trespasses, as we forgive those who trespass against us." She wondered if God had forgiven her for what she had done to Tom—or if she had forgiven Larry for what he had done to her. Maybe there was no real difference between Larry's affairs with other women and her desire for Tom. No, she could not believe it was the same thing. Surely God would know it was not the same thing at all.

At the end of singing "A Mighty Fortress is our God," the family led a procession out of the church, the remainder of the people walking behind them. In accordance with the funeral director's unctuously executed plan, Mallie and the boys got into the first black limousine with Joan Malcolm. Her sisters, Kye and Anne, Anne's husband and their children, followed in the second limousine. Policemen on motorcycles stopped traffic at street corners and through overhead red lights, ushering the long line of cars behind the limousines from the church to Elmwood Cemetery.

Within thirty minutes, the coffin was lowered into the ground and Samuel Malcolm joined his parents, his aunts and uncles, and his brother under the dated stone markers going back to the late nineteenth century. Stanchions of flowers—white crosses of lilies, daisies, and roses, as well as brilliant colors shaped into circles and squares—surrounded the small tent next to the grave. When the interment was over and Father Menefee had shaken each of their hands, Mallie whispered to the boys to take a rose from one of the wreaths and drop it, one by one, onto the top of the coffin. Her father had loved roses.

Many of the well-dressed crowd of people came back to the Malcolm house in Chickasaw Gardens to complete the ritual: an open bar, a sumptuous buffet of luncheon food in the dining room, and animated conversation. Sam Malcolm certainly had a proper send-off, someone said. There was an undercurrent of conversation about Joan. She was only in her early sixties, too young to be alone for the rest of her life. She would be married again, was the consensus—although there was only one Sam Malcolm. She would never find another man like him. Still, she was beautiful, smart, and she was rich—she was a catch for a single man. Neither Mallie, nor her sisters, could imagine their mother with another man.

Mallie stayed in the midst of the group as long as she could, always keeping an eye on the door for Tom or Larry. Neither of them came back to the house. In her conversations, in her movements throughout the house, she began to feel a creeping sense of isolation, as if in spite of all those people, she were completely alone. All of the important men in her life were gone.

Chapter Thirty-eight

"Hi Mallie," Terry said brightly on the telephone. "Tom wanted me to call you. He's with the bishop this morning—he's pretty stacked up with appointments today—but he wondered if you could come to the chapel at one thirty."

It was Monday morning. It had been four long days since the funeral, including an endless weekend. Mallie had picked up the telephone numerous times to call Tom and put it down. No matter what sort of urgency she was feeling, she knew she should wait for him to telephone her. He had promised he would call.

"Yes," she said to Terry, trying not to show her enormous relief. "I can do that."

She thanked Terry and hung up the telephone. Thank God! Renewed hope swept over her like a spring breeze. Tom wanted to see her. The timing was perfect. The boys would be at the Country Club all day. Sammy and Troy were playing in a round robin tennis tournament and David needed nothing more than a swimming pool to occupy him for hours at a time. A Pisces from birth, she thought he might be part fish.

She stood looking into her closet, wondering what she should wear, wishing some new outfit would magically appear. Every summer by the end of August her clothes looked old and tired. She would have to wait until late October to put her summer wardrobe away and take her winter clothes out of the attic closet. She wanted something simple. Perhaps her white slacks, her summer uniform—white slacks and a colorful cotton blouse or a knitted T-shirt. She picked up a red and white sleeveless blouse. Maybe pink would be better. Pink was softer.

Suddenly she had an idea. Suppose she brought Tom lunch. She could stop at the Woman's Exchange Café on her way to St. Michael's and have them package a portion of their wonderful chicken salad to go. If he had appointments all day, he would hardly have time for lunch. It would be a peace offering of sorts.

∽∾

As she drove into the parking lot at St. Michael's she noticed Tom's Chevy at an angle near the side door to his study. It was often parked that way, as if he had rushed in late for an appointment and not bothered to line up his car properly.

Next to Terry's familiar Ford Galaxie, Mallie recognized a maroon Dodge station wagon that she had noticed several times before at St. Michael's. She knew it belonged to Marilyn Jamison, an acquaintance of hers through Holy Trinity School. Her son was in the same class as Troy. Tom had told her once, months before, that he met periodically with Marilyn to advise her on her studies at the Memphis Theological Seminary. Everyone in Memphis knew that Marilyn's husband had been convicted of embezzling a large amount of money from a small bank in Jackson, Tennessee. It had been all over *The Commercial Appeal*. He had mysteriously disappeared at the time it was discovered, and after several years, Marilyn moved to Memphis and claimed abandonment. In the meantime, according to Tom, she had applied to seminary as a way of healing and to try to deal gracefully with the situation. All the people who knew Marilyn admired her, including Mallie.

Terry got up from her desk as Mallie walked into the reception room. "Hi there," she said, reaching out to put her arms around Mallie. "I'm so sorry about your father."

Terry had that rare combination of the appearance of a wood sprite—the green tennis shoes, the red hair with spit curls around her face—and the affectionate demeanor of a schoolmarm. Increasingly, she seemed genuinely concerned about Mallie, about whatever was going on in her life. Many times while Mallie sat waiting for her appointment with Tom, Terry inquired about the boys by name, or about her sisters or her mother and father. Several times recently she had delivered one of Mallie's frequent letters to Tom. Mallie felt that there was an understanding between them about her special relationship with him.

"I brought Tom some chicken salad for lunch," Mallie said, placing the small styrofoam container on the chair next to her. "I thought he'd probably skip lunch otherwise."

Terry sat down behind her desk. "How nice of you to do that," she said. "He rarely has time for lunch."

Mallie looked at her watch. Five after one. No sound from Tom's study. She began to feel anxious. A nagging voice in her head reminded her that except for a distant sighting across the church at her father's funeral, she had not seen Tom since he had abruptly left her house. She hoped that she could just walk into his study and he would be waiting as usual and everything would be the same as it was before the incident on the couch. She looked out the window.

"Is that Marilyn Jamison's car in the driveway?" she asked Terry, making conversation to fill the void. She already knew the answer.

Terry nodded slowly without looking at Mallie, or out the window at the car. Mallie's skin prickled. There was something about Terry's response, or lack of response, that set off a strange but familiar alarm. She tried to concentrate on the article she had begun reading in a *Psychology Today*, but she could not control the same creeping suspicions that had become so venomous in her last years of living with Larry. Little clues—like the earring in the couch, letters, odd telephone calls with no sound and hang-ups, Larry coming home hours after he was expected. She had never had any reason to be suspicious of Tom. Still, something nagged at her about Marilyn Jamison and her car in the driveway. The words blurred on the pages of the magazine. How silly! Tom was not Larry. And Marilyn Jamison was not the sort of woman who would flirt with other men, certainly not with Tom Matthews.

"How's your mother doing, Mallie?" Terry asked, breaking the silence. "Your father's passing must have been a terrible shock to her."

"My mother's so strong, she'll be fine. It's hard to imagine her without my father—but she'll be fine."

"Will she stay in Memphis, do you think?"

"I don't know. It's a good question. She'll probably spend more time in Vero Beach in the winter. They've had a house down there for years. She has lots of friends there."

Mallie looked at her watch again. One twenty. This was strange, even for Tom. Her appointment was for one o'clock.

Suddenly, out of the corner of her eye, she saw a figure, a dark-haired woman, walking quickly across the parking lot. The woman had obviously come from the side entrance to Tom's study—the same way that she always left. Before she could get a good look—surely it was Marilyn—the inside door to Tom's study jerked open. Tom stood in the doorway, shaking his head and putting out his hands toward her in a gesture of welcome, including his usual verbal protest.

"So sorry to keep you waiting, Mallie," he said. "Come in. Come in."

Mallie picked up the chicken salad and hurried past Terry, who barely looked up from her typewriter. As she walked through the door, Tom shut it quickly behind her and took her in his arms. In all of her times with him, he had never greeted her like that. Always, he had started their meetings with a brief hug, then talk, conversation, sitting across from one another—but instantly, this time, his mouth was on her mouth, as if he were hungry for her. She dropped her purse and the chicken salad on the floor. She felt transported out of all of her fears that her aggressive behavior might have wrecked their relationship. She felt the warmth of his face next to hers, his mouth searching her eyes, her ears, with its wet softness. She had never felt so wanted by him. She even dared to think that he had changed his mind about making love to her. She tried to imagine what could have happened in the past four days to make such a difference. For a split second, she wondered if he might have been kissing Marilyn Jamison, and that was why he was so instantly passionate with her. How absurd. She pushed the idea out of her mind. Tom was with her, loving her, with an urgency that she had never known from him. He led her to the couch, pushing a stack of books off onto the floor. Without words, they continued to kiss and stroke each other, Tom's hand touching her breasts.

"Mallie, Mallie," he finally said, sitting upright and withdrawing from her. "You're so beautiful, Mallie." He leaned back on the couch, as if exhausted. "You know that, don't you?"

Mallie could not think. She felt both exhilaration and panic. She felt as if she had come close to flying off a cliff with Tom.

"I wish things were different," he whispered. He looked at her with such intensity and caring in his eyes. But he was shaking his head. She knew without his saying anything further that he was trying to tell her that although loving her, he could not make love to her. Nothing had changed. As long as he was married, he would never make love to her. She would have to accept his decision or she would lose him.

"I love you, Tom," she said. "I know you love me. That's all that matters." He was a priest. She had always been aware of that. They came from different worlds, but in that moment she believed that someday they would be together. It was not possible that God had allowed her to find someone she trusted so completely and loved so deeply, and that he would not provide a way for them to be together.

Tom stood up and moved to the chair next to his desk. "Life is complex, Mallie," he said. "Love is complex—sometimes beyond our human understanding. That's why we need to have faith."

"Yes," she said, as if she understood exactly what he meant. "I know."

She felt a moment of clairvoyance, a moment as definitive as her mother's "knowing." She was sure of this: she knew he loved her and she knew his boundaries. She would not try to challenge them again.

Chapter Thirty-nine

The heat of the late summer dragged on into the middle of September. Mallie spent her time between her weekly visits to Tom and getting the boys ready for the fall semester at school, including all their after-school sports activities. In addition, her mother needed her to help sort out the choices for her new life without her father.

Joan Malcolm's big question concerned whether she should sell the house in Chickasaw Gardens and move away. To Mallie's immense surprise, she discovered that her mother had never really felt at home in Memphis. Rightly or wrongly, her mother believed that most of her friends were really Sam Malcolm's friends.

From Mallie's earliest childhood memories, her parents had always been social, their weekends spent entertaining or going out with friends. They were invited to every important social event. It had never occurred to Mallie that her mother did not love her life in Memphis. "I've always felt like a foreigner here," her mother confessed in one of their many conversations about her future.

One consideration was for Joan to buy a place in her child-hood home of Chicago. Her sister and only a few of her childhood friends were still living there. Also, her mother was well aware that Chicago had changed a great deal since she was first married and moved to Memphis. She knew she would not be going back to the place of her childhood. Whatever choice she made, she would still spend most of the winter in their condo in Vero Beach. There were many other widows and she had lots of new friends. She could have a bridge game there every day. Her married friends assured her they would include her in their dinner parties.

The more Joan and Mallie talked, the more her mother became convinced that she could live in Vero Beach full-time, and travel during the worst summer months. She could always visit Kye in New York. She loved going to the theater and shopping in the city. And, of course, she would go to Atlanta to see Anne and her family. Her only reason for coming back to Memphis, Joan made clear, would be to see Mallie and the boys.

One morning Mallie sat up in bed from her predawn musings, alert with the awareness that she had been spending all her energy worrying over her mother's life changes, denying her own. Her divorce would be final by the end of November. She had not come to grips with any concrete plans for what to do with herself—with her life—as a single woman. Like bingo balls rolling around in a wire basket, the possibilities had been tumbling over each other, occasionally spitting out the same bold message: *Make a decision based on something that will enhance your life*.

Every practical bone in her body told her that she needed to get a job, although she had the problem of no college degree and no work experience. There was no way she could find anything beyond an hourly wage position, and there was none she could imagine "enhancing her life." Before she went to England, she had briefly discussed with her father the possibility of returning to art school, and he had agreed to pay her tuition—if that was what she really wanted to do. She thought of her primary school teacher's comments.

"A natural talent," Mrs. Mackenzie had repeatedly told her parents in fifth grade. "Your daughter is very gifted. You should send her to the Saturday school at the Art Academy."

Mr. Dooley, Mallie's studio art instructor at Sweet Briar, had written an effusive letter to her parents about her artistic growth in Italy. "She has a wonderful life as an artist ahead, if that's what she wants—and if she will apply herself to it."

Mallie had so many regrets. She had refused to go to the Saturday school. She had chosen to go to the movies on Saturday with her friends instead. Only in college—and particularly in Italy—had the desire to make art lodged itself in her psyche. The pleasure had very little to do with the experience of standing in a room and looking with pride at one of her finished paintings. It was the process that thrilled her—the smell of the paint, the feeling of the brush in her hand, the emergence of something that had never existed before, the creation of images on paper or canvas that had come from her imagination and her hand. She wondered how it was that she had given up her art so easily. Larry never asked her to give it up. He even offered to buy her new brushes and canvas when they were first married. But, somehow, she couldn't justify giving herself to painting as she had in Italy. Her role as a wife and a mother, and as a community volunteer in Memphis, gave her the feeling that she was doing what she was *supposed* to be doing with her life. It was what her mother and her grandmothers had done with their lives, what all her friends did. Never mind that her thoughts wandered miles away from the bridge table or that she could not concentrate on her friends' problems with getting proper domestic help.

From the first time she told Tom about her student days as an artist—her love of the creative process—he had supported finding a way for her to take it up again. When she mentioned going back to school, maybe for a master's degree, he encouraged her.

"Most people would give anything on earth to have an artistic talent," he said. "Talent is God-given. Using it—being successful at it—is up to human motivation and persistence."

Mallie was motivated. She knew she could be persistent. But

she had no way of paying for school. Her father had assured her he would pay for it, but he was gone. It took all of her courage to sit down with her mother and explain why she wanted to go to art school—the concept of doing something that would enhance her life. Whether her arguments appealed to Joan Malcolm or her mother was simply using her psychic powers to discern what was best for her daughter, Joan listened and then said, "I think that's exactly what you should do." She agreed to pay Mallie's tuition for as long as it would take to get her master's degree.

Chapter Forty

The next day Mallie left her afternoon appointment with Tom at St. Michael's, riding high on the confidence he always gave her. She drove straight to the Memphis Academy of Art in Overton Park and left her car next to the curb in front of the building she had always loved. She sat for a moment, contemplating the award-winning Japanese design and the long, wide set of steps up to the entrance. How many times through the years she had entered that building, going to a board meeting or an exhibition.

It was time for her to resign from the board of directors. She would be a student and since her father's death, she no longer represented the same potential for fundraising. Even if the president of the board urged her to stay, she knew she needed to resign.

This time she was entering the building to become a student. As far-fetched as it seemed, maybe someday she would even have an exhibition of her own work hanging on the great white walls surrounding the center atrium.

As she stood next to the receptionist's desk going over the registration form—she had already read it many times—she felt awkward. Returning students milled around the main floor in their cut-off jeans and ragged T-shirts with slogans: "Fear No Art" and "Artists Do It Better." One pale, dark-haired girl wore a black

T-shirt that sported the bold, white letters: "A Man is to a Woman as a Fish is to a Bicycle." Mallie wondered if the girl knew that was a feminist slogan coined by some Australian woman years ago. She had learned about it at the Princeton reunion.

Many of the girls wore no makeup and had hair that appeared not to have been washed in a month. Mostly long, stringy hair or ponytails. Obviously years younger than she was, the girls ignored her as if she were an insurance salesman, or, perhaps, a matronly board member—which she was.

"It's too late to register for this semester, Mallie," the receptionist said. "Classes have actually already begun."

Mallie slumped in disappointment. She should have known better. She knew that most of the public schools in Memphis started at the end of August, but her boys had not yet started at Holy Trinity. Sammy had not gone back to St. George's. She had imagined that the Art Academy would be on the same schedule as the private schools. She should have paid closer attention. There had been too many things going on in her life.

"Why don't you sign up for one of the night classes," the woman behind the desk said. "Those classes are starting up next week—and they're taught by the same faculty members as the day classes. The only difference is you would get no college credit and there are mostly adults in the class." She handed Mallie the schedule.

A question immediately arose. What would she do about Troy and David? They would be at home at night. She couldn't go to school and leave them alone. She needed to be there to fix dinner and help with homework. In spite of her reservations, she glanced quickly at the schedule.

There was a basic drawing class taught by Bailey Smith, one of the most admired artists in Memphis and a revered faculty member. It was held on Wednesday nights from six to nine. That was a possibility. Wednesday was Larry's night to take the boys to his house for dinner. They never got home before nine. She felt a little snobbish about the idea of a basic drawing class. She was long past the basics. Still, that class might make sense. She had lost confidence in herself as an artist and she was certain that Bailey Smith would be a good teacher. His class might be the best way of getting back to work. Drawing, after all, was the underpinning for painting.

"Is Bailey Smith's Wednesday night class full?" she asked.

"It's always full," the receptionist said, "but I'll put you in it anyway—if that's the one you want. Someone in the night classes is always absent for one reason or another. Bailey won't mind."

"Would I have to pay today?" Mallie was embarrassed to ask. She would have to get the money from her mother. She was trying to be careful and not overdraw her bank account.

"No, no," the woman said. "It just has to be paid before you start next week."

Mallie was sure she could manage that. When she signed the form, she smiled. This was the first step into her new life.

Chapter Forty-one

"I can teach you to draw," Bailey Smith said in his opening remarks on the first night of his basic drawing class. "I can't teach you to be an artist."

He stood next to a blackboard, his long, lanky figure looming above his desk, one hand holding a newly sharpened yellow pencil, the other tucked loosely into the pocket of his worn khaki pants. In the stark basement room, Bailey Smith looked like an English don, his clothes clean and un-fussed, a lock of gray hair drooping over his forehead, his dark eyes impenetrable under thick horned-rim glasses.

He was a familiar sight to Mallie, although she had never had a conversation with him. He came to every art opening at the Academy. All of the exhibiting artists were either one of Bailey's contemporaries or one of his students. Unlike many artists who were also teachers and some of whom held jealousies, hidden or not so hidden, Bailey was known and loved for his generous encouragement to everyone.

Mallie was familiar with his work, although she didn't pretend to understand it. *Non-objective* was the term always applied to his painting. Sometimes, the term was *expressionistic*. His latest works seemed to have gone back to the figure. They were large colorful paintings with a strong architectural structure.

"Drawing is the closest you'll ever get to the mind of an artist," Bailey continued. "It's the first tangible mark of an artist's vision. That vision may change as it develops into a more finished drawing, or as it progresses into painting or sculpture—or some other form. But drawing is the core."

He seemed both earnest and at ease with his lecture. He had obviously given it many times before.

"Since the early sixties, most students have bypassed drawing to go directly into whatever they intend to do. They say they don't need to take the time to draw. The truth is they don't know how to draw. They don't want to take the time to learn. They want to build a building without studying engineering or architecture. They don't want anything that might resemble 'technique' to interfere with the emotion they want to express. They don't want any rules."

Bailey held a pencil up in the air as if it were a work of art itself. "My belief is that even if an artist never picks up a pencil again, he or she must first understand the construction of art. If you understand what the rules are and why they exist, you're free to break them. Eventually, if you're any good, it's important to break the rules and make your own."

He heaved a sigh and lowered his pencil. His eyes searched the room as if to see if anyone were listening—if his theory mattered to anyone.

For a second, Mallie thought his eyes connected with hers. She nodded, wanting to communicate her agreement with him. Internally, she said, *Yes, yes, you're right. That was the way I was taught nearly twenty years ago.* But she hoped she wouldn't give away her age and have to explain the gap between her college years and her return to school.

"So, let's take a break to go to the store for pencils and a large pad of paper," Bailey said. "Tell them you're in my class and they'll know what to sell you. We'll start again in about fifteen minutes."

It was a warm September night. Mallie had worn her old jeans and a cap-sleeved black T-shirt, hoping to blend in with the other fifteen or so other students. She stood near the back of the line at the Art Academy store, casually observing the group. Both men and women, all adults, none of them familiar to her. That suited her fine. She wanted to be anonymous. She wanted the experience to be hers alone without the complications of any other persons. No possibility of relationships.

For a few seconds she felt as if nearly eighteen years had vanished from her life, as if she were beginning again exactly where she had left off in Italy—not thinking about anyone but herself. At that point in her life, however, she knew that she had a marriage ahead of her—and children. She was so in love with Larry and she so wanted to have his children that she was willing to give up anything. This time around, she had no idea what might be ahead of her. She had Tom Matthews and she had her boys—and she was going to have her art again. At least for now, that would be enough.

When they took their seats, Bailey began an explanation of simple line drawing. He used straight lines to divide up the picture plane. "Take a direct line point to point," he said. "Go beyond the boundaries of the paper to see where the shapes connect."

Mallie made a mess of her paper in the beginning. She tore off the first sheet. She listened as he continued to talk about organic shapes: curvilinear, irregular, freeform, biomorphic. As she began each new page—two, three, four sheets—she loved the feeling of swirling her pencil, making organic, amoebic shapes on the paper. The two hours of class disappeared in seconds.

The following Wednesday Bailey began his weekly routine of setting up a series of objects in a still life composition, both geometric and organic shapes, as well as some type of soft, folded material. Usually there were three or four settings in a single night. With each one, he taught new principles. He began with the principle of perspective by first using a grid and showing his students how to create the illusion of space: an object becomes half its size every twenty feet. He explained the principles of line, shape, texture, and volume.

Mallie felt that her memory was coming alive as he talked. Her drawings improved with each new still life setting. She loved gesture drawing—quick statements of form and general character.

Gradually, Bailey introduced the class to nuances: shading and cross-hatching, all the principles familiar to Mallie.

"You've obviously done this before," Bailey said to Mallie one night, as he walked behind the students, checking their work. Smiling, he added, "That's a very good drawing."

Mallie was thrilled with his praise. In three weeks of classes, he had not spoken individually to her. She thanked him, knowing that her still life was good. Drawing in the class had been similar to getting back on a horse after falling. Feeling fearful and awkward at first, she had stayed with it, and the process had started to become instinctive again. Suddenly, she wanted to blurt out her whole life story to Bailey, tell him about her love of painting, her student semester in Italy, her marriage, her children, her divorce, her father's death, everything. *Stop*, she told herself.

"Thank you," she said without looking at him for more than a second. "It's been a long time coming."

He patted her shoulder. "Well, keep it up," he said and moved on to the next student.

Mallie could hardly wait to tell Tom about her class each week. For the first time since she'd begun seeing him in his study, she felt as if she were bringing something positive for him to enjoy with her, rather than something negative for him to fix. Her decision was made. She would apply for regular admission as a full-time painting student in the winter semester.

Chapter Forty-two

"Getting blood out of a turnip" was the analogy that John Bradford, Mallie's lawyer, used to describe his chore of working out a financial settlement with Larry on her behalf. There was just not much there to divide.

Larry had no savings account. His inheritance from his grandfather, the portfolio of stocks and bonds that he had proudly offered to show Mallie's father when he asked for her hand in marriage, had vanished. Sam Malcolm had waved off the idea of checking Larry's net worth, telling him that all he cared about was his prospective son-in-law's love and commitment to his daughter. As long as Larry worked hard, the rest would take care of itself, her father had said.

Mallie was certain that her father had counted on Larry's advancement at Malcolm Brothers to take care of all their financial needs. He could not have anticipated the problems he created by his determination to put Larry through all the tedious steps that he himself had gone through himself in learning to run the company.

The company had been very different—a small, regional hardware business—when Sam Malcolm started to work. Through the years he had helped it to grow into a national operation with distribution points as far away as California. Mallie's father insisted that Larry make sales calls in person every week to every small store all over the country that carried Malcolm Brothers products. He pur-posefully paid very little attention to him—an attempt to appear free from showing any favoritism toward his son-in-law. He also kept Larry's salary lower than any other salesman.

To Larry, his father-in-law's plan for him had been ridiculous—like teaching someone to run an airline by sweeping the hangar floor. The meager pay had forced him to spend his own capital, month after month, year after year, slowly leaching it away.

In recalling her arguments with Larry over the skiing trips they had taken as a family, Mallie regretted both her naiveté and her acquiescence. She realized over time that, of course, there was no possibility those trips could have been covered by Larry's salary. In her heart she knew they couldn't afford such luxuries, but when Larry had accused her of nagging him, she gave up and became complicit in his financial recklessness.

For so long, however, Mallie had been unaware of all the other drains on his financial resources: his business trips that included unexplained, extended weekends away from home, his "entertain-ment" expenses that she was sure he would not have dared to claim from the company. And the apartment he had rented in downtown Memphis, the one that she learned about from the anonymous letters.

She had no idea when Larry had reached the end of his inher-itance. But none of that mattered anymore. The puzzle at hand was how to divide Larry's income so that it would support two households.

"I don't think it makes sense to sell your house," John said. "Except for the mortgage, which is reasonable, it's pretty sound and the expense of finding anything today in a place you would want to live with the boys—at least three bedrooms—would be more than you could manage. Also, there are so many hidden expenses and difficulties in moving."

Mallie agreed that it was a good decision to keep the house, particularly for the boys. Even Larry understood that it was important to try to hold as much continuity as possible in their lives.

"The question is whether you can cut back on all your other living expenses," he added.

"All I want to do—besides take care of the basics—is go to art school," Mallie said. "I don't care about anything else. If I can pay the mortgage and I know the boys' education and health insurance are taken care of, I'll be fine."

John Bradford, Mallie's old friend from childhood as well as her lawyer, looked at her over his reading glasses. "Mallie, I've known you a long time. Can you really stay out of Goldsmith's and Levy's women's clothes departments?" He was not smiling.

Mallie felt squirmy. She was embarrassed that she had loved—and worn—beautiful clothes all her life. From her growing up years in Memphis, she had led an active social life that required beautiful clothes. But she would no longer need them.

"Clothes don't interest me anymore," Mallie said, the squirm diminishing under the anticipation of her changing life. She already had plenty of jeans in her closet from her summers in Watch Hill. "I'll live a different life, John. I've got enough dressy clothes in my closet to last a lifetime." She smiled. "I may never wear any of them again."

It was true. Mallie had already replaced the importance of Cotton Carnival parties, symphony balls, and Country Club Saturday nights with art classes and movies with friends. School functions with the boys and St. Michael's chapel on Sunday mornings did not require a special wardrobe. She had replaced her previous life with Larry with dreams of a different life. Somewhere deep in her mind she kept the possibility of some future connection with Tom Matthews. Meanwhile, she would be alone. She could not see herself entertaining as a single woman in her house on Walnut Grove.

"I can live on a lot less, John," she said.

Chapter Forty-three

Occasionally Mallie began to see Tom at St. Michael's on Saturday mornings. One morning in late October, she arrived to find him in a particularly ebullient mood. "It's such a gorgeous day," he said. "Let's take a walk outside."

"What a wonderful idea!" Mallie was ecstatic. His suggestion was a sign of their growing intimacy and ease with one another. For many months, her relationship with him had been cloistered in his study. Taking a walk was such a normal thing for couples to do on a beautiful fall morning.

The air outside was soft and warm in the sun, but as they passed under the shadows of shade trees, Mallie felt a crispness that she knew meant the coming of winter. The leaves of the great oaks and the sweetgum trees had turned red and yellow—some had already fallen into multi-colored piles on the ground.

The area around Victorian Village was a perfect place to walk. So many preserved pre-Civil War houses stood close together like dignified old soldiers still in uniform. The Mallory-Neely house was the most prominent, an elaborately decorative, three-story building with turrets and a tower. When the last family member died, the house had been turned over to the Daughters of the American Revolution to maintain and use for its headquarters. On that

Saturday morning no human presence was apparent, only the silent houses with their draperies still pulled shut.

When they walked back into Tom's study, Mallie sprang an idea of her own. She held her breath as she spoke. "Tom, how would you like to take a picnic out to Shelby Forest this afternoon?"

Taking a picnic out to the pristine woods that surrounded the lake was something she had often done with Larry and the boys. About twenty miles outside of Memphis, Shelby Forest was one of her favorite places. The day would be perfect for the colorful leaves and, perhaps the last bright, warm afternoon before the bleakness of November. Also, she knew that this was the Saturday afternoon that the boys spent with their father, so she would not have to be concerned about them.

Tom immediately responded with an apology. "I wish I could, Mallie," he said in his most sincere voice, the same one he used when he arrived late for an appointment. "I'd love to do that—really, I would—but I promised my wife I'd take her to the Pink Palace Crafts Fair for the whole afternoon."

Mallie had forgotten about the Crafts Fair. The annual event had grown increasingly popular through the years and become a big deal in Memphis.

"She's really counting on it," he said, as if he needed to confirm his commitment. "I'm so sorry."

Mallie said she understood. She was reminded of Tom's burden with a wife who was ill. She wondered if he would have to take a wheelchair, or if his wife would be able to walk on her own. There was so much that she didn't know about his life and so much that she had to leave unasked. She contented herself with his response that he loved the idea of the picnic with her in Shelby Forest.

After an abbreviated kissing session on the couch—"I really have to go now," he said, pulling away from her—Mallie drove home. Full of the excitement of their walk and her time with Tom, she sang along with the music on the radio in her car. "*Volare, oh, oh. Cantare, oh, oh, oh, oh. Nel blu di pinto di blu.*"

She had not heard that melodic Italian tune since before she and Larry were married. It took on new meaning. She was truly flying. Nothing, not even her dashed hopes that she would spend the afternoon at Shelby Forest with Tom, was going to get in the way of her fantasy: someday she would have the whole day with him.

Turning up her driveway, she was happy to see the familiar crew working in her yard. Twice a month, Henry Mathis, who had worked for her mother for years, and his two teenaged sons came with his truck and cleaned her yard, mowed the grass, trimmed the bushes, and hauled away the brush. Her mother had given her the gift of Henry's bi-weekly yard service for a Christmas present.

Watching them at work as she walked toward the house, Mallie was struck with an idea. Suppose she gave up part of her time with Henry and took the crew over to St. Michael's for the afternoon to clean up the chapel yard. It was always a mess. It would be a surprise for Tom. She created a picture in her mind: Tom would come to officiate at the service on Sunday morning and the yard would have been magically been restored. She would not tell him that she had been responsible, but he would eventually find out—and he would be grateful to her. Such a perfect idea!

Henry agreed to go. Mallie suggested that the crew stop for lunch, and, as soon as she changed clothes and finished her lunch, they could follow her to the chapel.

∞

She left her car down the street from the parking lot at St. Michael's, just in case someone might drive by and recognize it. She wanted her project to be a complete surprise. Henry parked his truck right behind her car. She walked around the grounds of the Chapel, showing Henry and the boys what she thought needed to be done. Once they got started, she went to the back yard to weed the flowerbeds herself.

Within minutes after Henry began clipping the hedge and the boys were raking up leaves, Mallie heard a car drive into the parking lot. She stabbed the sharp end of her weeding tool into the ground to remember where she had stopped and walked around the building to see who the visitor might be.

Instantly, Mallie recognized Marilyn Jamison's Dodge station wagon. She felt a gasp in her throat. What was Marilyn doing there? After catching her breath, Mallie marched over to the car and stood on the driver's side staring at Marilyn through the glass. Marilyn rolled down the window and looked quizzically back at her.

"Tom's not here," Mallie said flatly, as if Marilyn had brought wares to sell and no one was at home to buy. A heavy smell of flowery perfume floated out of the front seat.

"I'm a little early," Marilyn said, raising her wrist to check her watch.

"No, I mean he's not coming here today," Mallie said emphatically. "He's taking his wife to the Crafts Fair for the whole afternoon."

"Oh," Marilyn said.

They stared at each other like two ticket holders for the same seat.

In a matter of seconds, another car drove up and parked at an angle on the other side of the parking lot. Tom Matthews got out and strode across the pavement toward the front entrance of the chapel.

Mallie felt stupefied, as if she must be dreaming, as if what she had seen could not possibly be real.

Without looking directly at either woman, Tom acknowledged their presence with a simple nod and a barely audible greeting. "Hello, Mallie—Marilyn." He walked past them, up the steps, and through the front door.

Marilyn opened her car door and said, "Excuse me" to Mallie, as she followed Tom across the parking lot and into the building.

Conflicting thoughts collided like bombs in Mallie's mind.

Impossible! This is impossible. This can't be. Tom had lied to her. He had not gone to the Crafts Fair. He had come to the chapel to see Marilyn Jamison. She had come to see Tom. It had all been planned.

Instinctively, Mallie charged up the steps to the front door of St. Michael's. The door was locked. Setting her jaw, she walked around to the side door of Tom's study. That door, too, was locked. The only sound breaking the silence surrounding the chapel was coming from the power mower in the back yard. Mallie stood transfixed, staring at the door to Tom's study, as if it were the door itself that had locked her out of his life.

Blinded and sickened by stabs of nausea and dizziness, Mallie staggered across the parking lot and closed herself inside her car. She felt her body swelling up with rage, torrents of confusion and anger crashing over her in the enclosed cavern of her car. Never in her life, not even in all the years of Larry's women, could she have imagined that she would be in such a place, that she was capable of feeling such fury. Tom. Over and over in her mind, she heard the detachment in his voice saying "Hello, Mallie," as if she were a mere acquaintance who just happened to be standing in his parking lot. She had stood there, next to Marilyn's car, watching him walk past her—a completely different Tom from the man who had taken a morning walk with her only a few hours before. She saw Marilyn Jamison, her face heavily made up and the scent of her perfume still lingering in Mallie's nose. Marilyn had followed Tom into the Chapel, as if it were a familiar routine. Mallie felt the cold locked doorknob of Tom's study in the palm of her hand. She squeezed her fingers shut as if to strangle it. The word *hate* pounded on her brain like the blows of a hammer. *Hate*, the word she had been taught from childhood never to use. *Hate*, the emotion she had been taught never to feel. She could not control herself—she felt hate like fire burning in every pore of her body. She curled up in the front seat of her car and buried her face in her hands, trying to stop thinking, to keep from blacking out.

Nearly unconscious, Mallie was startled when Henry knocked on her car window. "We're finished, Miz Vose," he said. "We'll be off now."

She sat up and rolled down her window to thank him. She could barely see him, or the work he had done in the yard. She mumbled a few words of gratitude, then watched him pile the rakes and mower and tools in the back of the truck and drive off.

There was still no sign of life inside St. Michael's. The two cars were still in the parking lot, across from each other—Marilyn's car purposefully pointed toward the entrance to the building, Tom's car skewed at an angle. Mallie recorded the scene as if for evidence at a trial. But there would be no trial. No objective verdict could alter the betrayal she felt. Nothing could change what she had witnessed. She had trusted Tom Matthews. Believed in him. Loved him. She had spent so many Sunday mornings in the third pew of St. Michael's Chapel, listening to Tom's voice reciting the opening prayer of Rite II: "*Almighty God, to you all hearts are open, all desires known, and from you no secrets are hid.*" She had believed that God shared her secret love for Tom, and somehow she was certain that he approved. Sunday after Sunday she had tried to imagine that, as Tom said those opening words, he might be sharing the same secret with God about her.

Mallie stared blankly through the glass of her car window, her mind's eye roaming the pews of the chapel during all of the Sunday services she had attended. Occasionally Marilyn Jamison and other single women whom she did not know were present. At the time, she had not given Marilyn—or any of them—a suspicious thought. Seeing them in her memory, she felt another wave of nausea. Perhaps they were there for the same reason she was there. Tom had been her only secret, but, obviously, she was not his only secret. He had Marilyn Jamison—that was clear. Maybe others. *No, surely not.* She could not bear to think there were others. For a brief second the thought crossed her mind that she—Mallie Vose—was no different from Marilyn Jamison or any of those women. But that could not be true. Her love for Tom—his love for her—was different. She had truly believed that it was different. In England, Father Jon had said that she had been "blessed" by having Tom in her life. She thought of the passage about "love and betrayal" from Martin Israel's book. She had loved and she had been betrayed. According to Martin Israel, she was supposed to learn something about herself from that experience. In that moment, Mallie could not imagine what she might learn about herself. She hurt too much to care what she might learn.

All of her circuits jammed. Mallie could no longer think. She felt weak, limp, as if every muscle and nerve in her body had collapsed, and she was left helpless, immobile. She knew that she should drive away from St. Michael's. Go home. She should never see Tom Matthews again.

Chapter Forty-four

The last thing on earth Mallie wanted to do was to take Troy and David to a movie after dinner that Saturday night. Ideally, she would crawl into a dark cave somewhere. See no one. Talk to no one. All the way home from St. Michael's she tried to think of ways to get out of it. Tell them she was sick. She was certain that she looked sick enough. But she had promised them. She had even bribed them to get their homework done before Saturday night and she would take them. She had no choice. It was their second—maybe third—viewing of *Star Wars*.

Mallie lost herself in the darkness of the theater and the cosmic universe of Luke Skywalker and Darth Vader. As if in solitary orbit, she floated out of her beleaguered known world into a fantasy place where the events of the day held no consequence and required nothing from her. With an unexpected jolt to her complacency, the face of Tom Matthews jumped out from behind the black mask of Darth Vader. She instantly closed her eyes. His deep, dark voice encircled her as if he were locking her in a steel girdle. Her body tightened. Her heart lunged against her chest, taking her breath. *Stop it!* She forced herself to open her eyes. Tom was gone. Darth Vader was gone. The scene had changed to another planet with Luke Skywalker and Obi-Wan Kenobi, the wise and comforting, godly man, speaking to each other. Their voices sounded garbled. As if double reels were playing simultaneously, Mallie found it was difficult to concentrate on the screen. The nightmare of her real life was every bit as dramatic and frightening as the film. She saw herself as Princess Leia, both of them playing the role of a struggling, naive young woman trying desperately to do good in the world—the forces of evil against them. But she was not in a movie. She was not Princess Leia.

Mallie thought about the letter she had received from her father-in-law at the time of her separation from Larry—the first and only letter he had ever written her. He had begun the letter by telling her how deplorable he found his son's philandering behavior and then he urged Mallie to forgive him. He wrote that, perhaps, if she examined her own heart, she would find a Jezebel somewhere deep inside. Mallie had been outraged at the suggestion. Jezebel? She was not a Bible student but she knew the implication of Jezebel. The woman was a seducer. A harlot. Mallie was horrified that her father-in-law could have implied such an accusation. Whenever she, as a married woman, had been attracted to another man—and certainly she had felt desire for other men—she had denied it and never acted on any of her impulses. But that was before she had known Tom. She was still married to Larry and she had fallen desperately in love with Tom Matthews. A married priest. She realized what little thought she had actually given to Tom's wife. Mallie had even been willing to try to seduce Tom in her own home.

Mallie's mind was as scrambled as the screen full of planets and robots and space ships. Her world was out of control. She kept having surges of violent hatred—hating Tom, hating Marilyn Jamison. Maybe she truly was Jezebel. She no longer had any idea of what or who she was.

Periodically, throughout the two hour movie, tears flowed down Mallie's face. When the lights came on, she felt as if she had been on a binge, but instead of being filled, she had been emptied, depleted of all the emotional liquid in her body. She could barely focus her swollen eyes. She walked quickly ahead of the boys and threw cold water from the tap in the ladies' room sink on her face. The stiff brown paper towels stung her cheeks, nearly raw from tears.

"I think I'm getting a cold," Mallie told Troy, who asked matter-of-factly what was wrong with her. When she finally fell into her bed that night, she passed into oblivion from the emotional exhaustion of the day.

David knocked on her door Sunday morning. "Mom? Are you awake?"

For a moment, Mallie was not sure where she was, or even if David's voice was real. Was she dreaming?

"Are we going to church?"

No, absolutely not, she wanted to say. Mallie couldn't bear the thought of going to church. Certainly not to St. Michael's. Or even to Holy Trinity. She couldn't bear the thought of getting out of bed—of facing the day. Sleep had been a refuge. The recollection of the day before—the *locked door*—made her head throb.

"No," Mallie said just loud enough for her son to hear. "Sorry, David. I don't feel well."

"Anything I can do?" he asked.

So like David to be concerned about her. "Thanks, darling. No. I'll be okay," she said. "I think I just need a little more sleep. Will you get yourself some cereal? And don't forget to feed Bingo."

"Sure, Mom," he said. "Hope you feel better."

When Mallie woke again, she felt groggy and confused. Was it still Sunday? The blackout shades were pulled down to the window ledge and it was hard to tell whether it was day or night, morning or afternoon. There were no sounds in the house. She punched the illuminating button on top of the clock on her bedside table. Twelve thirty. The boys had probably not had lunch, or if they had made something, there would be a mess left in the kitchen. She would have to force herself get out of bed. She would have to get through the rest of the day. On Monday morning she would try to figure out what to do about what had happened with Tom. Maybe she would call Terry. Or Jenny. No, she should not call Jenny—at least not yet. Terry was the right person to know what to do.

Chapter Forty-five

On Monday morning Mallie fixed the boys breakfast and waited until nine o'clock before dialing the number of the chapel.

"St. Michael's, Terry speaking," the familiar voice said.

"Thank God you're there," Mallie said, sinking down on the floor of the kitchen with the telephone in her hand, unsure of what to say next.

"Mallie? Is that you? Is something wrong?" Terry had clearly recognized the distress in her voice. When there was no response, she said, "Are you still there?"

"Yes," Mallie said simply. "I'm here. Is there any chance we could meet someplace? I need to talk to you."

After a moment's hesitation, Terry said, "Actually I was on my way out the door to go to the post office. Tom's not in the office this morning. Where would you like to meet?"

Mallie couldn't think of any appropriate place near St. Michael's. She wanted to make it convenient for Terry. "Any place that's easy for you," she said.

"How about the Dobbs House on Union Avenue across the street from the Methodist Hospital? Have you had breakfast?"

"Not really," Mallie said. Other than a lukewarm bowl of Chicken and Stars that she had made herself finish the night before, she had not eaten more than a few cookies since Saturday lunch. She had no appetite. "The Dobbs House is fine." She had passed it many times and knew exactly where it was located.

"How soon can you get there?" Terry said.

"I'll leave as soon as I get dressed. It should take me twenty-five minutes or so."

∽⊘

Terry was already seated in a booth when Mallie walked into the restaurant. Her smile and the smell of fried bacon and waffles provided momentary comfort. Since she was a child, Mallie had gone occasionally to The Toddle House on Saturday mornings with her father. He loved waffles but her mother wouldn't allow him to have them at home. Bad for his weight problem, Joan Malcolm said. Going out for breakfast had been a special treat for Mallie and her father.

Mallie slid into the cracked, red leatherette seat across from Terry without removing her dark glasses. She didn't want to reveal her swollen eyes right away.

"Mallie, whatever has happened?" Terry spoke in her softest, most nurturing voice.

"Coffee, hon?" An older waitress, wisps of her coarse blondish hair sticking out of her nylon hairnet, stood next to Mallie with a small pad in her hand. "You having breakfast?"

"Coffee. Yes. Thanks. No breakfast." She was grateful that words came out when she opened her mouth. She had been afraid that she would try to talk to Terry and choke with tears—assuming that she had any tears left.

"How about you, hon?" The waitress turned to Terry.

"I'll have some orange juice, whole wheat toast, butter on the side, and coffee. Thanks."

The waitress trundled off with a minimum of notes written on her pad.

Mallie looked at Terry for a few seconds without words. She had to trust her. There was nowhere else to turn. In spurts, she blurted out the whole story of Saturday's experience at St. Michael's: her morning walk with Tom, his declaration that he was taking his wife to the Crafts Fair, her idea of cleaning up the church yard as a surprise for Tom, Henry, his sons, the truck—and then Marilyn Jamison meeting Tom—and the locked the doors. *The locked doors.*

Terry listened without changing her expression. When it was over, she reached across the table and took Mallie's hand. "I was afraid something like this was coming, Mallie," she said. "I'm sorry it happened this way."

"What was coming?" She knew the answer without asking, but she needed for Terry to say the words.

"I saw you falling in love with Tom," she said. "You and the others through the years."

Mallie felt a stab of anger in her stomach, a nauseating, bitter taste in her mouth. "The others? There are others besides Marilyn Jamison?"

Terry leaned slightly forward. "He's been close to Marilyn for years—actually from the time she had all that trouble with her husband and decided to go to seminary. I can't tell you how close. I don't know. He sees her a lot and I know he cares about her. I also know he cares about you, too, Mallie."

"But—others? There are others?"

Terry did not take her eyes from Mallie, penetrating the blackness of her dark glasses. "Yes, Mallie. There've been periodic complaints to Bishop Wagner from women who counseled with Tom. Two years ago a rejected husband threatened to sue the church with all sorts of wild claims against Tom. So far the bishop's backed Tom in every situation." She hesitated. "I have to tell you—I know Tom's meeting again with the bishop this morning.

Something must have happened recently. This is the first time the bishop's asked to see me."

"The bishop wants to see you?"

"Yes."

Mallie had an instant sense of panic. In spite of all the pain, all the rage of the prior day and a half, she realized in all of its absurdity that what she had wanted Terry to say was that there was nothing to her suspicion of Tom's romantic relationship with Marilyn Jamison—and there were no other women in his life but her. But, of course, she knew that was not so.

Maybe she had called Terry because she subconsciously wanted to punish Tom, to get back at him for lying to her, for choosing Marilyn Jamison over her—for locking her out. Was she telling Terry the story to hurt Tom, to destroy him in her eyes? What a vile thought. Mallie had never been vindictive in her life. Not even with Larry. From childhood, her father always told everyone that his daughter Mallie did not have a mean bone in her body. But that was not true. There were no human beings without a mean bone. It was a matter of being tested. Mallie thought of Palm Sunday, how as a response to Pontius Pilate asking whether to crucify Jesus in the dramatized Gospel reading, she was part of the crowd in the congregation that shouted "Crucify him!" She had shocked herself then. Maybe that was what she was doing now. Crucifying Tom. But Tom Matthews wasn't innocent. He was not Jesus. In spite of all of her belief in him, her trust, he had betrayed her. He wore a collar, but he was a man, a man no different from Larry.

"What do you think the bishop wants to see you about?" Mallie asked Terry.

"Last week, just before time for me to leave on Thursday, there was a huge scene in Tom's study," she said. "It was so loud I could hear the voices at my desk." She hesitated. "He was with that young woman, Julie Mason—the one who started counseling with your husband last year. She's been seeing Tom alone quite a bit lately."

Mallie took her glasses off and squinted in the light. The shock of Terry's revelation about Julie Mason made her want to look directly into Terry's eyes. She had forgotten Julie's last name—had not thought of her in months. At the time of her separation from Larry, Tom told her that he was counseling both Julie and Larry. His simplistic explanation had been that Larry needed a younger woman to make him feel superior, and Julie needed a father figure. Tom was working with them, separately as well as together. It had not occurred to Mallie at the time that Tom's revealing any details of those he was counseling was an unforgiveable breach of professionalism. Mallie had been flattered that he shared the information—as if it were a clear sign of trust between her and Tom. She had not asked and Tom had not mentioned Julie in many months. She had heard through the grapevine that Larry was seeing other women as well as Julie. Mallie had stopped caring, or even thinking, about either one of them. She tried to picture the scene with Julie in Tom's office.

"My God, Terry, what was the scene about?" A crazy thought entered her head. Maybe there was something going on between Tom and Julie—Larry's girlfriend, Julie. No. It was not possible.

Terry ran her fingers through her curly red hair, raising her chin. "Your guess is as good as mine," she said. "I couldn't hear specific words. But whatever the trouble was, you can bet she didn't plan to keep it to herself. She slammed the side door shut and sped off in her car."

"Would she have called the bishop?"

Terry shrugged. "Well, he's concerned about something urgent. I'm sure of that. He called me right before your call and asked me to come in to his office this afternoon at two. He sounded very serious. Tom had already left me a message on the machine that he would be in late this afternoon, that he was seeing the bishop this morning."

Mallie felt dizzy with added confusion. Whatever was going on, she knew that Terry had been well aware of her feelings for Tom for a long time. Still, she recoiled at the idea that Terry might reveal them to the bishop.

"Terry, you wouldn't tell the bishop about me—about Tom and me—would you?" But, even as she asked the question, she felt torn. On the one hand she would love to march into the bishop's office herself and tell him everything about her relationship with Tom—about Tom's lies. She would love to see the bishop's expression, to see Tom punished for what he had done to her. On the other, she felt frightened, as if she would be the one who would somehow be punished for her involvement with him—as if it had been partially her fault.

Terry shook her head. "I don't know what he wants to talk to me about—specifically. But I certainly wouldn't tell him anything about you—not if you ask me not to."

Thank God. "What about Marilyn Jamison?" Mallie said her name as if it filled her mouth with rat poison. "Do you think the bishop knows about her?"

"I truly don't know what he knows or what he'll ask me. I know he's a good guy, a fair person. He's been proud of the success of St. Michael's and he has always supported Tom. But this time—I don't know." She reached out and took Mallie's hand. "No matter what the bishop says or does, Mallie, I would urge you to forget about what happened on Saturday. You need to understand that Tom—oh, what can I say? You need to try to forget about Tom, Mallie—as much as you can. Whatever it takes—you need to get on with your life."

The two women sat in silence for a few seconds. Mallie withdrew her hand. *Get on with your life*. What life? Her divorce would be final in a matter of weeks. Tom had become her life.

"You have those wonderful boys," Terry added, "and haven't you started going to art school?"

Mallie nodded. The Art Academy seemed so small, so far away from where she was, as if it were only a tiny piece of her life. But no, that wasn't true. The Art Academy was so much more than a tiny piece of her life. When she was in her drawing class, time stopped. She lost track of everything. She knew that she was completely absorbed in her work. During one of her recent sessions, Bailey Smith had spent more time with her than with any of the other students. He had used Mallie's work to demonstrate chiaroscuro to the class. What Mallie had done instinctively, he explained from a technical point of view, was the correct solution. Mallie had floated out of class, convinced, for the moment, that she really could be an artist.

And yes, she had her boys. Her boys were certainly more than just a piece of her life. They were vital to her sense of herself as a person. Through them, she was part of a continuum, a link from one generation to another. She loved all three of them. She talked to Sammy at St. George's every Sunday night. He was becoming a young man who thought for himself. "Mom, I met Senator Edward Brooke tonight," he recently told her. "He came to school to speak at Vespers—he's so smart! I really admire him." She thought it was a sign of his education and development that, in spite of living with the racial divide in Memphis all his life, Sammy did not even mention that Senator Brooke was black. Troy and David still took an inordinate amount of her time. She provided meals and drove carpools and went to a basketball game at Holy Trinity for one or both of them at least three days a week. She did homework with them every night—except for math. She had no idea what they were doing in math. But she knew that they needed her to be there. "Being there" was a part of love, she was certain of that. At Faith at Work, Dave Stoner had written those very words in his definition of love. But she suddenly remembered that Tom had often told her that he would "always be there." Once again, he had lied. She fought back tears.

"Mallie, you must stop and think about it. You have so much to be grateful for in your life, so much ahead of you," Terry said. She spoke as if trying to coax Mallie back from some distant planet. "It's in that scripture passage about faith, about believing in *that which we cannot see*."

Mallie dropped her head without responding. How could she explain to Terry that she had believed in Tom? How could she believe in something that she could not see—or touch?

"Do you have a good friend you can talk to? I think you should be with a friend today," Terry said. She reached over to take Mallie's hand again. "I'm so sorry about all of this—and I hate to leave you, but I do have to go back to work. I'll call you later, after I've seen the bishop. Will you be at home this afternoon?"

Mallie nodded again. She squeezed Terry's hand and mouthed the words, "Thank you."

Chapter Forty-six

Mallie avoided her usual route home. She consciously forced herself to drive on the other side of town, as far away as possible, from St. Michael's Chapel—and the cathedral. The thought of possibly seeing Tom in either place turned her stomach. She planned to call Jenny the minute she got home. She could not bear to be alone.

"Of course, I'll come over," Jenny said immediately. "Are you okay?"

"I need you," Mallie said. She had dialed her friend's number as if calling the fire department. Her mind was in flames.

"I'm coming right now."

Just hearing Jenny's voice had a calming effect. Mallie put water on the stove and took two mugs out of the cabinet. At least she could offer her a cup of tea. She turned on the small television on the kitchen counter, anything to break the oppressive silence of her house. It was just before noon, time for the news and weather. She had no interest in either. The voices, the urgency with which they reported a local traffic accident annoyed her. She turned it off. The box of Fruit Loops from the boys' breakfast sat gaping open on the counter. The milk carton, left out of the refrigerator all morning, was already at room temperature. She thought of her unmade bed, her damp towel in a wad on the bathroom floor. She was a messy person. Her life was messy.

It was Monday, the beginning of a new week, the day she usually felt that anything could happen, anything was possible. Normally, she would be looking forward to seeing Tom on Tuesday, making preparations for what she would wear, what she would say, how she would feel when he kissed her. But there would be no more Tuesdays in Tom's study. No Tom.

She had a class at the Art Academy on Wednesday night. She wondered if she would have the energy to go. She wondered what was happening in Tom's meeting with the bishop. What did it matter? Actually nothing mattered. Maybe her class mattered. The boys mattered. She absently closed the cereal box and put it on the shelf, the milk in the fridge. She walked up to her bedroom to make the bed.

∽⌒

"Mallie?"

From her room upstairs Mallie heard the side door slam and Jenny's voice calling to her. "Where are you?"

In the twenty minutes that it had taken Jenny to get to her house, Mallie had made her bed and straightened up her room and her bathroom.

"Be down in a minute," she said. "Would you turn off the kettle in the kitchen?" She could hear the steam whistling. She glanced in the mirror. Her eyes could barely focus. They were rimmed in red and squinting. Her skin was colorless. She looked away. She knew Jenny wouldn't care about her appearance.

"What on earth has happened?" Jenny reached out with both arms when Mallie came into the kitchen. "Are the boys okay?"

"They're fine," Mallie said. "It's not about them." She hugged Jenny and let go quickly before the tears started again. She took a step toward the stove. "Let's make a cup of tea." It was difficult to know where to begin to tell Jenny her story. They had been together so much, talked about so much, and yet, she had kept the biggest piece of her life a secret from Jenny.

They took the tea to the library, the same room where she had seen Lee Harvey Oswald shot on television, where Larry had told the boys he was leaving, where she had stripped off her blouse in front of Tom. She told the story straight through, as if it were about someone else. In that moment, it felt as if it were about someone else. The Mallie Vose she described was a naïve, foolish woman who had jumped from a life of lies with her husband to a life of lies with her counselor—her priest.

Jenny listened without flinching or saying a word. Finally, when Mallie paused after telling her about Marilyn Jamison and the locked door, she said, "Mallie, I can't believe you think I didn't know about some of this. I've watched you and I could see this happening. I'm hardly surprised."

"Why didn't you tell me?" Mallie said.

"I had to wait until you were ready to talk about it before I mentioned it. What do you think would have happened if I'd warned you about what was going on? Would you have believed me? Would you have stopped seeing Tom?"

That was a question Mallie couldn't answer. She thought again about Father Jon and her conference with him at the church in Arundel on that Saturday afternoon. "You have been blessed by your priest," he had said. She thought of Martin Israel's words about "being a fool for love"—about learning about oneself through betrayal. "It just hurts so badly," she said. "Oh Jenny—I've been such a fool."

"What you need, my friend, is to wake up to the truth," Jenny said. "You're right that your life is out of control. You're in a mess. You tried to make your marriage perfect. It wasn't. You tried to make a relationship with Tom Matthews perfect—and it certainly wasn't. Maybe it's time for you to have another counselor—a real counselor—and get your life straight. This is not about the men in your life. It's about you."

Mallie shook her head. The truth was that since she could remember, she had tried to be perfect—to do everything right. The fear of not being loved if she were not perfect had driven her to be a performer throughout her life. Only with Tom, in the intimacy of his study, had she been able to let go of the fear. Her desire for him had allowed her to forget everything else. She had been *a fool for love*.

Jenny got up and put her arms around Mallie. "You've become human, Mallie. I don't know why so many of us are born not knowing what it means to be human. We seem to have to learn it the hard way."

Jenny's words felt like soft rain. Merciful. Real. Mallie suddenly had a flash picture of Tom in his meeting with the bishop. "What's going to happen to Tom, do you suppose?" she said.

"*Nothing* is my guess," Jenny said. "Whatever might be his problem now has been his problem all along, and I'd bet the bishop's been aware of it. I doubt anything will change at St. Michael's. It's you who has to change."

Mallie slumped in her chair, depleted. The lively energy that her secret life with Tom had provided for months was gone.

"How do I do that?" she asked. Suggesting that she change her life made her feel like a child asking for someone to help her learn to tie her shoelaces while she was walking. Or maybe, it was more like telling her she needed to learn to swim as she was falling out of a boat.

"I have an idea," Jenny said. "There's a new pastoral counseling center that just opened in East Tennessee—near Knoxville, I think—in the mountains. I've met the man who started it at a Faith-at-Work Conference several years ago. He's trustworthy and smart. I think you should go over there."

"What about the boys—and my art classes?"

"Mallie, they'll be fine. They'll still be here when you get back. This is something you need to do for yourself. Now. It'll be important for the boys, and maybe for your art, too."

What Jenny said made sense. Mallie knew she would need to give up Tom and all that he had meant in her life. She didn't want to talk about her situation with him to any other counselor in Memphis. It would be impossible to find someone in town who didn't know him. "Do you think the place could take me right away?"

"I don't know. I'll call you when I get home and give you the number. It's worth a try."

Chapter Forty-seven

I t was nearly seven o'clock when Mallie received the call from Terry. She had finished cleaning up the kitchen after the boys' dinner. Troy was in the basement working on a science project. David was doing his math homework upstairs.

"It's been a long afternoon," Terry said, the cadence of her voice slower and more deliberate than Mallie had ever heard her speak. "A very long day."

"What happened? What did the bishop say?"

"I'm not talking about my time with the bishop," Terry said. "That was brief and to the point. I spent most of the afternoon with Tom in his study."

Mallie felt her pulse rise, her mind race. "Tom?" She said his name as if she might be referring to someone who had died and unexpectedly reappeared.

"The chapel's going to close its doors, Mallie. Tom's resigned as chaplain."

Mallie felt an enormous weight on her heart, as if someone truly had died. In spite of what had happened only two days before, St. Michael's Chapel had been her life's blood. She felt certain that she could not have survived the trauma of her humiliating rejection by Larry and her divorce if it had not been for the chapel—if

it had not been for Tom. She knew the place had been important to many other people too. Something catastrophic must have
occurred for the bishop to want to close the chapel. She waited for
Terry to speak again.

"This is to go no further than you—at least not until I speak
with the bishop again and it's all finalized. You understand that?"

"Yes, of course."

"That young woman, Julie Mason, has accused Tom of 'improper
sexual advances'—that's the term the bishop used with me."

Mallie felt sickened. Dear God, surely Tom could not have
made sexual advances toward Julie Mason.

"What did Tom say to the bishop?" Mallie asked.

"Tom walked out of the bishop's office without really defending
himself," Terry said. "All he said was that it was not true—that
if the bishop believed that young woman's story, he had nothing
more to say to him. He resigned on the spot. He came back to St.
Michael's and we talked for the rest of afternoon. He was distraught,
Mallie. He told me that her charges were ridiculous, absurd—that
the girl had been rejected by her own father. Tom had been seeing
her twice a week trying to help her get over a final rejection by your
former husband. She had actually tried to seduce Tom in his study.
When he tried to stop her, she screamed at him, accused him of
leading her on. I guess that was all the commotion I heard from my
desk on Thursday." After a brief silence, Terry said, "I have to say,
Mallie, I believe him in this case."

Mallie closed her eyes. She could not imagine Tom Matthews
with Julie Mason trying to seduce him in his study. She saw the
scene in her own library when she had tried to seduce Tom. That
had been months ago. It was all so confusing. As angry as she was
at Tom, she struggled to exonerate him from the charge by Julie
Mason. She believed his story too. Mallie had never met the girl,
but she knew enough about her and her rashness—the affair with
Larry, the phone call, and the attempted suicide—to know that she

was capable of extreme drama. "What did you say to the bishop?" Mallie asked Terry.

"I told him I thought the girl was lying—that she was off-balance," Terry said. "He said it didn't matter, the time had come to close the chapel. It's become an expensive operation and the diocese can't afford to keep it open and pay Tom's and my salary any longer."

Mallie had wondered from time to time how St. Michael's survived without taking in any annual parish pledges and still giving free counseling to anyone who came to see Tom. Certainly, it couldn't survive on donations in the plate on Sunday mornings by the medical students and nurses and the small group of Tom's followers. She had never given more than five or ten dollars on a Sunday morning herself.

"What will happen to you, Terry?" Mallie asked.

"The bishop offered me a new job at the cathedral. He said that the chapel would probably be sold before the year was over."

"Well, thank heavens you have a job," Mallie said. "What will happen to Tom?"

"The bishop called him this afternoon while I was still in his office and suggested he take the summer off. He said the whole business of Julie Mason was unfortunate, but that on rethinking the situation, he understood the girl was 'somewhat off-balance.' He said he would like to have Tom join the staff at the cathedral to teach Bible study classes in the fall. He assured him no one would ever know what happened at St. Michael's. The explanation for closing would be the prohibitive expense of running the chapel. Opening St. Michael's had been the bishop's idea. He would take full responsibility for the decision to close it."

"What did Tom say to that?"

"Well, thank God, he'd calmed down enough to tell the bishop he'd think about it. I was afraid he'd explode on the phone."

"And what about Julie Mason? What did the bishop say to her?"

"He didn't tell me specifically, but it seemed to me that he apologized for 'the church.' It sounded as if he told her how very sorry 'the church' was for anything negative that happened to her at the chapel—that he was personally sorry—that she could come to talk to him anytime she felt she needed to talk to someone—that he would take care of Father Matthews. She apparently left his office satisfied. Who knows what it was really all about for her."

Mallie stiffened. The response of the bishop felt so phony, so trivialized, such a pandering to both Julie Mason and to Tom Matthews. Was the reputation of the church and one of its priests worth the protection of the bishop's office—worth his telling lies? She wondered what the bishop would think if she told him her own story—about the months of personal turmoil that she had lived through with Tom Matthews. And what about Marilyn Jamison? Or maybe he did know about Tom's involvement with women in his study. Maybe if she went to talk to him, he would apologize to her as well. She had no use for an apology. An apology would change nothing at this point. Mallie had wanted nothing in her life beyond being with Tom—nothing beyond believing that he loved her. But she finally understood that the love he professed for her was not the kind of love she thought she needed, certainly not the kind of love she felt for him. She felt deadened, as if the world as she knew it had ceased to exist.

"Are you still there, Mallie?" Terry had waited for a response.

"I'm here," she said quietly, not sure where she really was.

"I've been so concerned about you all day," Terry said. "Did you call a friend?"

"I was with Jenny Bolton this afternoon," Mallie said. "She's advised me to go to this new counseling center in East Tennessee—it's run by a man she knows from Faith at Work. I called them a little while ago. Luckily, they had a cancellation for next week and they have a place for me." She stopped to take a breath. By saying the words aloud, she was admitting that she had really committed herself to going to a counseling center for an entire week.

"Good, good," Terry said. "And the boys—can you make arrangements for them?"

"I called Larry. He's keeping the boys. That's as far as I've gotten."

"I'm so glad you're going," Terry said. "So glad. That's a good solution. Perfect timing."

Nothing about it was perfect in Mallie's mind. She hated asking Larry to keep the boys, even for a night, much less for a week. She hated asking him for anything. And in some ways it felt like she was running away. She should be able to figure out her life on her own—her mother would never rely on anyone else to tell her how to fix the problems in her life. She wasn't sure she had the energy, or the courage, to go alone to an unknown place at the other end of the state and put her life in the hands of unknown people. A week at the center was expensive. She was not sure how she was going to pay for it. The only thing she knew for sure in that moment was that she had to make some major changes in her life or she would die.

Chapter Forty-eight

The drive on Sunday afternoon to the James A. Preston Pastoral Counseling Center in eastern Tennessee took six and a half hours. Mallie followed the directions to the old horse farm situated in the rolling countryside just outside of Knoxville. She could see the blue haze of the Smoky Mountains in the distance. Large oak trees lined the driveway and punctuated the pastures; white picket fences cordoned off fields where groups of horses and cattle were grazing. She felt as if she were in a museum looking at a Corot painting. There was a comforting serenity about the place.

At the end of the driveway, manicured vegetable and flower gardens surrounded a large, white clapboard house and several outbuildings. Before Mallie could get out of her parked car, a middle-aged woman in high-heeled shoes and a short, flared skirt waltzed out the side door of the white house and waved to her.

"Hi there! You must be Mallie Vose," the woman said, smiling.

Mallie was instantly put off by her shiny red lipstick and fingernail polish. Not at all what she had expected to find at a pastoral counseling center. For the whole trip from Memphis, alone in the car, she had been anxious, grimly persevering, as if preparing herself for an arduous mountain climb. Whatever was ahead of her would be difficult, but she would stay the course. Her need was serious. She expected the place to be serious. Surely the woman who greeted her was not a counselor. She was too made-up and too cheerful.

"I'm Angie," the woman said, her voice high and chirpy. "I'm the receptionist here. Let me help you with your luggage." She opened the rear car door and reached for Mallie's suitcase. "How was your drive? A lot of traffic?"

Mallie panicked and put her hand up to stop the woman from taking her suitcase. "Could I have a few minutes by myself?" she said. "I'd like to just be here alone for a few minutes. It's been a long drive."

Angie shut the back door and took a step away from the car. "Of course," she said. Her demeanor changed quickly. "You just take your time. No one's in a hurry here. Stay as long as you like. I'll be inside if you need me." She turned and walked toward the house without looking back.

Mallie scooched down into her seat, looking over the fields where the puffy white clouds almost touched the earth in the distance. The serenity she felt when she drove in had been replaced with dread. She wanted to start the car and drive away. But where would she go? She couldn't go home. The situation at home was the reason she was there. There was nowhere else to go. It had been her decision to come, her desire to change her life. She thought of Tom's words to her on her first visit to his study. He told her that by coming to see him she had made "a decision to live—whether or not she could save her marriage." She had been unaware of the scope and the consequences of such a life-changing decision. Well, this time she was aware. This time she knew she was not there to save her marriage. This time she needed to save herself. She had her boys and her art—and she wanted to live. This place, this pastoral counseling center, as she understood its mission, was supposed to offer her another chance. She closed her eyes. *Please dear Lord,* she whispered, *if you are there, help me. I need you.*

After taking a deep breath, Mallie opened her eyes, got out of the car, and reached into the back seat for her suitcase.

Angie stood waiting for her at the side door. "We're glad you're here, Mallie," she said softly, an entirely different tone from her original greeting. "I'll show you to your room. You're in Cabin B." She pointed to one of the smaller houses. "There'll be a group session here in the White House—that's what we call this build-ing—with James at five o'clock. That'll give you a little time to relax and meet your roommate."

They walked silently together to Cabin B. Angie held the screen door for Mallie and spoke to the woman inside. "Helen, this is Mallie Vose, your roommate for this week. Mallie, meet Helen Brady."

Helen Brady was propped up on her bed with pillows behind her, a book in her hands, half-glasses down on her nose. She spoke to Mallie in a lifeless voice, a stark contrast to Angie's cheerleader greeting.

Mallie put her suitcase down and looked more closely at her roommate. The woman had to be nearly her age, obviously not a young bride, but she was pregnant. Helen Brady had large streaks of gray hair and swollen, crusty bare feet. Mallie immediately felt that something was wrong. The woman was depressed. Was the pregnancy a mistake? Or maybe Helen Brady wasn't married. Instinctively Mallie felt compassion for her.

"We'll see you all at five. Okay?" Angie said. She closed the door quietly behind her as she left.

Mallie checked her watch. Four twenty. Not much time to relax. "Is this your first time here?" she asked Helen Brady.

"Yes," the woman said, placing her open book upside down over her swollen stomach. "I'm from Charlotte, North Carolina. This is my third child. My husband was killed in a small plane crash six months ago—it was his friend's plane—they were going to Las Vegas. I begged him not to go. I didn't—we didn't—know I was pregnant when he left." She took off her reading glasses, as if to make the final point. "I'm forty one years old."

There it was—all the facts out there at once. Mallie sat down on her bed. She wasn't sure what to say. "My God," she said. "I'm so sorry. How terrible for you."

"Thanks," Helen Brady said. "I'm here to figure out how to get through this for my other two kids. I've got a boy fifteen and a girl twelve. They need me and I'm a mess." Her eyes had dark circles underneath them and there was a sense of despair about her. "I know I should want this baby—it's Lennie's baby too. Lennie was my husband. He never even knew about it." She swallowed audibly, as if a huge burden were stuck in her throat. "Oh, I'm so sorry. I'm just blurting out everything to you and I don't even know you."

Mallie walked over and put her arms around Helen Brady. "We'll get to know each other. I'm a mess too."

Helen looked startled. "Really? You look beautiful to me."

"Well, don't be fooled by looks," Mallie said, a statement she wondered if she could have made a year ago. She checked her watch again. "I guess we'd better get ready to go on over to the White House for the meeting. I have no idea what to expect in this place. Do you?"

Helen shook her head. "Not really. I know James was the head of an alcoholic rehab place in Charlotte before he came to Knoxville to found the center. Some friends of mine in Charlotte think very highly of him. One of my friends is on the board of directors here. She said all of the counselors, particularly James, are people to trust."

That confirmed Jenny's assessment to Mallie. "Well, we're here. We'd better be able to trust them," she said.

Helen carefully put on her obviously new leather shoes, a painful experience for Mallie to watch. Her hands were also swollen, the skin around her wedding ring puffed up. Mallie washed her own hands—no wedding ring—in the bathroom and changed from her wrinkled khaki skirt into her black slacks and a long-sleeved cotton blouse. A few minutes before five, the two women walked on the path together without talking.

Angie opened the door. "Come on in," she said. She took them into a large sunroom filled with twelve or fourteen people, some standing near a table filling coffee cups or lemonade glasses, others seated in chairs and along a long window seat. Mallie was surprised at the diversity of the group. There were both men and women of all ages—one girl appeared to be still in her teens. Angie suggested that they get something to drink before sitting down.

As Mallie was pouring her lemonade, she spotted James Preston—she assumed he must be James Preston—talking to a younger man in the corner of the room. He was tall and gray haired, the only man in the room who was dressed formally in a coat and tie. He stood as erect as a preacher in a pulpit. The young man was listening to him with a sort of reverent, puppy expression.

"Okay, folks," James Preston broke from his conversation and raised his hand. "Let's get started." He walked over to the raised brick hearth in front of the fireplace in the center of the room and sat down. Everyone else found seats around him. Mallie and Helen sat together on the window seat.

"I'm James Preston," he said. "I want to welcome you here. Let's take a few minutes for each of you to introduce yourself—nothing formal—just your first name and anything you want to say about why you're here."

Mallie sighed. Another experience like the one in Arundel, England. Once again, she would have to go through the public exercise of explaining herself. Suppose she just stripped off her blouse and shouted to the group: "I'm Jezebel! Who are you?" She knew it was not a time for jokes, but then, it wasn't really a joke.

One by one, the individuals stood and spoke briefly. The youngest girl was named Betsy. She couldn't have been over eighteen. She told the group that she had flushed the last of her cocaine stash down the toilet when she got to the center. Her parents had forced her to come, but after she got into her room and her mother left, she decided she would try to make it work. The group applauded and she sat down. One couple wanted marriage counseling. They had been married seven years—the classic seven years, Mallie thought—and they were having trouble. An older, balding man had lost his wife to cancer and was bereft. He couldn't seem to get on with his life. Mallie followed Helen Brady who stilled the room with her sad plight of her dead husband, her teenage kids, and her unwanted baby. Without embellishment, Mallie recited her list of reasons why she was there: "I'm in the process of getting a divorce after eighteen years, I lost my father this year, I fell in love with my married counselor who is a priest and I need to put all this behind me. I need to figure out how to start a new life." Her voice, her words, sounded positive, so different from the desperation that she was feeling inside. She sat down avoiding eye contact with anyone.

"Thank you all," James said. "It's good to have you here." He leaned forward, still sitting, with his elbows on his knees and his hands locked under his chin. Mallie thought of Rodin's sculpture *The Thinker*.

"Now, here's what I want to tell you about this week—what to expect. Tonight I want each of you to write a history of your life up to the point of your decision to come here—concentrate on what has been most important to you through the years. No less than five pages, no more than ten. Starting tomorrow morning, you'll work mainly with an assigned counselor, according to a schedule. Take your history to your first session. You'll also have group sessions, sometimes with me in this room, sometimes with others. You'll meet with resource men and women—individuals who live in the area and who've been through our process here. They'll share some real life experience with you. Your only responsibility is to follow your schedule—and to be fully here. While you're here, you need to forget about what's going on at home or what's happening in the rest of the world. This week is for *you*. It may be the most important week of your life. Take advantage of it. Be here."

And that was that. He stood up and announced, "Let's eat. There are sandwiches and desserts in the garden."

Mallie and Helen fell into a sudden and quiet alliance; whatever was to come, they would be together. They ate ham and cheese sandwiches and met the others before going back to their room to try to condense each of their forty years of life experience into less than ten pages.

Chapter Forty-nine

Mallie started her assignment at least ten times. She wrote. She erased. She scratched out. She tore up the pages. She started again. James had instructed the group to write their life history up to the point when a decision was made to come to the center—and to focus the writing on what was "most important" in their lives. Mallie had no clue where to begin or what to focus on. There was so much to say about her life. All of it was important to her. She knew she wanted to pick the thread that might unravel the puzzle that her life had become. Maybe that thread would become apparent as she went along. She would begin at the beginning. The beginning was her given name: Valeria.

Mallie had explained the derivation of her name a thousand times to people who asked. She was named for her grandmother and her father's sister, her Aunt Valeria, an artist who was killed at a young age by a reckless Italian on a Vespa in Rome. From the start of school, Mallie had disliked her name. It made her different. All the girls in her class had names like Dixie and Susie and Betty Jane. She remembered, as if it were yesterday, the voice of the bully in first grade who said her name sounded like some exotic bird. He flapped his arms and croaked out every syllable slowly—"Va-lee-ri-a"—as if he were imitating a creature in its last dying moments. Then he laughed. She had felt humiliated.

Fortunately, one day at recess the handsomest boy in the class forgot her name when he was the leader of one of the teams of Red Rover. All he could think of was her last name. Instead of calling her Malcolm, he somehow shouted out *Mallie*. She had been the last girl chosen, but she had instantly loved being called Mallie. She went home that day and told Anne and Bernice that she had a new name, a nickname. She wanted to be called Mallie. Eventually, the nickname stuck. After a number of years of resisting, even her father dropped his determination to call her Valeria.

As she wrote about her first grade experiences, Mallie was reminded of the day she wore her WAVE uniform. World War II had started and her father had given her the patriotic uniform as a going away present when he left to join the navy in California. She had been so proud of it before the day she wore it to school. That day she found herself in the most embarrassing moment of her life (so far). It all began because Freddy Neale, the freckled-faced nerd, whom no one liked, chose to wear his army uniform. Everyone started teasing her and saying that she and Freddy were a couple. "Soldier girl loves soldier boy!" they chanted. At recess, two of the boys held her and made Freddy kiss her. She thought she would die of embarrassment. She never wore that WAVE uniform again.

So many stories of her childhood came to Mallie's mind. So many memories of being with her father: good, happy memories of the early mornings in a duck blind in Arkansas with him—bad, scary memories of his drinking and yelling at her. The confusion lay in never knowing exactly what would dictate his behavior toward her. She had been honored that he wanted her to go on hunting trips with him, even though she never really liked firing the gun and killing the birds. She just wanted to please him. The hunting paid off when she won an art prize at the Mid-South Fair for her watercolor painting of a sunrise on one of the ponds. Her father was so proud of her.

From her second grade year, Mallie remembered her recurrent nightmares that her father would not come back from the war. He had been overseas for two years. No matter how much she feared his temper, she adored him. At the end of every Mass in the Catholic Church, she put a nickel in the metal slot, lit a candle, and prayed to the Virgin Mary that nothing bad would happen to him.

She recalled the night she and her friends were playing spin the bottle when she fell and broke her ankle, trying to run from a boy who was trying to kiss her. Her father praised her and began his lectures on how important it was for a girl to "be a lady" and to "be chaste." All men want to date the fast girls, he said, but they want to marry a lady. She needed to be a lady and to save herself for her husband. Even when she was engaged to Larry, she heard her father's voice in her head telling her to "wait" for her wedding night.

Once she started writing about Larry, she couldn't stop. As if she were watching a film of her courtship and the early days of her marriage—before all the women and the lies entered her life—so many scenes came back.

The night she met Larry at the debut party in New York, dancing together like Fred Astaire and Ginger Rogers. The times he came to Sweet Briar for weekends, never without a present in hand: a box of lily-of-the valley soap, chocolate turtles or thin mints, a gold heart pin with a single tiny diamond in the center for Valentine's Day.

She thought of their picnics in the woods on spring weekends, spreading a blanket near blooming rhododendron bushes and dogwood trees. Lying next to each other on the blanket, they had watched the clouds through the tree boughs and talked about books. He had been reading Hemingway—someday he wanted to run with the bulls in Pamplona. She had discovered Mary Renault—she wanted to visit the Acropolis and the Peloponnesus in Greece.

Her happiest memory was the weekend they went to New York

to buy her engagement ring. They had stayed in separate rooms at Larry's grandparents' apartment on 72nd street. He surprised her with tickets for *West Side Story*, the big musical hit of the Broadway season. From the moment the orchestra hit the first stirring notes, Mallie was transported into the world of the Jets and the Sharks. Nothing in her experience related to the tension of the gang warfare—yet her heart sang with every word. In those precious moments, Larry was Tony. She was Maria. Throughout the love duet "Tonight," she and Larry pressed each other's hands as if they were drawn together by magnetic force. Nothing on earth would ever separate them.

Her happiness was magnified with the birth of each of her boys, particularly her last son. Once Mallie learned of the Lamaze method of natural childbirth, when she was pregnant with David, she was determined to try it. She wanted the sense of accomplishment that one of her friends described to her after her child was born without anesthetic. When David finally came into the world, after nearly twenty-four hours of labor and no pain relief, Mallie felt that she had reached the top of Mount Everest. In that moment she believed there was nothing she couldn't do.

Mallie put her pen down. She knew there were many things she couldn't do. She couldn't bear any more lies or any more loss in her life. There had been so much loss. Her beloved Bernice, her surrogate mother who had been so important to her growing up. Even though Mallie was a grown woman when her father died, she still lived with his words—both real and imagined—of praise and criticism, as if she were tethered to his opinion. And then there was the loss of her trust in Larry, the lies, the loss of her marriage.

She put her head in her hands. She would have to write about her attempt to get help for Larry at St. Michael's, and the story of how she fell in love with Tom Matthews. She would have to describe his heartbreaking betrayal by lying to her and then locking her out of his office, her feelings that she had lost God himself.

The real truth was that she had lost herself.

Chapter Fifty

Mallie tried not to show her surprise when she was introduced to her counselor, a petite, blonde woman named Saralynn. The woman seemed younger and was even more cloyingly cheerful than Angie. She could not have been over twenty-five and wore no wedding ring. Mallie imagined the counselor's shock when Saralynn read her "Life History." What could an unmarried woman in her twenties possibly know of marriage and children, of affairs and divorce, of suddenly losing your father when you most need him, and worst of all, falling in love and trying to seduce your counselor—a married priest?

After their initial greeting and a warm handshake, Saralynn was all business. "My office is upstairs," she said. "Follow me."

Mallie gripped her notebook and her "Life History" under one arm and dutifully followed the counselor up the stairs. She felt increasingly doubtful that anything productive would come from the experience.

Saralynn's office was a small room in one corner of the second floor—open windows, bright blue and yellow flowered wallpaper, two large chairs facing each other with a child's chair off to one side. There were fresh garden flowers, colorful zinnias and marigolds, and a crystal bowl filled with smooth, round stones on a rectangular table.

Some sort of professional degree was framed simply and hung on the wall between two posters, one of them a beach scene—possibly by Eugene Boudin, a French Impressionist Mallie recognized—and the other a rainbow-filled landscape by an unknown artist.

"Have a seat," Saralynn said. "Either one is fine. Did you bring your 'Life History?'"

At least the counselor wasn't wasting any time, Mallie thought. She chose the chair by the window and tried to hand Saralynn her sheaf of papers.

"I want you to tear up those pages," the counselor said with authority.

"Tear them up? Now?"

"Now," Saralynn said, smiling. "Then throw them in the wastebasket."

Mallie was stunned. She had worked on those pages for hours, well into the night, writing and rewriting about all the events she thought were important in her life.

"Are you serious?" she said.

"That 'Life History' is the way you are programmed to see your life," Saralynn said. "You've come here to learn to make new decisions. You can't make changes as long as you're hanging on to your old habits and your old stories. It's time to let them go."

Mallie liked that idea. Maybe Saralynn was smarter than her appearance indicated. She tore up the papers and tossed them in the wastebasket close to her chair.

For the next ten minutes or so Saralynn spelled out the center's principles and methods of counseling—how the counselors use transactional analysis, Gestalt and Jungian concepts to help individuals understand their decision-making process and how to learn to make new decisions for the future.

"It works," Saralynn assured Mallie. "But only if you're completely honest and if you're willing to do the work it takes to be successful. That's the key."

That first day, Mallie met with Saralynn twice. Neither time did the counselor mention Larry, the divorce, or Tom Matthews. Those were the pressing problems—particularly, Tom—that Mallie thought she had come to the center to resolve. Instead, Saralynn introduced her to the Gestalt method of role-playing to uncover the engraved impressions made by those people—living or dead—who still bore some form of control over her life. Those impressions, Saralynn explained, subconsciously had been dictating all of Mallie's decisions. To rid herself of those influences, she must relive her actual experiences and recognize her role in allowing them to control her. The first step was a confrontation with each of her parents.

Saralynn placed the child's chair a few feet in front of Mallie's chair. After she sat back down in her own chair, she said, "I want you to close your eyes and picture your father exactly as you remember him when you were a child. When you can picture him, I want you to imagine becoming your father."

"How do I do that?" Mallie asked. The idea of being in her father's mind seemed an impossible task.

"Picture him in your mind's eye—see the place in the house where he's sitting, exactly what he looks like, what he's wearing, what he's doing."

Mallie closed her eyes and tried to imagine her father. Initially she thought she could see him at a distance, as if behind a scrim on a stage. She tried to get closer, lift the scrim. She began to envision him sitting in his library chair, reading his newspaper and sipping his evening drink. He was still dressed in his three-piece suit from work. "Okay," Mallie said tentatively. "I think I have him."

Mallie wondered where all this was going. As strange as she thought it was, she was determined to follow her counselor's directions.

"Now, picture yourself as a child in the room with your father," Saralynn said. "How old are you? What are you doing?"

Mallie immediately saw herself on the floor in the library, next to her father's chair, drawing on a large pad with an ink pen. She was six years old. To her amazement, she felt tension, as if something bad was about to happen. Her expression became tense.

"What is happening?" Saralynn asked. "Is your father angry?"

The suggestion of her father's anger triggered Mallie's memory of his yelling at her. In the scene in her mind, she had inadvertently bumped the little table next to his chair and spilled his drink all over the rug. At the same time, she knocked over the blue ink that she had been using to draw the pictures. The ink spread like blue octopus fingers across the light-colored tan rug. Her father was reacting with fury at her. His eyes were bugged out like a wild animal and his hand was raised against her as if he wanted to strike her. Her memory recalled his exact words: "Valeria, you God-damned stupid little idiot! Look what you've done! Get out of here! Get out of my sight!" Mallie automatically winced at the sound of his voice in her head.

"Get up and sit in the child's chair," Saralynn said quickly.

Mallie obeyed, and in two steps she was seated in the little chair.

"Now," Saralynn said, "let yourself experience what you felt as a child. Look at your father in his chair in front of you. What were you feeling as he said those words to you?"

"Frightened," Mallie said. It was easy to remember exactly how she felt as the child in front of her raging father. "Terrified."

"What do you want to say to your father?"

"I want to run out of the room—get away from him."

"Stay there. Tell him what you're feeling."

Mallie hesitated. She tried to mouth words but no sound came out. She saw herself running up the stairs to Bernice, getting as far away as possible from her father's anger.

"Say it, Mallie," Saralynn ordered her. "Don't run away this time. Say exactly what you are feeling."

With her eyes closed, she gripped the arms of her little chair. She whispered, "I hate you. I didn't mean to spill the ink!"

"Say it louder so he can hear you."

"I hate you! You're mean. I'm terrified of you," Mallie said, firing the words at him, as if they were bullets that could obliterate the angry look on his face.

"Now, get up and sit back in your father's chair," Saralynn said. "Become your father again. Think about what the child has just said to you. How do her words make you feel?"

Mallie closed her eyes. She tried to imagine herself in her father's mind, hearing his own child say: "I hate you. I'm terrified of you." He must have been shocked at himself. He must have wondered: *What have I done to her? How could I have been so angry?* As if Mallie could feel the emotion creeping up inside of him, the color of the anger turning from fire-engine red into deep blue, she dropped her head in remorse. She felt her father's self-loathing. He wanted to take back his words—he wanted to tell the child he was sorry, that it didn't matter. *The drink wasn't important. The ink wasn't important. She was important.*

"Say it," Saralynn said. "Say what you're feeling."

"I want to say 'I'm sorry,'" Mallie whispered. "I want to say 'I love you.'"

Back and forth, from chair to chair, from father to daughter, Saralynn led Mallie through countless painful memories. At one point, when Mallie was in her father's head, revelations came out about his own painful childhood, his mother's bipolar disorder, his father's polio that left him disabled and incapable of being a normal father. Sam Malcolm had felt rudderless as a child and took an authoritarian control of his own life. That authority became stronger and verged on violence later when coupled with alcohol.

In the end, as Mallie sat in the child's chair, the counselor asked, "Can you forgive your father now?"

With tears in her eyes, Mallie said, "Yes." She felt the burden of her father's own childhood pain. She felt her father's remorse and his love for her. Her childhood fears—the fear of her father's anger, the fear of failure—none of her report cards were good enough—the fear that when he yelled at her she was not loved—all of it flew away.

Saralynn explained that it was important to forgive her father and say goodbye to him—actually goodbye to her childhood perception of him. When Mallie reached that point, he would no longer hold the same subconscious influence over her. "It is that unforgiven influence that holds the hand of control over all your relationships with men," Saralynn said, "including your husband."

Dealing with Joan Malcolm was different. It was far easier for Mallie to get into the mind of her mother and envision: dark, perfectly coiffed hair, her sea-blue eyes, her Revlon true-red lipstick, her long thin feet in black suede high-heeled shoes. So many times in Mallie's childhood she had clomped around the house in her mother's high-heeled shoes pretending she was actually Joan Malcolm.

When Mallie first sat in the child's chair, she relived the mother and daughter experience that occurred in Goldsmith's department store when they were looking at dresses for Mallie's eighth-grade dance. Mallie knew what her friends were wearing, either an off-the-shoulder or a strapless dress, mostly taffeta and shiny. Joan Malcolm picked out a black velvet dress with a white lace high collar and long sleeves for Mallie. In the child's chair, Mallie recalled all her emotions about that dance, the pain of wearing that buttoned-up black velvet dress. Everyone had teased her and said she looked like a pilgrim. She had been humiliated and hated her mother for making her wear it.

In the child's chair, Mallie recognized that her anger toward her mother came from her belief that her mother tried to control every aspect of her life. When she became her mother, she began to understand the motivation behind her mother's actions. Some of the stories Mallie had heard and dismissed about her mother's childhood became real.

When Joan Malcolm was four years old growing up in Chicago, her mother, Mallie's Montell grandmother, took her for a walk on Michigan Avenue. It was her nurse's day off and the first time they had ever been alone together. At one point when they stopped for a red light, Joan realized that she was no longer holding her mother's hand. Actually, her mother was nowhere in sight and she was alone on the busy street. What was she to do? She decided to retrace her steps down Michigan Avenue looking into stores along the way. Toward the end of the second block, she peered though a large window to see her mother sitting in the back of the showroom trying on hats. Joan walked calmly into the store, realizing that her mother had not even missed her. At that point, Joan took control of her life and was determined to grow up and take better care of her own children. That care felt to Mallie like unfair control.

In the end, Mallie readily forgave her mother and said goodbye to her.

On the second day, Mallie had to put Larry in the chair and experience their married life through his eyes, as well as through her own unfiltered lens about herself. The objective was to discover how blind she had been to much of her part—her 50 percent—of the failure of their marriage.

In one of the Gestalt visualizations, Saralynn led Mallie back through the experience of reading the letters she had found in Larry's suitcase, the letters from so many women all over the world. In Mallie's own state of insecurity involving the other women in Larry's life, she had not been open to hearing her husband's underlying fear that he would lose his job if he criticized her father or anything about Memphis. She did not suspect that her husband was worried that he had severed ties with his family's connections in Rhode Island, and that if he lost his job in Memphis, he did not know how he would support his wife and three boys. She'd had barely a glimpse of the lack of trust that was building between her father—the president of Malcolm Brothers—and Larry, or the teasing Larry endured from the other employees of the company. It was not that he had not told her lies about the other women in his life or that he had not had multiple affairs, but for the first time, Mallie could see that she had gone deep into herself in defiance of Larry and raised walls around herself he could not penetrate. She had tried to protect her own insecurities and not understood his insecurities. She did not understand at the time that his pride was as wounded as hers. She did accept the fact that the damage which had been done through the years by both of them had left the marriage in irreparable shreds. Eventually, after many trips back and forth inside of Larry's head, Mallie was able to forgive Larry and say goodbye to him.

At the end of the first three days of counseling and all of the Gestalt experiences, Mallie was exhausted. She had relived and rethought many of the defining experiences with both of her parents and with Larry. Saralynn had saved the last Gestalt session for her confrontation with Tom Matthews.

In a rare moment of teaching negative visualization at the end of the session involving Tom, Saralynn suggested to Mallie that she envision a coiled, poisonous snake in the corner of the priest's study. The idea had made Mallie's skin crawl. "That will help you stay away when you're tempted to return to that place," Saralynn said. "It's not that the snake was always there. There was an element of support and a positive experience for you for a time. You learned a great deal about yourself. You began to see yourself as an attractive, vital woman again. But there's a deadly snake there now, and you must protect yourself."

Mallie assured Saralynn that she would not go back to St. Michael's. Ever. Besides her resolve never to see Tom Matthews again, she knew the chapel might not even exist for much longer.

Chapter Fifty-one

I n the group meeting on the third afternoon, James wrote a list on a blackboard. "These are your life priorities," he said, "the proper order of your responsibilities."

1) Yourself
2) Your spouse
3) Your children under eighteen
4) Your children over eighteen, parents, siblings, and friends
5) Your job or your occupation.

"These priorities can change from time to time, depending on the urgency of the need. You may have a sick child who requires immediate and exclusive attention. You may have a parent or a friend in trouble. Or you may have a crisis in your job. Those situations take precedence over everything else until they are resolved. But when the crisis is over, you must go back to taking care of yourself first."

In his words, Mallie heard echoes of what she had learned at Faith at Work and at St. James in England. But they still sounded so selfish to Mallie. *Me first?* It was a difficult concept.

Someone in the group asked the question: "Isn't that the opposite of what the Bible teaches? Aren't we supposed to think of God first? And then of others?"

James responded with a question. "Who do you think *you* are?" he said.

No one spoke.

He waited several seconds before he answered his own query. "The first commandment says: 'Love the Lord thy God with all thy heart and all thy soul.' If we are sons and daughters of God, then, just like our earthly parents, we carry God within us. We are not God—not a single one of us—but in a very real sense, we are a *part of God as God is a part of us.* It is that divine part of ourselves—our higher self, our creative self, our soul—that must be our first priority."

Mallie remembered that Bruce Larson at the Faith at Work had spoken about the *creative spirit* as the deepest part of ourselves, a wellspring that poets and painters instinctively know, whether they call it God or not. James was confirming the truth of that idea.

Each new day at the center, in addition to her counseling sessions with Saralynn and the group meetings with James, she spent time with volunteer resource women from Knoxville. These women talked openly about life before the process at the center and life afterward. Every woman made her feel more comfortable, less judged—her greatest fear about coming to the center in the first place.

One of the resource women was an English teacher at the Maryville High School near Knoxville. She had been married to an alcoholic for twenty-five years before she came to the center. After her week of therapy she discovered her own worth and made plans to divorce her husband. She was happily remarried. Another woman had grown up with an older sister in an "iron lung" from a childhood polio attack. She had felt guilty and responsible for her sister all through her life—she had been the one who wanted to go swimming in the city pool where her sister apparently contracted the polio. She discovered that she had tried to atone for her action by locking up her own life with her sister in the iron lung. She broke that chain of guilt and began a new life. Listening intently to their stories, Mallie heard the word "free"—as if those women had been birds confined to a cage where they could not fly. Whatever cage Mallie had lived in, she decided that "free" was what she wanted to be, and she would do whatever it took to achieve it.

In the group session on the fourth afternoon, James and Saralynn worked together, showing examples of the dynamics of a marriage. The first exercise included four volunteers from the assembled group, two women and two men. The two counselors knelt on the floor in front of each other and instructed a man and a woman to stand behind each of them.

"How many people are there in a marriage bed?" James asked the group.

No one spoke. Finally someone said, "Two?"

"Try six," James said. He pointed to Saralynn and himself on their knees and then to the couple standing behind each of them. "One man and one woman and two sets of parents. That's a pretty crowded bed!" He laughed, a big, expansive, easy laugh. "Not only do a bride and groom bring their parents into their marriage bed, but also into every aspect of their lives: how to celebrate Christmas properly—how to raise children correctly—how to fight—and how to deny one another. Those carefully programmed, ingrained responses are always there, all just beneath the surface."

Mallie thought of her marriage to Larry. She could imagine that he had expected her to be like his mother, Edie. He adored his mother. Mallie adored Edie, too, but she was not Edie and never could be. She realized that she had expected Larry to behave like her father—to be as admired and successful as Sam Malcolm. But he was not her father. She had tried to be a wife like her own mother, as clearly as she had understood Joan Malcolm—a totally inappropriate wife for Larry. The theory made sense. Her blindness to his and her own expectations had been a part of her failure.

"Why do you think Saralynn and I are down on our knees?" James asked the group.

Before anyone could answer, Saralynn spoke. She turned her head to look up at the couple looming above her. "Because this is the place—the height—where I viewed my mother and father when I was a child. This was my position of powerlessness. This was where I learned my first life lessons, and unless I consciously learn to make new decisions based on experience, I will remain subconsciously chained to those ideas I formed as a child. They will follow me wherever I go and whatever I do."

The cage, Mallie thought—that's the psychological cage that I have lived in since my childhood and the place I have been struggling to escape.

Chapter Fifty-two

When the teaching session was over on Thursday afternoon, Mallie decided it was time to speak to James. She had not had an opportunity to work with him or have any personal conversation with him since she arrived on Sunday. Partially out of her mother's politeness training, she wanted to express her gratitude for her time at the center.

"Excuse me," she said, after he finished speaking with a couple and appeared to be leaving the room. "James?"

He turned to look at her. She suddenly felt spotlighted. His intense blue eyes that often laughed during a session were serious and focused on her with curiosity.

"Yes?" he said.

"I'm Mallie Vose." She put out her hand and spoke quickly, surprised at herself that she felt uneasy. "I just wanted to thank you for starting this counseling center. This week has meant so much to me."

He took her hand in both of his and smiled. "Thank you," he said. Then he gestured toward the back corner of the room. "Come, sit down with me for a minute."

She felt hesitant. He always seemed so busy and here he was asking her to sit down with him. She followed him to two empty chairs in the corner. There were people still milling around the room and talking in groups.

"Tell me why you came here," he said.

Mallie took a deep breath. She had spoken so quickly—perhaps flippantly—at the introductory meeting. That experience seemed so long ago. Obviously, he did not remember anything she said. She would tell him again, this time more forcefully. "I'm on the brink of a divorce after nearly eighteen years. I have three boys, three teenagers, and I fear for the loss of their family center. I lost my father to a stroke this year. I fell in love with my counselor, a married Episcopal priest who betrayed me. I knew I had to get away from him." She hesitated, then added, "I was afraid if I didn't do something—something different in my life—I would die."

James Preston did not register any emotional response to her litany of reasons for coming to the center. "And what have you learned since you've been here?" he asked her.

"Well, I've forgiven myself for my 50 percent of the failure of my marriage and said goodbye to both my parents and to my husband—and to the priest." As she spoke she thought, of course, that he would be pleased with what she had done. She was pleased.

He looked at her with steely eyes, not with damnation, but certainly not with praise. "So, if you've said goodbye to all those people, how are you going to replace that loss in your life?"

She felt sick to her stomach. She had not expected him to question her accomplishments of the week. Saralynn had told her that she had done good work. At that moment, in front of James, she felt like a threatened child again. Fearful. Helpless. She had no answer. "I don't know," she stammered.

He took her hand. "I suggest you find out before you leave here. Keep working. This is your best chance." He stood up and smiled at her. "I trust you *will*." He let go of her hand and walked out of the room.

Mallie stumbled out the back door to the hammock, the special place she had discovered hidden in the oak trees behind the White House. She needed to be alone before she and Helen Brady went into town for dinner. She felt as if she had been kicked in the stomach, that same devastated sense of fear and inadequacy and failure that had been her shadow through her life. She was still in *the cage*. She sat on the edge of the hammock, letting her body sink into the ropey center, lifting her feet off the ground. What now? The familiar critical voice began a familiar inner dialogue. *You have been kidding yourself to believe that you have really learned a new way. You are in the same old trap of being threatened by letting an important man in your life tell you what to do. Are you going to let James Preston undermine all that you have learned at the center? He obviously accused you of learning nothing.* But Mallie knew that was not the whole truth. She knew her mind had been opened in ways she could never have imagined. Still, she had felt like a butterfly pinned to a board when he spoke to her. He seemed to be looking at her with a laser, seeing things inside that she had not seen herself. She had not come to this place and spent the past four days struggling so hard to accept and forgive her past for one man to undermine her success.

The anger she felt at his question slowly turned in her mind. The more she thought about it, the more she knew in her heart that his question was valid. She had suffered many losses in her life—acknowledging them in front of her counselor had initially felt liberating, but she had more work to do. The vacuum left by saying goodbye to all of those people in her life would produce another form of loss. If she went home without knowing how to fill that loss, she might be tempted to go back to Tom Matthews. Or to jump into another relationship that could be equally destructive. How would she fill the inevitable emptiness when she got home? That was the real question James Preston was asking. That was her challenge. She had one more day at The Center to figure it out.

Chapter Fifty-three

At dinner that night, Helen told Mallie she had had a remarkable day: she had been through a Gestalt exercise with her unborn child. Mallie could see that Helen's eyes, so dark and forlorn at the beginning of the week, had come alive. She couldn't talk about it, she said. She wasn't sure she understood how it happened—but she was filled with gratitude for the baby. She felt a new sense that her husband had not left her and that he, too, was grateful for the baby. Mallie was genuinely happy for Helen.

Mallie chose not to talk about her day. She needed to keep it to herself, to think about her encounter with James, to resolve the challenge he had given her. As she fell asleep, his voice echoed in her mind: "I trust that you *will*."

Dawn could not come fast enough. As soon as the clock reached seven thirty and Helen stirred in her bed, Mallie jumped up and dressed. "I've got to see James," she said. "I'll meet you later for breakfast."

She knew James came in early every day to spend time alone in his office.

The White House was unlocked. She raced up the stairs and hesitated before she knocked on his door. The whole building, normally bustling with people, felt like it might still be sleeping. With her heart pounding, she knocked and called to him, "James?"

"Who is it?" he asked. His voice was soft, distant, as if he had been in meditation.

"It's Mallie Vose," she said. "I need to speak with you."

He opened the door quickly. "What is it? Are you all right?"

"I have the answer to your question about filling the losses in my life," she said.

"Come in," James said. He reached for her hand and guided her toward the sofa in his office. "Tell me."

Mallie barely sat down before she began her story. "I woke in the night with a vision. It explained a dream I had when I felt extreme panic that my marriage was over. I knew the dream was important, even prophetic, but I didn't really understand its true meaning at the time."

She could feel James actively listening to her. His expression was entirely different from the day before. There was no accusation in his eyes, only curiosity and compassion.

"All these months I thought the dream was mainly about a tidal wave that hit the little sailboat I was on with my husband. It was terrifying. I was certain I was going to drown. When I was washed up on the beach and realized I was alive—I felt a sweep of gratitude. At the same time, I knew I had to climb a rugged cliff in front of me. When I got to the top, there was an old woman sitting on a rock with a baby in her arms. She held the baby out to me and said, 'Take this child. Care for her and you will be fine.'"

Mallie barely stopped to breathe. "The next morning when I woke up, I focused on the tidal wave and the cliff. I saw the tidal wave as a perfect metaphor for what had happened—my life, like the boat, had been splintered. To survive, I would have to climb the cliff in front of me. I was never really clear about the old woman and the baby."

James nodded, a tacit sign for her to continue.

Mallie momentarily paused and closed her eyes, as if to recreate the vision in her mind. "Last night in the dark of my room, the old woman came back to me. She stood at the foot of my bed as plain as day. Once again she reached out and offered the baby to me. This time she did not have to say a word. I knew."

From Saralynn's explanation of the Jungian theory that all the individuals who appear in dreams represent a part of the dreamer, Mallie knew the meaning of the gift. She felt tears in her eyes as she spoke. "I knew what that child represented in my life."

James waited silently for her to finish her story.

"The child is my soul," Mallie said. "It's the core of my being, my connection to my deepest self, to God and to all living things. The old woman is also a part of me—the wise and caring Mother I've neglected to listen to for so long. She came to give me *the gift of my creative self, my spiritual self.* Caring for her will fill any emptiness in my life."

"Yes," James said. "Yes." His blue eyes radiated warmth and approval. He reached over and took both of Mallie's hands in his. "There's no substitute for all the work you've done this week. All that you've been taught and all that you've learned will serve you well. They're valuable tools to understand your responsibility for the decisions you've made in the past and those you'll continue to make in the future. The truth is that to really live your life fully, you will need to go beyond knowledge and your rational understanding. No one can teach you who you are as a spiritual, creative being. To know that comes from within. It's the gift of grace, something beyond all reason." He squeezed her hands. "I'm happy for you."

Mallie felt as if James had given her a benediction, a final blessing. She was grateful, but at the same time she knew that she did not need it. She was assured in herself that she had been given what she needed within herself. No man, no person, could add to her gift of grace—or ever take it away.

She floated through breakfast and into her last session with Saralynn. When she finished telling her counselor about her vision, Saralynn smiled and said, "Congratulations, Mallie. You've got a new life." Then, she leaned forward and said, "How do you plan to keep it?"

At another time, that question might have troubled her. But she knew the answer. She told Saralynn that like her mountaintop experience at Faith at Work, she knew the euphoria of the moment at the center would fade. But her gift of grace would not leave her. She had accepted it and it was hers to keep.

"You might think about doing something that would clearly signify you've made a major change," Saralynn said. "Cut your hair—or maybe dye it red." She laughed when Mallie looked puzzled. "I'm serious," she added. "Do something tangible as a reminder that your decision to change has had real consequences."

Mallie had been thinking periodically throughout her time at the center about her drawing class and wondering if her art would change because of her new insights, her sense of freedom.

In Saralynn's office that morning it occurred to her that during her last class at the Art Academy, she had been so surprised when the substitute teacher called her Valeria—her legal name, as it was written on her application. Unlike the experiences of childhood when the sound of her name made her feel uncomfortable and different from all the other girls, she liked the way it sounded. She liked the idea that she was different.

Suppose she took back the name that she had been given at birth: Valeria. Her real name. How would it feel to give up the name "Mallie," a nickname offered to her in fourth grade by a boy whose name she could not even remember? Choosing to be called Valeria Vose would certainly be a tangible reminder of a major change in her life. Once the divorce was final, she would no longer be Mrs. Lawrence Vose, her married name. She could go back to her maiden name: Valeria Malcolm—but that name did not feel like the person she had become. For half of her life, as a wife and a mother of three sons, Vose had been her legal family name. Surely it was hers to keep. How would she feel to be Valeria Vose, the artist, the woman with a new life? It was a place to start.

Acknowledgments

Gratitude for the encouragement to write and publish this book has its genesis in the late 1990s with my introduction to Joan Zabarsky, the founder of the Literature Forum and the Wordsmith program in Boca Grande, Florida. She took me under her wing and convinced me I was a born southern writer with a story to tell. And to Roxana Robinson, whose fiction class at the Wesleyan Writers Conference in June of 1995 has remained an inspiration.

Of vital importance in the process was my introduction to Sena Jeter Naslund by our mutual friend, fellow writer, and brilliant editor, Lucinda Sullivan. Sena's description of founding a low-residency MFA in Writing program at Spalding University in 2001 lit a fire in my heart. Her willingness to accept me into her program in my sixties without a college degree opened doors of creativity and opportunity I had barely dreamed possible. The teachers and mentors in her unique mandate of nurture and critical challenge were each a priceless gift: Dianne April, Robert Finch, Cathleen Medwick, Roy Hoffman, Elaine Orr, Crystal Wilkinson, the incomparable Molly Peacock, my critical and creative thesis advisor, and Robin Lippincott, my friend and perceptive editor, without whom *Valeria Vose* would not have been born.

So much gratitude to the thoughtful and supportive manuscript readers: Penny Schmidt, Lila Saunders, Dede Reed, Tamara Lloyd, Judy Gardner, Erin Reed, Sandy Lohnes, Deborah Begel, Kim Hume, Margot Finley, Mary Beth Schneider, Phoebe Megna and Mary Vickers. More than a reader, Candy Hooper has continued to inject invaluable positive energy and advice. Special thanks to wonderful Lee Smith and to Eleanor Morse, Elizabeth Stuckey-French, and Bill Roorbach for their generous blurbs. Deep appreciation to my life-saving counselor friends Marion Sue and John DeFoore and to my theological reader/advisors in the Episcopal Church: The Rev. Buddy Stallings, The Rev. Susan Flanders, The Rev. Lyn Brakeman, and especially The Rt. Rev. Chilton Knudsen.

Also from the beginning, the wisdom and support of Patricia Reis, author and therapist, has been essential. Her introduction to Brooke Warner and She Writes Press based upon the success of her memoir *Motherlines* paved the way for this publication. The whole team at She Writes Press from Brooke, Samantha Strom, Crystal Patriarche and Taylor Brightwell to Julie Metz, the masterful cover designer, Maggie Ruf, the creative web designer to Jennifer Caven, the meticulous copyeditor—professional, caring and exceptional individuals, each one. They have changed my world as they are changing the publishing world.

Last but never least, my heartfelt gratitude to my family: my mother Alice Berry Condon Hoguet and my husband Aubrey Gorman, both of whom have left this world but have never left me. I hear their voices of conviction and support. My sisters and my brother—Kate, Louisa, Dodie, and Martin—are always with me. My cousin Connie, the best and most gracious proofreader in the world. Most of all, I am forever indebted to my beloved children: Eleanor and Tom Mallory, Grace and Michael Ott, and Charles Bingham, each of them, along with my six amazing grandchildren—Mike, Daniel, Louis, Miles, Curtis, and Bliss—have believed in me and inspired me to follow my dreams.

About the Author

Photo credit: Patricia Christakos

Alice Bingham Gorman is a writer of fiction, nonfiction and poetry. She earned an MFA in Writing from Spalding University in 2005 and received an Honorary PhD in Fine Arts from the Memphis College of Art. Her writing has been published in *Vogue, O, the Oprah Magazine, O's Little Book of Love and Friendship, The Louisville Review* and countless regional periodicals and art publications. Born and raised in Memphis, Tennessee, she divides her time between Maine and Florida. *Valeria Vose* is her first novel.

SELECTED TITLES FROM SHE WRITES PRESS

She Writes Press is an independent publishing company founded to serve women writers everywhere. Visit us at **www.shewritespress.com**.

Fire & Water by Betsy Graziani Fasbinder. $16.95, 978-1-938314-14-8. Kate Murphy has always played by the rules—but when she meets charismatic artist Jake Bloom, she's forced to navigate the treacherous territory of passionate love, friendship, and family devotion.

Play for Me by Céline Keating. $16.95, 978-1-63152-972-6. Middle-aged Lily impulsively joins a touring folk-rock band, leaving her job and marriage behind in an attempt to find a second chance at life, passion, and art.

The Wiregrass by Pam Webber. $16.95, 978-1-63152-943-6. A story about a summer of discontent, change, and dangerous mysteries in a small Southern Wiregrass town.

What is Found, What is Lost by Anne Leigh Parrish. $16.95, 978-1-938314-95-7. After her husband passes away, a series of family crises forces Freddie, a woman raised on religion, to confront long-held questions about her faith.

Appetite by Sheila Grinell. $16.95, 978-1-63152-022-8. When twenty-five-year-old Jenn Adler brings home a guru fiancé from Bangalore, her parents must come to grips with the impending marriage—and its effect on their own relationship.

A Tight Grip: A Novel about Golf, Love Affairs, and Women of a Certain Age by Kay Rae Chomic. $16.95, 978-1-938314-76-6. As forty-six-year-old golfer Jane "Par" Parker prepares for her next tournament, she experiences a chain of events that force her to reevaluate her life.